DETECTIVE JACK MILLS: As the department's unofficial "Poster Cop" and #1 jock, he's spent his career chasing golf balls and chasing skirts, scoring with ease in both fields. Now he's chasing a cop-killer—and all he's catching is hell. Seems Jack is getting too close to the truth . . . close enough to kiss his brass good-bye. . . .

DETECTIVE CLAIRE WILLIAMSON: Tall, brunette, beautiful, she's been named Jack's partner on the case. As far as her fellow officers are concerned, she's just another hot tuna swimming with the sharks. But Jack knows that while he may be her equal in looks, she's certainly a better cop . . . and if he tries any quick moves on her, he's the one who will be eaten alive. . . .

SWEET DEAL

"John Westermann has hit his stride and is running on a very fast track. *SWEET DEAL* is a novel not to be missed, a compelling examination of human values in the new American epicenter, the suburbs. . . . Pick up a copy and enjoy crime writing as it is meant to be written."

—*New Orleans Times-Picayune*

"Westermann is the only cop writer who can dance the high wire between humor and hell. This is the real thing."

—Andrew Vachss

ARTIE BACKMAN: A recently retired Nassau County police captain, he set out one morning to spend a day at the track and ended up a big loser, tortured to death and buried in a shallow grave. For Jack and Claire, the question is: What kind of sweet deal was he mixed up in? It's not every career cop who can salt away two hundred grand in a secret bank account. . . .

LOUIE ALLESI: A Long Island wiseguy who might provide some interesting answers to the $200,000 question. He runs a profitable business in hot cars, pornography, prostitution, and dirty cops. Artie Backman, once an asset, may in retirement have turned into a liability . . . not only to Louie, but to all the other members of the force currently on his payroll. . . .

SWEET DEAL

MICHAEL BACKMAN: Artie's hot-shot lawyer son with connections to Long Island's powerful political machine, including the Nassau County Executive and his Senator brother. It's the kind of machine which doles out patronage to friends and which could easily chew up a couple of flatfoot detectives who push the wrong buttons. . . .

ANGELA CORTELLI: A skinny blonde waitress over at the Spartacus Diner, she was Artie's main squeeze. Word is, this is a girl with a pair of handcuffs tattooed on her backside, and where cops are concerned, she's always ready to offer service with a smile. A one-woman Department of Internal Affairs, Angela has an intimate knowledge of Long Island's finest. . . .

SWEET DEAL

"Westermann, one of the few crime writers to realize that America is now the suburbs and that criminals live in ranch houses too, uses the sprawl outside New York to great effect. . . . Good stuff. Westermann paints people rather than types and puts them into a palpable world of strip malls, frontage roads, and postwar subdivisions. Gangsters in the townships are as creepy as their brothers in the boroughs."

—*Kirkus Reviews*

"A funny, profane, hard-boiled police mystery. . . . tough but very entertaining. . . . this is very good writing, indeed."

—*Wilson Library Bulletin*

Books by John Westermann

Exit Wounds
High Crimes
Sweet Deal

Published by POCKET BOOKS

SWEET DEAL

JOHN WESTERMANN

POCKET BOOKS

New York   London   Toronto   Sydney   Tokyo   Singapore

This book is a work of fiction. Names, characters, places, and incidents are either products of the author's imagination or are used fictitiously. Any resemblance to actual events or locales or persons, living or dead, is entirely coincidental.

POCKET BOOKS, a division of Simon & Schuster Inc.
1230 Avenue of the Americas, New York, NY 10020

Copyright © 1992 by John Westermann

Published by arrangement with Soho Press, Inc.

ISBN: 0-671-79170-2

First Pocket Books printing April 1993

10 9 8 7 6 5 4 3 2 1

POCKET and colophon are registered trademarks of Simon & Schuster Inc.

Cover art by David Jarvis

Printed in the U.S.A.

FOR LISA

Many thanks to Larry Fisher for his technical assistance, and to First Lieutenant Robert Capriotti, 14th Regiment, New York Guard, for his technical advice.

And thanks again to Jessica and Jake.

". . . You could be just another white-tailed baby
stranded on my brights . . ."

Just a Little Light, The Grateful Dead

SWEET DEAL

1

THE BILLBOARDS never failed to disconcert Detective Jack Mills. His ruggedly handsome face was suddenly plastered all over the county once more. The billboards were cropping up again, as they did whenever a police department recruiting drive was under way: on the flank of a southbound county bus in New Hyde Park, on the side of a high-rise bank, on an overpass.

The photograph, taken seven years ago, had permanently joined Detective Jack Mills and County Executive Gilbert Otto in the minds of Nassau County residents. The county exec and he were shaking hands, looking bravely to the future. COP A GREAT LIFE, it said across the bottom in bold letters. CALL THE NASSAU COUNTY POLICE DEPARTMENT FOR DETAILS.

Jack smiled. Not a bad poster, if somewhat dated. His sideburns were too long, Gil Otto's tie too wide. But nobody had come through the academy since who tempted anyone into replacing Jack. He was tall enough to be the starting small forward on the PBA basketball team. His hair was sandy

1

blond and his nose and chin were straight, photogenic.

Jack's well-maintained body and handsome face also occasionally appeared in law-enforcement magazine ads for executive body armor, and in public service antidrug commercials. Jack was one of the few who did not think this notoriety had gone to his head, because he knew that in a month he and Gilbert Otto would be sporting Magic Marker moustaches, blacked-out teeth, and anatomically inaccurate sexual organs, while saying unspeakable things to each other in cartoon bubbles. A month after that, they would be torn down by snickering civil servants.

The county seat where Jack Mills worked, and to which he was driving through the warm September afternoon, was located in a busy lawyer's town with the silly name Mineola, which sounded to Jack like a small record player but was actually an Indian name. Jack pulled his unmarked black Dodge sedan into the parking lot of Nassau County Police headquarters, a block-long three-story structure of tan brick with big windows that made it look more benign than it was.

"Hey, Poster Cop," said the guard at the front door. "We got about five calls for you today from broads that want to unload your gun."

"Pass 'em out to the rest of the men," said Jack. "Tell them I said, 'Well done.'"

Dressed in his wrinkled khaki suit and well-worn deck shoes, he climbed to the second floor and flopped down at his desk in the homicide bullpen, three hours before he was scheduled to go off duty, one hour after Sergeant Rodney Lomack had expected him back from an interview.

This was evident from the snarl he got, along with a fresh trough of paperwork, which landed on Jack's desk with a thump. Lomack rolled back to his windowed office.

Rodney Lomack was a dapper little black man with a moustache as thick as a broom. Because he spoke intelligibly, the brass thought they knew him. Lomack was teaching Jack the homicide ropes and filling in the monstrous gaps in his police education, lessons he had missed at his soft post in community relations.

Rod Lomack was a patient man. Jack had known almost nothing about police work when he got to the squad. He was qualified to stop by management seminars, Rotary luncheons, public schools and hospitals, and to ramble on ad nauseam about his all-American lacrosse career. When it came to crime, he had only recently gotten over being as shocked and flustered as the average rookie.

"You take the scenic route?" asked Lomack, reappearing, pointedly looking at his watch.

"No, boss.

"Two hours for a simple deposition?"

"I got lost."

Lomack shook his head. "You never bring me presents, your reports are always late. It takes you a month to solve cases I could crack in twenty minutes, and I have to take calls from your fucking agent. Why do I like you?" Lomack sauntered toward his office again. "I swear if I didn't need you for the basketball team, I'd toss your honky ass."

Jack ran his tongue over his teeth. In a conference room down the hall an argument erupted, followed by the sound of flying furniture and loud promises to inflict great physical pain. No one in the bullpen flinched; just someone doing business.

The walls were a grayish institutional blue, the color of suicides, of Seattle. Chief of Detectives David Barone had ordered the color for just that reason, to depress suspects, never mind the effect on those who worked there every day. In self-defense, Jack had decorated his own work space with the *Sports Illustrated* swimsuit issue and with pictures of Amen Corner at the Augusta National Golf Club. His off-again girlfriend, Katy, and daughter, Jennifer, smiled up at him from photos beneath his plexiglass blotter. But it was still a depressing place to sit. His desk had an iron ring welded on the side for handcuffs. Happy people never shook hands over it; he never "did lunch" with a client.

Jack shared his small cubicle with Detective William Eats O'Day, a 380-pound asthmatic with gout who led the homicide squad in sick time. A sensitive soul, unlike most of the squad's swaggering cowboys, Eats was absent again— home, where he could not be yelled at. Jack missed him. They could have talked about the Mets for the rest of the day, kept their minds off the unavenged dead.

Jack's phone rang and he wondered if it was Lomack calling to badger him some more.

"Hi, Jack."

He waited a moment, gathering himself. "Hi, Katy."

"Would you like to come over and talk this thing out? My folks are away for the night."

"What's the matter with our house? You remember our house?"

"I'd rather be on neutral ground."

"Fine."

"Let's make it dinner."

"Okay," Jack said, suddenly buoyant. "I'll pick up a couple of lobsters."

Jack hung up and stared into the dark blue space over the bullpen.

"Got a date?" asked Al Trankina, a polyester busybody who sat across the aisle.

Jack would not call an evening with the woman he had so recently lived with a date. He would call it an exciting obligation. "Sort of," he said.

"So get lost," said Trankina. "I'll cover for you here."

Jack hit the fish store on bustling Woodcleft Canal in Freeport for a couple of lobsters and some littleneck clams, the Bay Shack liquor store for champagne, and then drove to Katy's parents' waterfront co-op. He parked his black county car at the edge of the landscaped circular driveway and rode the elevator up to the third floor.

She was waiting for him in ambush, dressed in skintight cutoff jeans and a skimpy white halter, nails and lips red, her blond hair flowing like she had just strolled out of the beauty parlor. She wrapped her arms around his neck and kissed him full on the mouth. Her perfume overwhelmed him. He dropped the lobsters, held onto the champagne bottle, pressed himself hard against her.

5

"Horny?" she asked.

"And hungry too."

She forced one of her legs between his. "What do you want to eat first?"

Jack smiled. "Shouldn't we talk?"

She looked up at him as if he were crazy. "Is this the same Jack Mills who screwed me in the bathroom of an airplane?

"I don't know. Are you the same Katy O'Brien? Two weeks ago you come home and announce that life with me is terminally degrading and—"

"Let's have a drink," she said. "Maybe we need time to decompress."

Katy sashayed into the kitchen for champagne glasses and Jack wondered who else had seen that wiggle lately, wondered why he cared. He studied the silver-framed pictures on the credenza, some of Katy as a child. Waving from a canoe. In her maroon high school graduation cap and gown. In a sexy bathing suit on the hood of her older brother's black Corvette. Jack did not miss knowing her back then, felt no nostalgia for her youth. The phone rang and he wondered who was calling her.

She came out of the kitchen without champagne flutes, but with that look of hers that he hated. "Al Trankina."

Jack took the phone. "Mills."

"I hate to do this to you, Jack, but you gotta come back. We got an inquiry about H-eleven-eighty-nine."

"Okay. On the way," he said.

"Sorry," Trankina said. "I owe you a blow job."

"Keep it."

Katy was sitting on the living room couch when

he turned, her face flushed as if she had just been working out.

"Honey—"

"Forget it," she said. "I should have known."

Jack dropped to one knee in front of her. "Katy, listen, there's an emergency."

"There's always an emergency these days. Remember when you used to go to work at eight and were home to start the barbecue by four? You had a dream job. So of course you screwed it up. Didn't anybody ever tell you? Only assholes volunteer."

"But—"

"Homicide, and *you* hate the sight of blood."

"I'm thirty-six years old, Katy. I figured it was time to grow up."

"Oh," she said, "I see. Does that include accepting responsibility and acting mature, maybe getting married and settling down?"

Jack looked away. "This was my last chance to be a real cop."

"Twenty-four hours a day? How stupid do I look? You're having the time of your life."

"It's nothing but work. I don't have a bimbo, and the time of my life was years ago."

She folded her hands as if in prayer and said plaintively, "The commissioner is a rabid fan. You could tell him that this was a mistake, that you'd like to—"

"Honey . . ." Jack felt the argument slipping away from him. "You're flipping out again."

Katy narrowed her eyes and said, "If I accepted this bullshit situation I'd be a bigger fool than you."

"That's not true," Jack said.

"Yeah, you're right. You'd still be the bigger fool."

He stared at her, wondering what he might say to end this conversation on a more positive note.

"Go ahead," she said. "What are you thinking?"

"I was thinking I should have a warning stamped on your forehead for the next guy: Manipulative. Has to Have Her Way."

"Fuck you, Jack, okay? Just fuck you." Katy pushed him aside and picked up a lobster. She snapped the rubber bands off its claws, marched to the balcony and chucked it into the drink. Her ass, he noticed, did not wiggle once.

"What about this guy?" asked Jack, holding up the other lobster.

"Stick it down the front of your pants."

He dropped the creature. "This is forever," he warned.

"Thank God for small favors."

Lobster number two crawled under the railing and followed its mate off the balcony.

Katy burst into tears.

Jack tried to put his arms around her.

"Get out of this house before I call your fucking buddies on you."

Jack left. He rode the elevator down to his car empty-hearted. He keyed his mike and let headquarters know he was on the road, then took a lap around the circular driveway to check the open lobby, to see if she had followed him down, to check if it *wasn't* forever, that her tears were real.

He saw only plastic palm trees flanking elevator doors that were closed like a vault. He smiled and took a second lap, faster, yelling into the lobby as he roared past again, "Good-bye, you beautiful bitch!"

Mr. and Mrs. Carl Ryan were in their fifties, but tired-looking in their rumpled clothes. Mrs. Ryan carried a briefcase, Mr. Ryan, a box of files. Jack knew what they wanted.

H-11-89. A case six months old when he inherited it. A case going nowhere: The victim, Jane Doe, probably sweet sixteen, with the bruised face of a damaged angel. Found naked on Super Bowl Sunday staring at the heavens, preserved in ice in a swimming pool behind an empty mansion in Woodbury. No jewelry, three fillings. Work done in America, according to the report of the first case agent, who was now retired.

H-11-89, dead from repeated blows to the head, and dumped. Never identified, never reported missing. Network TV true-crime shows had run her picture to no avail. Someone's daughter swallowed whole. No one even to grieve for her passing, unless it was him.

She frequently weighed on him, invaded his peace of mind. When things at the office were slow, he would look for her among lists of young women who let their learners' permits expire, orphanage rosters, porno movie credits. He showed her morgue photograph to every pimp in the tri-state area, spent time inventing her character, imagining her life and how it ended. He thought of her murderer, scot-free perhaps. Just one of maybe eighty annual Long Island murders. With fifteen unsolved. Forever. To let it go would be to let her go. He was all that she had, officially.

"We're looking for our daughter, Libby," the man said. "Have been for the last three years."

Mr. Ryan laid out his research on Jack's desk, handed him a high school graduation picture. Libby Ryan was a normal teenage girl with a happy face and a future. "She was last seen in Columbus, Ohio, at a frat party."

Jack studied the photograph. "I don't think I've seen her," he said. "I'm sorry."

"Maybe someone else around here . . . ?" said Mr. Ryan.

"I'm pretty current on our files. And I know what you're going through. I have a daughter of my own."

His sad visitors showed no reaction, simply stood up and began gathering their briefcase and carton of files.

"Would you be able to direct us to the Suffolk County Police Headquarters?" asked Mr. Ryan.

"I'd be glad to."

After Jack told them how to get there, he asked if they planned on visiting every police department in the country.

"What would you do?" asked Mr. Ryan. "You're a plumber with a growing business. Your only child is a high school senior. Her dippy boyfriend loses track of her at a toga party. And she is never seen or heard from again. What the hell would you do?"

"I'm not sure," said Jack. "Probably what you're doing."

"We nailed fliers on telephone poles, then took calls from creeps demanding ransoms, threatening to mail us body parts if we didn't pay. I've gone to

10

more bogus 'meets' than I can remember, and still nothing."

Jack looked at Mrs. Ryan.

"I've told him," she said helplessly. "Computers do this much faster than we can, and cheaper too. He can't sit still. Home is worse than the road."

"Leave me a picture of Libby for our files," said Jack. "You never know."

"Thank you, Detective. Our number is on the back."

After they left, Jack sat scribbling at his desk for a moment, a memo to the files to justify his time.

"Nothing?" asked Trankina. "No connection?"

"Nope."

2

DAVID BARONE'S wood-paneled corner office, on the top floor of Nassau County headquarters, commanded a handsome view of tree-lined Franklin Avenue and the Dale Carnegie Institute across the street. There was soft gray carpeting, a private bathroom, an air conditioner that worked and furniture that had been polished during the current fiscal year.

Chief of Detectives Barone had gathered his subordinates there for the weekly review of open cases or, as they referred to it, the weekly review of open sores. Blots on the great man's record.

Eats O'Day went first, as he was senior man and anxious to dispose of his cases before Barone got himself really worked up.

"Body of a mummified male Indian uncovered by house builders in Muttontown. The medical examiner sets the time of death around seventeen fifty. No available witnesses. Recommend we close and ship the body to the county museum."

"Very good, Eats," said Barone. "Nice of you to make it in today."

"No problem."

Sergeant Izzy Goldman reported no progress investigating last year's murder of a young seminarian whose body was discovered on the grounds of a convent.

Al Trankina went next, followed by everybody else with more time in the squad than Jack, which was everybody. All in all the squad was doing a nice job. Most were pulling their weight.

Then Jack Mills laid out his paperwork, the evidence of time and expense taken on behalf of H-11-89 and the people of the state of New York.

Barone was suddenly very unimpressed. "You've got to be kidding."

"Nothing solid yet," Jack admitted.

"That's why God made detectives, Mills. To solve what on the surface appear to be mysteries."

"Yes, sir."

Barone said, "Do you understand that I am tired of telling people that nothing new has come up, that we still don't even know who she is. The people of this county pay me very good money to announce that arrests are imminent, not to appear befuddled and confused."

"Yes, sir."

"I was wondering if you'd like to get off this case. You're good at public relations; maybe this one calls for experience."

"I'm not afraid of a challenge."

"That's commendable, so long as you *are* afraid to fail. You've been at this almost three months now."

Jack said he did not think he would fail.

Chief Barone let loose an exasperated sigh and

made a show of gazing out the window. "I understand you're having some personal problems."

Jack looked at Al Trankina. "Nothing I can't handle."

Barone and Sergeant Lomack looked at each other in a way that made Jack recall the special assignment that had finally made him bail out of community relations.

There had been a drug bust planned for a nasty Hempstead saloon. Senator Thomas Otto, older brother of the county executive, was expected. The cops moved into position and waited. The senator was late, unavoidably detained at a family wedding. The bad guys in the bar noticed that their steady flow of traffic had stopped. They packed up their wares and tried to skip out the back, where they were promptly arrested. The senator arrived, three sheets to the wind. While the assistants to his assistants strapped him into a flak jacket, his aide-de-camp tried to convince the strike force to uncuff their fleeing felons and reenact the caper. He settled for Jack Mills and his community relations colleagues, who were ordered to respond to the bar forthwith. That night on the eleven o'clock news a clip ran showing the armored and exercised senator standing on a milk crate whining about heinous animals poisoning America and his personal commitment to wipe them out. In the background, Jack Mills and the rest of the humiliated actors held newspapers over their faces as they were led handcuffed from the front of the bar.

No, thought Jack, smiling weakly at Barone, he was not ready to go back on the tit. A bad day in homicide was still better than a good day at a flower show. "I'm not ready to toss in the towel." he said.

Rodney Lomack gave Barone a humble smile.

"Make it happen, Sergeant." Barone pushed himself away from the conference table as if it were covered with dirty dishes. "I know this office owes you a couple of favors, Rod. I just want you to know you're burning one now."

For the remainder of the morning, Jack worked the phones at homicide, logging in the four unsuspicious deaths reported by the precinct squads around the county, making notifications. He updated his memo book. He oiled his five-shot Smith & Wesson Chief and combed his hair twice in the men's room. His lecture agency called with a speech date in Albany, an offer Jack declined. At three o'clock he called his daughter. No answer on the first ring or the second.

Jack called his daughter every day. He coached her Catholic Youth Organization basketball team. Took her to dinner, shopping, PG-13 movies. Taught her to play tennis and golf and lacrosse. And prayed it would be enough, that Jenny would never wind up an open case in a cop's bottom drawer.

She was fourteen now, able to beat him at Scrabble, still interested in Mets tickets but angling for Maybelline's Cosmetic Bag Day giveaways at the stadium, instead of Glove Day.

This change was inevitable. He'd seen it coming that spring, during a softball game. Jenny had drilled a shot off the pitcher's shoulder. The pitcher fell in pain. Jenny stopped halfway to first to check on the guy's condition. She was thrown out by a second basegirl with different priorities. Jack had never been so proud of her. When he told her so, she had burst into tears. Jenny the shortstop, goalie, point guard, was about to become a woman.

For which he had Babe to thank, now an impossible task. Babe Downey had been as good a wife as a guy could have asked for, but he had been young and horny and dumb when he got married in college at age twenty-one.

Third-team lacrosse All-American at Syracuse. His handsome Irish face in the paper, upstate and down. At home in a world where it was acceptable to hurt and be hurt. Guys knew him; girls knew him. Every bartender at every decent Long Island night club knew him. He believed the hype and reveled in the recognition, went so far as to encourage the nickname General Mills, until Babe pointed out to him that the only other people she knew of named after breakfast cereals were Buckwheat and Farina.

And then he graduated—into thin air.

There were no professional lacrosse leagues that paid a living wage, only summer leagues and alumni games, the laid-back atmosphere of cricket. For Jack it was a period of mourning, and a string of bartending jobs. One year later Jenny was born, and Jack was still saying yes to any girl who asked. At age twenty-eight he joined the police department and doubled his pleasures. Babe, when she caught him, might have forgiven him had she found evidence of only one transgression. But as his lies unraveled, she saw she'd been played for a fool. The lawyers moved in and Jack moved out. Now it was daily phone calls and three weekly visits and a guilt that would never go away, a certain stability in its irrevocability.

On the fifth ring Babe's answering machine came on and he remembered that Jenny had tennis practice. The tape beeped.

"It's Daddy, honey. Just checking up on you. I'll talk to you later. I love you. Hi, Babe."

Jack made coffee and kicked back in his chair. He reread H-11-89 for the two hundredth time and wondered why he was so fucking dumb. Al Trankina suggested a late lunch but Jack was too agitated to eat. He was dreading telling Jenny that Katy had left him, afraid she might see him naked in the light of failure. Again.

He thought about the summer Saturday afternoon he and Jenny had gone to the Yankee game with the Emerald Society. Forty-three armed men and their sons and daughters rode a bus through the Bronx, watched a win and returned to Nassau County. Then for some reason he remembered the night of horror back in May when he had put his flashing red light on the roof of an unmarked car and raced for the south Baldwin address he'd been given, down streets he knew intimately but that now looked different, past schools that seemed useless, stores that were ridiculous.

A Nassau County patrol car was parked in front of the large modern house made of redwood and glass. The front door was open, the living room empty and dark, a room with a vaulted, stucco ceiling with skylights, modern art on the walls.

"Hello," he called out.

No one answered him.

Next to the master bedroom was a bathroom with clear glass walls. Jack ran for the rear of the multilevel house.

"Hello!" he cried.

"Yo!" A young cop's theatrically bored voice. "Down here."

"Okay."

The patrol cops were standing in the den with hands on hips. He did not know them, though they acted as if they knew him. The four kids sat on couches, wrapped in beach towels, shivering.

Jenny stood up and ran to her father. "Daddy, I'm so sorry."

Jack hugged her and fought back tears. He clutched her, rocked her.

It took a while for Jack to recover, and he decided, while his knees were still shaking, that he would forgive her whatever she had done, because she was still alive, still breathing, still his—and not about to be trundled on a gurney into the morgue in a gray rubber bag to be torn apart like meat by Dr. Corning. He blinked away his crystal vision of her pretty hands folded, surrounded by flowers in her casket, slowly lowered into the earth next to his grandparents.

Not yet, he prayed. Please, not before him and Babe and most, if not all, of her contemporaries.

Over her shoulder he sized up the boys. They were older, maybe a year or two. High school kids, he figured. Scared. Good.

One of the cops was explaining that the house belonged to one of the boys' fathers, a divorced man on vacation in Myrtle Beach. The boy lived with his mother, several blocks away. He did not have permission to be using the father's pad or frolicking in the outdoor heated pool, possibly skinny-dipping, the cops weren't sure. A neighbor had called 911.

Jack held Jenny at arm's length. "Skinny-dipping?"

"We weren't," said Jenny, opening her towel to show him her bathing suit. "Honest."

"Where are you supposed to be?" Jack asked her.

"Sleeping over Becky's."

"Where are you supposed to be?" he said, glaring at Becky, knowing full well that her parents would never allow the girls out at this hour.

"Sleeping over Jenny's."

"So where were you actually going to sleep?"

The girls looked at each other and did not answer.

Jack said, "I see."

"No, you don't see," said Jenny.

"Mind if I have a minute alone with this boy?" Jack asked the cops.

"Sure," one said. "Just don't mark him up."

"Daddy!"

"Which one of these fine lads is your date, Jenny?"

"I am, sir. David Dawkins. This is my father's house."

He was tall and well built, a nice-looking kid. Jack put his arm around the kid's shoulder and walked him out on the deck by the pool, fighting the urge to snap his neck. The water shone bright with underwater lights.

"Okay if I throw on my clothes? I'm cold."

Jack released him. "No. You just answer my questions."

"Yes, sir."

"How long have you known Jenny?"

"A little over a month."

"You like her?"

"Very much."

Jack saw David's wallet on the chaise longue, scooped it up and opened it. Inside were two ten-dollar bills, six credit cards and the telltale circular outline of a condom. Jack's right hand balled into a fist, and he wondered how many blows he might land before the precinct cops could pull him off.

"You planning on fucking my daughter?"

David paled, turning as blond as his hair. "No, sir. I just . . . carry that.

"In case you're gonna cheat on her?"

"No, sir."

Jack stared into the steaming water of the pool, then up at the stars, then around the deck. Several beer cans were stacked up on the diving board. He had not smelled alcohol on Jenny's breath.

"I'm sorry about this, Mr. Mills. It's really not as bad as it looks."

Jack said, very softly, "You seem like a nice kid. So I'm even gonna let you date my daughter. If you fuck her, you die. Do you understand?"

"Oh, yes. Don't you worry about that."

"I mean it, motherfucker."

"Yes, sir."

There was a commotion from inside the house. Becky's mother had arrived angry, a pretty brunet in a pink sweatsuit, swearing to spank her child's butt until it bled.

"I'm Jenny's father," Jack said, reentering the den alone. "Seems our girls are no longer to be trusted."

"You got that right," she said. "I'm surprised at you, Jenny Mills. I really thought at least *you* had more sense."

While the girls got dressed, Jack thanked the cops for their discretion, suggesting that the less they said back at the shop the more he would appreciate it.

"Not to worry," the shorter one assured him. "We got daughters ourselves."

Jack sent Jenny out to his car to sit and stew. He walked Becky and her mother to their car and said he would have Babe call in the morning to coordinate whatever action they took against their suddenly wayward girls.

"Fine," she said, "if Becky's still alive in the morning."

He slid behind the wheel of his own car and looked at Jenny.

"Why me?" he said.

"You're my father."

"I'd have thought you'd have given them your mother's number."

"I was going to. David gave them your name and told them you were a detective. They recognized you. After that they didn't want to hear about Mom."

Jack nodded gravely. "Do you have any idea what you've just put me through? I got a desk full of pictures of stupid little girls like you."

"We weren't gonna sleep here."

"Bullshit, Jenny."

She began to cry, and said softly, "I don't do those kind of things."

"What? Skinny-dipping? Drinking beer? Having sex with a boy you barely know?"

"We had our suits on."

"You can wreck your *life* on a punk like David Dawkins."

"He's not a punk, Daddy. He's a straight-A student and the captain of the lacrosse team."

"Lacrosse?" Jack slammed the dashboard. "He's not gonna live to graduate high school if he ever goes near you again."

Jenny's face screwed into tears and she pressed her face against the side window while Jack drove the few short blocks to Babe's house.

A light was on in the kitchen. Babe was alone, reading news that had nothing to do with her.

Jack followed Jenny into the house and told Babe what had happened, his voice choked with anger and fear. "Fourteen goddamn years old and she's out for the night with a man."

Jenny jumped in with her side of the story but got so upset and excited she couldn't finish. She sat down at the table and stared at her untied Reeboks, her chest heaving with sobs.

Babe calmed them both down, then issued a comprehensive list of punishments: "You can go out at night only to babysit or play supervised sports. No phone, except in dire emergencies. No television. Your allowance is history. And you can kiss that leather jacket you wanted good-bye."

Jenny accepted her fate without comment.

"Now get," added Babe.

Jenny left the kitchen. Jack took her seat at the table and covered his face with his hands. "Jesus."

"Okay, Jack. That ought to be enough. David is a good kid, especially considering how screwed-up his father is."

He looked up at Babe in amazement, then a rapidly expanding anger filled his chest. "But our—"

"Tell me the truth: What's got you more upset—that David's a lacrosse player or the straight A's? That he's like you or different? That she's warming up to womanhood and is attracted to jocks? Could that possibly be because you remember how spoiled jocks tend to treat their women?"

He shook his head and his eyes filled. "That's not fair, Babe."

"Oh, no?"

"I couldn't bear to lose her."

Babe paused, staring. She patted his hand. "I know that. Believe me. No one's ever doubted that you love her."

"Sorry."

"Go home and get some sleep."

Jack had wanted to say that he was home, but he wasn't, so he didn't.

Shit. It was four o'clock. He suppressed the memory, put on sunglasses and left the squad room.

He drove his unmarked black Plymouth to his daughter's bus stop in Baldwin and staked it out. Saw in *Newsday* that the prime rate was up, housing starts way down. He couldn't pay his portion of the national debt if he wanted to. He read the sports, his horoscope, "Doonesbury" and "The Far Side," then closed the paper. Tuned in "Mike and the Mad Dog" on WFAN. Learned that three more Big Eight scholarship athletes had been arrested and charged with rape. And that his alma mater faced NCAA sanctions for recruiting violations.

He smiled, remembering the play Syracuse had made for him. A Father Donohoe had arrived without an appointment one afternoon his senior year, just knocked on the door and said he had a great idea. Jack's family was not interested at first. They had been wined and dined for six months, by North Carolina, Rutgers, Johns Hopkins, Maryland. Enough was enough. Jack was going to Chapel Hill. It was all over but the phone call. Then Father D said the only two words that could have changed John Mills, Sr.'s mind: Roosevelt Raceway. Father D sprang for the valet parking, dinner and drinks for the whole family, even gave everybody fifty bucks to get them started. Before the first race, he excused himself and said he had to go chat with the boys. Ten minutes later he returned with his card marked. It took three winners before Jack's family trusted Father D enough to bet big. Then they quietly cleaned up as if they were robbing a bank. Father D left them that night with such an embarrassing pile of cash that Jack had no other choice but to star for Syracuse.

Which was not the worst thing that could happen to a kid. Not by a long shot.

The square yellow school bus ground along the shady suburban street at five miles per hour, slamming into overhanging branches and squealing to a stop at the corner. Rodney Carter, a chubby kid Jenny detested, got off first, then Amy Littleton, then Jenny. She was wearing tight gray jeans, pearl earrings and an oversized U2 sweatshirt (for which he had shelled out sixty bucks). Her light brown hair was cut short, and she carried her red nylon backpack over her shoulder, her clarinet case and tennis racket in her hands. When she noticed his car, her face lit up and his heart felt warm and lucky.

"Daddy," she cried. "What are you doing here?"

"Playing hooky."

She leaned in the window and kissed his cheek. "You're bad," she said. "How come you're not playing golf?"

"Wednesday," he said. "Big tournament."

"And?"

"I figured I owed you a shopping trip. School clothes and notebooks, right?"

Jenny smiled, but did not explode with joy as she used to over a trip to the Roosevelt Field Mall. She was getting older. It was not entirely cool to be seen with your dad, even if he was a down dude.

"I'll wear a bag on my head if you want."

"Funny, Dad." She got into his car and plucked the microphone off his dashboard. "Hey, everybody," she said, without keying the mike, "Detective Mills is goofing off with his daughter again."

"They know," he said, "they're used to it."

"That reminds me. I have to call Becky and Jackie and tell them not to come over. We were gonna work on our science project, the one I told you about, with the frogs?"

"I remember," he lied.

"You know what, Dad? Mom says sometimes you don't listen."

Babe Downey was home early from her job as a tech rep for Canon, still dressed in her light gray suit and red bow tie, looking pretty and competent, a grown-up woman of the world. Her briefcase was open, her work spread out on the kitchen table of the neat split-level house they had bought together. She wore her dark brown hair to her shoulders, and aviator eyeglasses. She said she didn't mind if Jack took Jenny out, but prior notice of his visit would have been nice. She could have gone bar-hopping, maybe found herself a decent man.

"Sure, Mom," said Jenny. "We believe you. Can me and Dad pick up that magazine I want to get?"

"Which magazine?" asked Jack.

"Seventeen," said Jenny.

"But you're only fourteen," said Jack.

"Mom?"

Babe always said that Jack had a rubber backbone at happy hours, conventions and when Jenny had him trapped in a store. She looked at him and smiled. "Don't spoil her, Jack. She won't have a wife to take care of her when she grows up."

"Mom says no, Jenny."

As they backed out of the shady driveway, Jack experienced a tiny but familiar pull of regret, a sense of some critical task undone.

"We still going to the beach with Katy this weekend?" Jenny asked.

"I doubt it."

"Why?"

Jenny said nothing while he explained, merely stared through the windshield, picking at her cuticle. Her ankles were crossed, her sneakers churning. Jack knitted his brow as he dissembled.

"So, basically, Katy is back at her mother's, and I'm holding down the fort at the house."

"She thinks you have a girlfriend?"

"Yup."

"Do you?"

"Nope."

"Then why does she think that?"

"She thinks she knows me."

Jenny gave him a rueful grin, wise beyond her years. "You really don't have a bimbo on the side?"

It amazed him that she understood about girlfriends, that she might actually know what a man would do with a girlfriend. "I said I didn't, and I was telling the truth."

"You and Mommy broke up because you had girlfriends."

"That's true. Back when Daddy was wild and—"

"So it wouldn't be like *totally* unreasonable for Katy to think that you—"

"No way. Not after all the pain I've caused you, your mother, my parents."

Jenny looked out the side window at the stores on Hempstead Turnpike. Within a block they passed a McDonald's, a Burger King, then a Roy Rogers, TCBY, Carvel, another McDonald's. Fast food for fast dudes, he thought. Jack knew he had botched this. Jenny had every right to have that look on her face.

"Mom is gonna *love* this."

An interesting point, one he had not fully considered. Babe might even start making eyes at him again, now that he was living alone.

"What do you mean exactly?" he said.

"You doing to Katy what you did to Mom."

"But I didn't."

"That's what *you* say."

She thought he was lying. His own little girl. On a subject of great importance.

She said, "I hope this doesn't make Mom go crazy."

"What makes you say that?"

"Give me a break, Dad."

"Right now the worst thing I could do would be to lean on her."

"Or the best."

"Trust me," said Jack. "You don't understand."

The kid was wishing. You couldn't blame her for that. She knew her parents liked each other.

They stopped at a traffic light behind a school bus. A high school boy made a face through the dirty glass. Jenny pulled down her sun visor, as if she did not want to be recognized. In her father's cop car. Lover Boy's car. The Jack of Hearts.

The light changed and the lady behind them honked.

"Jen?"

"Could we just go home now. I don't feel like shopping anymore."

"Sure."

She leaned her head against Jack's arm, as if she were sleepy, so he draped his arm around her and drove one-handed, treasuring the moment. He knew he did not deserve her, that her fine character was not his doing. Jenny had his eyes and his legs and her mother's heart.

When they pulled into the driveway, she sat up straight and he brushed the hair from her smooth tan face.

"You okay?" he said. He was surprised to see Jenny this upset. She got along okay with Katy, but they were not what he would call close.

"I'm fine," she said. "I was worried about you."

"Thanks a lot, Jen, but I'm okay. It's not like we haven't seen this coming, right?"

"Are you gonna tell Mom or should I?"

"I will."

"I want to be there."

"You know," said Jack, getting out of the car, "I think I want you there."

Babe was in the wood-paneled den watching Oprah chat up homosexual grandparents. She had a Hofstra sweatsuit on and slippers, a glass of iced tea by her side. Her face barely changed expression when he sat on the couch and told her Katy had moved back to her mother's, as if it were news she had long expected.

"What happened?"

"Katy thinks Dad has a girlfriend."

Babe said, "No! What is she, crazy? Where would she get a dumb idea like that?"

"Funny," said Jack.

"No . . . it's not."

He turned to Jenny. "Don't you have something you ought to be doing?"

"Yes," she said. "Watching my parents interact."

"Upstairs," said Babe. "Right now."

Jenny gave Jack a hug and a kiss. "I love you," she said, "no matter what."

Babe said nothing more until they could hear her walking the bare floor above them.

Jack stared at pictures on the wall that did not include him, marveled at how quickly Babe had got on with her life: finishing college, finding a job that paid more than his, dating people with IQs in excess of one hundred, causing him to wonder just how bad a husband he had been, how much he might have held her back.

"So how does Katy like it?" asked Babe, as if she were glad he'd been burned, glad he had finally confirmed that his adulteries weren't her fault.

Jack made things instantly worse by insisting that he hadn't been cheating, that he'd learned his lessons, albeit at her expense.

"That will comfort me in my old age," she said.

As a gesture, he admitted he had been getting friendly with one of the booking clerks.

"Like almost cheating? What's that mean—only oral sex? I'll give you credit, Jack. You could always laugh while your life was sliding down the tubes."

"Why is that, do you suppose?"

"You're a child. You picked an age you liked and stuck with it. It's gonna cost you."

3

AT TEN minutes before noon, Artie Backman kissed his wife Eloise on the top of her gray-streaked head and told her he was going to the off-track betting parlor on Hempstead Turnpike. He liked a couple of horses in the fourth race, a couple of "Speeder Rican jockeys."

She did not look up from her magazine; Artie Backman always liked a couple of horses.

It was three days after his retirement from the Nassau County Police. He was fifty-eight years old, with a smoker's cough and a trick knee he had picked up in Korea. Aside from his perpetual scowl, he wore carpenter's blue jeans, an Emerald Society windbreaker and a snub-nosed Colt revolver in an ankle holster. After toting a gun for a quarter of a century, he was not about to relinquish the privilege, nor was he confident contemporary lawmen could protect unarmed citizens. Artie Backman blamed liberal Jews for letting the Spanish and blacks run wild, but most of all he blamed the guinea governor, who year in and year out vetoed capital punishment.

"I might stop off for a beer," he added from the kitchen door. "See what's doing in town." The screen door closed behind him with a rattle and his work shoes scuffed the concrete driveway.

Eloise heaved a sigh of relief. She was not ready to share the house with him during the daylight hours. Bad enough he came home every evening.

But Artie Backman—as far as she knew—had few friends and few interests outside the job. The phone rarely rang with offers of boat rides or golf outings or tickets to Yankee games, nor had it when he was in a position to dispense department patronage. Now that he was powerless, she feared she would become his only diversion, the object of all his attention. For better or for worse, she thought, but not for lunch.

Artie, Eloise noticed, had left his half-empty PBA coffee mug on the wooden kitchen table, next to a napkin sprinkled with sesame seeds, and she thought how all the years as a cop boss had spoiled him, turned him into an inconsiderate slob. Nothing would change him now. Not Artie. She knew if she scolded him later for leaving a mess, he would tell her what he'd been telling her since the small family party Friday night: that it was his retirement, not hers, and she'd damn well better not forget it.

Eloise Backman busied herself around the house for the rest of the afternoon, smoking cigarettes, watching "All My Children," "General Hospital," then the private-eye shows on Channel Nine. During commercial interruptions, she made her daily call to their only child, Michael, at his Mineola law office, then whipped up a tray of ziti and a salad for dinner. The mail arrived, the newspaper deliveryman, to collect. A sleepy summer day on a quiet suburban street. Alone.

He left when? she thought, wondering whether to set the dinner table for two. Noon? How long does it take to place some bets and drink some beers? Five hours? She wondered if this was his idea of establishing new guidelines, what he would call breaking her in. Screw Artie Backman. She ate by herself, grimly enjoying her anger.

By eleven o'clock that night Eloise knew something was wrong. She thought about calling his friends and co-workers, but she could only think of one: Richard Mazzarella, a captain on the homicide squad, a man who had worked on the side with Artie for years, and who no longer troubled himself to stay in touch.

She considered dialing 911, but what would she report? He said he was going drinking. The precinct cops would think her foolish. And Artie would scream bloody murder when he heard. He might have driven to Hempstead or Great Neck; he might be in New York City stuffing twenties into a G-string. He was a bellicose drunk, full of arrogant opinions. He could very well be in jail. Then a thought struck her out of the blue—that Artie had simply walked out of the house with the clothes on his back and was never, ever coming back. It had happened to other wives she knew, women who thought their men were going out for a pack of cigarettes, only to discover later that the smoke shop was in Dry Tortuga.

He had opted for the lump-sum pension, $293,000 after taxes. The check from Albany was due to arrive any day now—unless Artie had beaten her to the mailbox, or had given the pension board a different mailing address and was planning on spending his golden years with someone else, far away.

She twisted her wedding ring around, thinking that would be just like Artie to knife her in the back, totally in character. She had given him the prime of her life and his only son, and now he was giving her the shaft, snatching her financial security out from under her, leaving her disgraced, to an old age of poverty and loneliness.

She picked up the phone on the bedside table and called her son at his oceanfront condo in Long Beach. "Michael," she said. "I'm worried about your father. I think he's run out on me."

Michael Backman laughed out loud. "You should be so lucky."

"Go ahead and laugh."

"Mom."

"Who'll take care of me? Who'll mow the lawn?"

"Wait . . . Ma? Don't worry so much. Remember when we used to hide in my room and wish he was dead?"

"You always know just what to say to me, don't you? I wonder where you got that particular trait?"

Michael said he would have some of his people check around. A one-track personality like his father should not be hard to find.

Eloise got into bed. She said a full Rosary, then petitioned St. Jude on Artie's behalf. Numb, her lips still moving, Eloise fell asleep and dreamed about Artie getting gas on I-95 somewhere in the

Carolinas. He had a case of German beer in the front seat and a sleeping go-go girl, wrapped in an army blanket, in the back. But in the morning he still wasn't back.

At 1313 hours on September 7, Eloise Backman reported her husband Arthur missing to Fifth Precinct police officers at the station house on Dutch Broadway in Elmont. She furnished them with detailed information: everything from his Social Security number to the name of his dentist. She gave them a picture of Arthur in his captain's uniform.

A report was filed, an alarm sent out nationwide. The cops assured her that everything would work out fine.

"Lots of guys bean out when they finally pull the pin," said the fat desk sergeant, who told her he knew Artie from way back. "It's like going through a divorce, or smashing up your favorite car. These things take time."

The sky was clear for the annual Superior Officers' Association golf tournament, the Long Island Sound a comforting blue. Next to the pro shop stood rolling bars, golf carts holding shelves loaded with booze and ice, each bearing the logo of its corporate sponsor.

Captain Richard Mazzarella, in his complimentary Bluff Point ensemble, streaks of sunblock all over his shiny bald, shaved head, was chipping to the manicured practice green. His red visor reminded Jack of the rings around Saturn.

"You sleep here?" asked Jack.

"Very funny."

Jack had been roped into running the tournament, to free up Captain Mazzarella so he could enjoy the "company of his peers."

Jack owed the man. Dicktop Mazzarella had made his promotion and transfer happen with one well-placed word. Mazzarella had clout and loved jocks.

"Everything ready?"

Jack nodded. "We got food, we got booze, golf balls, prizes. I got the stripper lined up for six o'clock, between the clambake and the cocktail hour."

"Good. You're playing with me, in a group with Charlie and Eats."

"I didn't pair Charlie with Eats," said Jack.

Eats O'Day was a terrible golfer. The year before, his cart had broken down on the twelfth hole, its gears ground to smoking dust.

"I made the switch," said Captain Mazzarella. "They're supposed to be such good friends, right? *Everybody* loves Charlie O'Connell."

Jack Mills moved to the scorer's table to welcome the players as they arrived in their sweat suits and Air Jordans, their sleeveless T-shirts and cutoff jeans, and straw hats with beer cans and lobster claws on them. The assistant pro looked at Jack and rolled his eyes.

"Wait," said Jack. "The county executive's entourage has yet to arrive."

"I think I'll get these guys out on the course as fast as I can."

"I think that's a very good idea."

The lead-off group assembled on the first tee, made their side bets and had at it. Twenty minutes later they finished the hole. The second group was worse, causing the backed-up golfers on the tee to howl at their whiffs and worm-burners.

Gilbert Otto, the Nassau County Executive, arrived with Police Commissioner Wild Bill Foley. Dicktop Mazzarella personally walked them through the arduous registration process, emphasizing how much their participation meant to the men.

Jack left the sign-in table to warm up. He had a good chance to win, along with Mazzarella and Charles O'Connell, and maybe Sergeant Peter Agassi from Highway. He had butterflies in his belly, usually a good sign.

The first tee was still mobbed, which greatly bothered Mazzarella. He had his game face on, swinging his weighted driver. Charlie O and Eats parked their cart at the end of the line. They had beers in their hands and their feet up, not at all concerned. Eats was wearing kelly green Tip O'Neill knickers and argyle socks. He was telling Charlie a joke about a penguin.

"Quiet on the tee," Mazzarella said. "We got golfers here."

Peter Agassi addressed his ball, waggled, wound up and ripped. The flight of his ball, while long, was decidedly left to right. He cut loose with an obscene stream of commentary. The ball landed on the roof of the gazebo at the entrance to the parking lot.

"Good!" he cried. "I deserved that!" Agassi lifted his leg, bent the club over his thigh, snapped the shaft, then whipped both halves into a nearby pond. "Come on," he said to his partner. "I can still get back in this thing."

The final group was up. Jack Mills, Charlie O and Richard Mazzarella all hit good shots. Then Eats waddled onto the tee. He used his club as a crutch to bend over, set his ball a good two inches in the air. In spite of his girth he made a full half-swing and, as he did so, from the fence near the gazebo came another colorful riff from Peter Agassi. It must have disturbed Eats: His ball traveled all of twenty-five yards. But he shrugged, smiled and said, "Nothing wrong with *that* baby."

After nine holes of very slow golf, Jack, Charlie O and Mazzarella were tied at three over par. Eats was on his way to shooting whatever. (It was difficult to record the score of a man who said, "Put me down for the max.") Eats did not count lost balls or provisionals, using instead a separate category of "contingency shots," the contingency being that he needed them. Yet he did not seem to have a deleterious effect on Charlie O's game. Their cart was having fun. Jack Mills, in Mazzarella's cart, was not. The Dicktop was grim as a death march.

On the tenth tee the foursome found the shaft of a golf club stuck in the ground, like a sword. A self-adhesive note was attached: HAVING A GREAT TIME AT YOUR OUTING, MILLS. DRINK POISON AND DIE. LOVE, PETE.

"I think we can count Pete out," said Mazzarella.

A rolling bar drove up. Charlie asked Jack what he was drinking.

"Beer."

"Dick?"

"Nothing."

Eats turned to the bartender. "You got shots of Jack Daniels? Put me down for three."

During the wait to hit, Eats chugged the shots and chased them down with big boy Buds. When it came his turn he was plastered. One swing, two swings, three swings, four. . . . Eats said he couldn't take much more.

"Me either," Mazzarella said through his teeth.

"Your idea," Jack reminded him.

"So was your promotion."

Jack said nothing. Mazzarella had backed him for the gold shield because he wanted to surround himself with winners, high-profile cops with ready-made reputations. Not because they were buddies.

"Hey, Charlie!" yelled Eats. "Why do dogs lick their balls?"

"Because they can."

"Nope," said Eats. "Because they can't make a fist."

Mazzarella shook his shiny head. "I hope he's driving Charlie O bonkers."

Jack said, "Doesn't seem to be."

"We gotta get rid of him. He left me a crater to putt through back there, stomping on my line. He belched on my backswing."

"You want me to tell a three-hundred-pound man, who's having the time of his life, that he's out of the parade?"

"He's killing me, Mills. That swing, those pants. Think of something."

Jack thought of something. He asked Eats for a

favor he could not refuse, and handed him a slip of paper. "I'm sorry, Eats. We don't get to see each other enough as it is."

"No problem." Eats patted Jack on the back and walked off in the direction of the clubhouse.

"Hey!" said Charlie O.

Jack told him to relax. Everything was fine.

"Where's he going?"

"To pick up the stripper. He said to tell you 'Good luck.' "

Charlie O raised his Irish eyebrows. "I hope we see him again. Eats don't get out much."

"He don't like to get too far from the fridge," Mazzarella sneered.

Jack birdied twelve to take the lead. Leaving the green, he watched a squall line rolling in from Connecticut.

On the thirteenth tee, as light drizzle began to fall, they found Agassi's putter snapped in half. The note said: THE BITCH JUST WOULD NOT BEHAVE. MORE COMING. LOVE, PETE.

Jack took a two-shot lead to the soggy seventeenth tee, where Mazzarella said, "Jeeze, you're playing good today. What a shame you can't win."

"What are you talking about?"

"You're not a boss. You're not a member of the organization."

"I'm ineligible? For even the unofficial prize? The one that's not in the rules?"

"Five grand and a weekend in Vegas?" said Mazzarella. "How would that look to the others?"

"It wouldn't bother me none," said Charlie O.

Jack flapped his hands around helplessly. "But

you told me I could play when you asked me to run it."

"I'm really sorry," said Mazzarella, feigning sincerity. "I thought you knew."

"No . . . I didn't."

Mazzarella smiled at Charlie O. "It's you and me, Charlie. Still tied. Your honor."

"But—" A beeper went off on Jack Mill's waistband.

"Aw, now ain't that a bitch," said Mazzarella. "Duty calls."

4

TRAFFIC ON the eastbound expressway was moving and the late afternoon showers had stopped. Driving to the crime scene, Jack found himself in surprisingly good spirits. He had his window open, smelling the green wet earth of the last Long Island farms, happy to be on authorized overtime, working what he knew would be a big case, a cash cow. There would be leads he could follow, concrete tasks to perform, the construction of a homicide case against a person or persons unknown—which was more than he had on H-11 -89 and was better than sitting home alone.

The Long Island Lighting Company transmission lines ran parallel to the expressway; Jack had no trouble finding the crime scene in the scrub pines next to the earthen company road, just west of Route 112.

The Crime Scene Search Unit from the Suffolk County Police Department was present, a squad of diligent ferrets nosing through the Oldsmobile Cutlass, the shallow grave, the mud around it for clues. Outside the perimeter, local and network news teams were setting up feeds. Jack saw the Suffolk County commissioner in a dark rubber slicker huddled with both chiefs-of-detectives. He found Sergeant Rodney Lomack, a confirmed nongolfer, in the Nassau County command post, a blue-and-orange bus outfitted with a high-tech arsenal and space-age communication equipment. Sergeant Lomack was on a call to a chopper pilot. He was holding a copy of Arthur Backman's departmental photograph, which had only moments before arrived from Personnel on the fax machine.

Jack asked a cop he did not know, "Where's the body?"

"They took it away."

Lomack nodded when he saw Jack, and motioned for him to get within whisper range.

"It's half ours," he said softly. "The high muckie-mucks worked it out that the crime began in Nassau County with the missing person report, but the murder probably took place here. So we'll learn to share. You'll work with a Suffolk County dick."

"Whatever. Two heads are better than one."

Lomack stroked his luxurious moustache. "Whoever brought Arthur Backman to this ignominious end was one nasty motherfucker. The medical examiner said Backman died from a sudden loss of blood due to multiple gunshot wounds to the abdomen and gonads. I'd say rage was the motivating factor here, as opposed to profit. Seems like all we got to do is make a list of Backman's enemies, and check 'em out one by one." He raised his eyebrows. "Even a rookie like you should be able to handle that."

"I only got twelve years left on the job, Sarge.

Maybe we should toss this squeal to a younger man."

Rodney Lomack smiled grimly. "Was he really as big an asshole as I've heard? I mean, he never messed with me the couple of times we crossed paths."

Jack squinted, assuming a pained expression. "As soon as you left the room he called you a nigger. Bet on it."

"I see."

"You could honestly say most everybody hated his guts."

"Don't let the commissioner hear you say that. He just called from the country club. He's treating this as a departmental tragedy."

"Tell Commissioner Foley if they try to give Backman an inspector's funeral, they're gonna have to pay massive overtime. I knew him when I was a rookie at the One-Three. He wouldn't help a dying baby."

"A lot of victims are scumbags, Jack. That's how they get to be victims. We still got to investigate, and it don't hurt if we look sad. The honky fuck was one of our own."

Lomack and Jack stepped out of the command post to watch the Suffolk County tow truck solemnly winch Backman's Cutlass out of the mud.

Lomack said, "The crime-scene guys will tear it apart at the garage, the basic vacuum number. With the windows left open and all this rain, I ain't too sure we'll like what we get. That, plus the car has been partially stripped. The speakers are gone and the radio is hanging out."

"Where'd we find the corpus?"

Lomack looked over Jack's shoulder. "Next to those little scrub pines. A jogger noticed the car, then the top half of the head sticking out of the mud."

"Suffolk County dug him up?"

"Yeah. Around two-thirty. They didn't know he was our missing person right off. He still had his wallet in his jeans, a twenty-to-win OTB ticket on a horse that ran fourth and five hundred, twenty-two dollars in cash. We found spent rounds in the mud under the body. Looked like thirty-eight hollow-points, maybe from his own gun. He was wearing an empty ankle holster."

"Where's the body now."

"The medical center—ours. You can stop there on your way back to Mineola."

"Okay." He nodded. "Anything else I should do here?"

"You gotta meet your opposite number from the Suffolk County Homicide Squad. Everybody is cooperating with everybody else and making nice."

There was an ongoing rivalry between the cops from Nassau and Suffolk. They leapfrogged each other on labor contracts and fought to the death on softball diamonds. Nassau cops considered themselves harder workers because they served the same size population crammed into a third of the area. Suffolk was expanding, growing, and looked upon Nassau as its poorer cousin.

"A Detective Williamson," said Lomack. "She's over in their bus."

"Claire Williamson?" said Jack, raising his eyebrows. "You're kidding."

"Affirmative action, my man. Unless maybe she earned what she got."

Jack said, "I wasn't complaining."

Jack had met Claire Williamson at a Detectives' Association seminar where he had served as one of the guest speakers, holding forth on the merits of sport in guiding our youth, the cost-effectiveness of police boys' clubs. They had spent time at the bar after, telling war stories, toasting mutual friends, flirting. Jack had come very close to asking for a date, and surely would have if he had not been living with Katy O'Brien at the time. He remembered she had laugh lines around her eyes and mouth, straight white teeth you wanted her to sink into your flesh.

Jack followed Lomack through the muddy reeds to the Suffolk County command post and climbed into the other county's mobile investigation center.

Claire Williamson was preparing her preliminary report at a small gray desk. She was tall, beautiful, brunet, in her midthirties and blessed with athletic lines her HOMICIDE jumpsuit did nothing to disguise. No ring on her left hand. A cigarette hung from her lips.

"Long time no see," she said. "They trust you out on the streets now?"

Jack smiled. "My mascot days are over. I caught the squeal." He offered his hand, which she shook with familial vigor. Her perfume pleased him. Crime scenes were usually such unrewarding places.

"Wanna hear the tape of the call?"

"Sure," Jack said. He sat on the edge of her desk. "Sergeant Lomack." Someone called Lomack outside. Detective Williamson hit the PLAY button on a tape recorder.

They heard a 911 operator say, "Suffolk County Police Department," then:

"Yo, po-lice?"

"That's correct."

"Yo, listen quick. You gots to send somebody down to the Mo-bile station on Route One-Twelve at Horse Block. They's a head sticking out of the mud out back."

"A human head?"

"Yeah."

"Can I have your name please?"

"Whatya need my name for?"

"To assist the investigating officers."

Silence, then the sound of a truck rushing past. "My name is Reginald T. Hanes."

"Where are you now, Mr. Hanes?"

"I'm on a pay phone, officer. At the Mo-bile station by the powerful lines."

A pause, the sound of a barking dog.

"Excuse me?"

"The sign says Mo-bile. Underneath the powerful lines. I'll be waiting for you-all. Oh, Jesus. Send someone with a gun."

"Why a gun, sir?"

"One of the dogs has got me trapped in the booth. Jesus! Help!"

Claire Williamson shut off the recorder. "Our men saved him from the dog." She handed Jack a set of her reports, looked him in the eye. "Do you always wear pink pants to work?"

"No."

"Do you always work alone?"

"The guy I team up with rarely shows," Jack said.

"One of life's limited partners?"

"They're everywhere, aren't they?"

She wrote a number on her card and handed it to him.

"Home phone?" he said.

"Fax."

He grinned. "You ever date cops?"

Claire frowned. "You don't waste any time, do you?"

"Damn biological clock . . . always ticking. Sorry."

"My dad told me the day I was sworn in—stay out of their shorts and every cop on the job will be a brother. Sleep with just one and to everyone else you'll be a whore."

Jack thought this over. "So . . . then it's really just Suffolk County cops that you don't date."

"And married men. And guys who think because I'm pretty, I'm dumb. The list goes on."

"But you party now and then."

"You don't want to know."

"I really do," he said. "One all-American to another. And then I'll tell you how lonely I've been."

"Drop dead."

Jack smiled and said, "I forgot that your dad was on the job."

"Deputy Inspector Cliff Williamson, commander of uniform patrol. My big brother John is a cop in the Second Precinct."

"Only a cop?"

She cocked her head, as if ready to take offense. "He's a union delegate. Got my big mouth and Dad's honest backbone."

"Quite a combination."

"Of course his career path has gone flatter than Kelsey's nuts."

"So it fell to you to continue the family tradition of making rank?"

"I can handle it. Here, you'd better check these items." She pushed a large manila envelope toward him.

Jack opened the evidence envelope and slid out the inventory search list of Backman's car, wallet and clothing. He read the itemized list aloud:

"Key ring, two keys for nineteen eighty-two Cutlass, two house keys, one handcuff key. One wallet—brown calfskin—containing five hundred twenty-two dollars in U.S. currency, OTB ticket purchased September fifth at twelve forty-seven hours at Franklin Square. Twenty to win on 'Speed to Burn' in the fourth at Belmont. Assorted credit cards, bank cards and a police department identification card, stamped retired. Also a list of phone numbers."

Jack looked up. Lomack stepped up into the bus. He held up a playing card, an ace of hearts, covered with tiny numbers and initials.

"Backman's. I'd like to keep it confidential if I can, for his wife's sake if no one else's."

"Sure," said Claire. "Just between us boys."

Lomack gave her a look and popped out of the van again.

"I think you hurt his feelings," said Jack.

"Hey, Jack, cut me some space, okay? You happen to be a dumb-ass rookie when it comes to homicides. You should be thanking your lucky stars that I'm not. This is going to be a big case, the kind to make or break careers."

Jack leaned against her desk. "I relish the opportunity to learn at the knee of a master."

"Jack, Jack."

"What?"

"If you never leave Long Island, you'll never know you aren't famous.

"I don't understand."

"No shit," said Claire.

Jack Mills parked behind the massive Nassau County Medical Center in East Meadow and worked his way through a noisy emergency room crowded with mostly English-speaking cops interviewing victims who spoke Spanish and Arabic and Jive. Families were arguing, crying, smoking. Jack hurried down to the morgue. He got there in time to catch Dr. Julian Corning completing his initial report on Arthur Backman.

In the basement of the medical center, under bright fluorescent lights, the swollen corpse was laid out under a sheet on a silver table with a drain. Jack was thrilled that the cadaver had been resewn, the essentials reattached. Dr. Corning depressed the foot-activated recorder and signed off. He peeled off his rubber gloves and butcher's smock and led Jack to a coffee pot in the glassed-in office. He was rather cheerful for having just spent time in someone's chest.

"Wicked," he said, raising his cup as if in a toast. "The killer had himself a wonderful time."

"What do you mean?"

"I mean, from the marks on his wrists and blisters on his palms, Backman probably dug his own grave while handcuffed. He was beaten about the face and head; a tooth on the lower left side was cracked. And you know when bad guys say they're gonna shove that badge down your fucking throat? That's what the killer did. The safety pin passed clear through Backman's tongue and lodged in the back of his throat. Then our perpetrator emptied a revolver into his crotch. Hollow-point ammunition, where less is more. There was also dirt in his mouth and throat."

Jack sipped from his Styrofoam cup. "Any sign of sexual abuse? I mean, other than blowing his balls off?"

"The anus appeared undisturbed. He had rope burns on his ankles."

"What'd he have in his stomach?"

Corning wrinkled his nose. "Peanuts and beer."

"Was he drunk?"

"I'll let you know tomorrow."

"Time of death?"

"My first guess, about seventy-two hours ago, say the evening of the fifth, give or take. A lot of big maggots, but the weather was fairly warm. Depends on how long the head was exposed before he was found. As I said, more tomorrow. A little more the day after that."

Jack remembered the childhood rhyme about worms crawling in and out, eating guts and then spitting them out. "I don't have a lot of time," he said. "When you read the papers tomorrow it's gonna look like we lost a freaking saint."

"It always looks like that at first," said Corning.

"And after forty-eight hours our chances of nailing the bad guy drop dramatically, like almost down to nil."

Corning grinned and looked at his watch. "So get busy," he said. "Your time is already up."

5

JACK WOKE up early the next morning and ran seven miles along the Meadowbrook Parkway, over the bridge to the Jones Beach tollbooths—where poor Sonny Corleone got ambushed—and back. He wore slinky purple shorts and one of his Boys' Club T-shirts, and a baseball cap down low, as if he did not want to be recognized. It was already warm and humid and he worked up a healthy, cleansing sweat before returning to his small white two-bedroom cottage on a shady side street off Merrick Road. He did his push-ups and sit-ups on his living-room floor, felt like he was warming up for an important game.

As he was coming out of his shower, the phone rang.

"Hi," Babe said. "I need a favor. Can you take Jenny to the dentist this afternoon? My calendar says you're off."

"I was, before I caught this big case. Who knows now?"

Babe said, "I'll bet you wish you still ran those bullshit kids' clinics."

"I wish a lot of things, Babe. Nobody rides the gravy train forever."

"You could have," she said. "People still ask me, 'Hey, didn't he used to be Jack Mills?'"

"I got tired of feeling like a poster child."

Babe laughed. "So who killed Captain Backman?"

"I wish I knew. This case could be a royal pain in the ass," he said, the phone on his shoulder, pulling on a pair of powder blue golf slacks, the last of his clean clothes.

"Solve it quick and get out of the limelight."

Or do my laundry, he thought. "We don't have much to go on yet."

"The lab guys will solve it. Give 'em a chance."

"You mean, before I bring my extraordinary powers of deduction to bear upon the evidence."

"Let's hope."

"I don't think this'll be a lab solution," he said. "The rain on the scene, the length of time before discovery. No witnesses have come forward . . . I mean, hey, I'd love the lab to call me and say, 'Pick up Johnny Joy Juice. We got a DNA match from an eyelash in the wound.' I could bill my time to H-eleven-eighty-nine and hang out for the last little bit of the summer." He mopped at his hair. "Gotta go, Babe. Give Jen a big kiss and I'll call you later."

"Okay if we share?" asked Claire, nudging him aside.

"Huh?"

Jack had just closed his locker door in the corner of the dismal bullpen. He had not heard her approach.

"Sure. Feel free. I never lock it anyway."

Claire opened the door, took one look inside, then turned to Jack and said, "Very becoming. Evidence from a sex crime?"

Jack looked back inside, saw hanging from the center hook the black leather hood with zippers over the eye and mouth slots.

"No," he said. "My promotion party. Remarkably effective at interrogations too."

"Lovely. What else you got in here?" She rummaged through the back, finding a lacrosse stick and spikes, an outdated trooper's manual. Then the top shelf: "Cologne, soap, baby oil, bullets, knives, Tums. What, no French ticklers?"

"Fresh out," Jack said.

Claire hung her blue blazer on an empty hook. From her belted skirt hung a Glock nine-millimeter automatic with twice the firepower of his piece and four times more expensive. The sleeveless white blouse she wore showed her well-defined biceps and triceps. Jack knew guys who would have loved to have arms like that.

Rodney Lomack slid into Eats's broken chair. Claire stood, even though both men offered a seat.

Jack read the description of Backman's clothing.

"Skip down to the car," said Lomack. "The glove compartment."

"A withdrawal slip from the Franklin Square branch of Citibank for five hundred dollars. Ray-Ban sunglasses. Nassau County road map, property of Nassau County Police Department. What's the matter, Sarge? Are you pissed he glommed a map?"

"The withdrawal slip," said Lomack. "I always stick mine in my wallet with the card. I was wondering why Backman put his in the glove compartment."

Jack threw out his withdrawal slips as soon as he got them, but he knew better than to tell that to Rodney Lomack. He didn't want to hear about raising five kids on a flatfoot's paycheck, working two side jobs while finishing college, paying full price for everything because most merchants were white.

"See if this is a joint account or if Backman had a stash of his own," Lomack said.

"Right," said Claire, taking notes. Then to Jack, "Keep reading."

The report listed five distinct types of human hair in the car and three in the trunk. Lomack said the night men had been dispatched to get samples from Mrs. Backman and anyone else she knew who had ridden in the car. The report concluded with an item about some grease smeared on the fabric upholstery of the back seat.

"What kind of grease?" asked Jack.

"They're working on it."

Lomack showed them the blown-up color photographs of Arthur Backman's physical removal from the crime scene. The bloated hands were not cuffed, and Jack remembered that no handcuffs had been recovered. They studied the aerial photographs of the surrounding area, the dirt road through the forest strewn with tires and construction debris, the car tracks, the bicycle tracks, the muddy footprints of more than one jogger, more than one thief.

"What kind of canvass did we have?" asked Jack.

"A quick one," said Lomack. "Claire, talk to Suffolk about doing some more, like maybe a roadblock next Monday night around the time we think he went into the ground."

"You got it."

"Where do you want to start?" Lomack asked Jack.

Jack picked up the ace of hearts. "I'd say we gotta find out what Backman liked to do when he thought no one was watching."

"That makes sense," Claire agreed.

Jack said, "I'll stop by the One-Three to see if Backman had any cases pending against the really bad boys. Plus maybe someone down there has got some good ideas. Claire can talk to Mrs. Backman. Then we'll start calling the numbers on Backman's ace of hearts."

"Can you keep all these balls in the air?" Lomack said.

Jack said, "Give us forty-eight hours to lay it all out."

"I'd give you longer than that, but I don't believe Chief Barone will be so inclined. He'd rather keep us media stars unsullied by failure, if you know what I mean. If we can't show him progress by tomorrow night, he might panic and bring in one of the older hands."

"Like?"

"Maybe Dicktop Mazzarella. I hear he was one of Backman's many friends."

Jack winced. Captain Mazzarella was in charge of a different zone, but outranked them nonetheless.

"I don't like having jobs snatched away," said Lomack. "It would mean the boys don't trust my judgment."

"What do you care what the politburo thinks?"

"Don't give me heartburn. Go build me a scenario."

The desk officer at the ramshackle Thirteenth Precinct was holding a cheeseburger hero with one hand and talking on the phone. The signal monitor was bent over a Rolodex, checking an address for one of the radio cars. He looked up when the door closed, and waved Jack Mills through to the precinct commander.

Jack Mills had worked the One-Three right out of the police academy, suffering nobly through eighteen months of deadly chaos that drove him happily into community relations. It was downtrodden and dangerous. Down where human life was Third-World cheap. Civilians drove around it or their armed drivers made sure they had their doors locked.

Inspector Mad Mario Cullen was at that moment arguing behind the closed office door with Captain Oliver Notso Keene. Notso Keene was the late Arthur Backman's replacement and, from the sound of the argument, off to a rocky start.

Jack knocked on the wooden door, then turned the knob.

"Yes?" said Mario Cullen, as Jack entered. Inspector Cullen was a bowlegged Ichabod Crane type with good enough political connections to compensate for a lack of brains. He was seated at his big wooden desk, eating a container of raspberry yogurt. Notso Keene stood in front of him, fists balled and jaw clenched.

"Jack Mills, sir . . . from homicide? I'm here

about Arthur Backman. I need to talk to several people if I may."

"Talk to me," said Notso Keene. "I'm the one holding the goddamn bag."

"Excuse me?"

"The son of a bitch never did his job," said Captain Keene. "His desk drawers are filled with unopened mail, requests for evidence from the district attorney, subpoenas, medal of valor recommendations, overtime cards. And the fucking men are ready to mutiny."

"Relax," said Inspector Cullen, waving his hand. "They're always ready to mutiny."

The captain said, "I can't get any of them to be pallbearers. And if I order them, I gotta pay them. Most of them are happy as clams that Backman bought his lunch."

Mad Mario Cullen slammed his palm on the desk. "Are you telling me, Captain, that this simple little assignment has you buffaloed? I promised the commissioner a respectable turnout, and he shall have one, do you understand? Or you will be scrubbing the prisoners' latrine."

The color drained from Notso's face. His voice wobbled as he spoke. "Inspector, if you paid attention to what went on around here, you wouldn't be promising things you can't deliver."

"You, sir, are coming dangerously close to a charge of insubordination."

"Are you threatening me, Inspector?" asked Notso Keene.

"I most certainly am," said Mad Mario.

"I oughta kick your ass."

Mad Mario invited Keene to try it.

Jack Mills, who usually enjoyed warfare between superior officers, noticed that Notso Keene looked suddenly not so keen. He was struggling for air, clutching at his shield, then down on one knee he went and onto his back.

Jack threw open the office door and yelled for an ambulance. He knelt beside Oliver Keene, ready to start CPR, trying to remember the procedure—how many breaths to how many pumps? Two quick, then one to five? He tipped Keene's head back, then opened the mouth and cleared the frothy airway with his fingers. As he contemplated the coated tongue and yellowed teeth, the rancid smell of cigarettes, it occurred to him that Inspector Mad Mario Cullen should breathe life into Notso Keene and he should pump the heart. "Inspector?"

"Awkk."

"You want to give me a hand here?"

"Awk—ca't breathe."

Jack looked up. "Huh?"

Mario Cullen was tipped back in his swivel chair, grabbing his own heart, eyes begging for help, his face a healthy pink.

"Come on, Inspector!" Jack snapped. "Captain Keene's changing colors."

Inspector Cullen pointed to his own chest. "Heart attack," he said. "He gave me a heart attack. You saw it." The precinct commander closed his eyes and slumped onto his desk.

Jack rushed over and frantically searched for a pulse. He felt a strong carotid pulse and gave Cullen's bony body a shake. "Will you *stop* fucking around. Inspector! Help me?"

Inspector Cullen lifted his head off the desk. "Save Notso," he croaked valiantly. "Don't worry about me."

"Seriously?" Jack asked.

Cullen groaned and fell forward again, his hand knocking his phone off the desk. The signal monitor ambled reluctantly into the office, mumbling something.

"Motherfucker!" Jack cried out to the signal monitor for another ambulance and—if anyone was interested—a little help. He might have managed to resuscitate Notso by himself, but he had never heard of one man breathing for three, while manually pumping two hearts.

Fortunately for Jack, Mad Mario Cullen, when lowered to the floor, made clear his intention of refusing mouth-to-mouth by clamping his jaw shut and whining. So Jack and the signal monitor knelt on the carpet and saw to the cardiopulmonary needs of Notso Keene until medical personnel arrived.

While a pair of stretchers were being rolled into Inspector Cullen's office, Jack went downstairs to the locker room, rinsed out his mouth, and washed his face and hands. He was standing at the sink, staring, when he heard a familiar voice say hello.

In the mirror, Tommy Bledsoe, a tough old salt, was grinning at him. "I heard you just gave Notso head."

"It's okay. I didn't swallow. How ya been?"

"Other than this lousy job I got, everything else is going good. I'm back with the wife."

"This place is still a zoo, I see."

"I think it's something in the air." Tommy shouldered past Jack to the urinal. "Any idea yet who blew Backman's balls off?"

"Nope."

"I heard upstairs that a task force was being assembled to solve the case."

"Lomack said things would get hot."

Tommy stepped back and zipped his fly.

Jack said, "Tell me about Backman, would ya? I always tried never to have anything much to do with him."

"I don't like to speak ill of the dead, especially other cops, but in Artie's case I'll make an exception. He was a motherfucking dog. If he liked you—meaning, if you kissed his ass—he'd give you free rein. If he sensed the smallest streak of independence in you, he spared no effort to make your life miserable, to drive you out. Constant squad changes, the worst posts, the worst assignments. Your mother was dying and you needed the day off? Too fucking bad. An hour, for a teacher's conference? Get bent. If you called in sick, he came to your house in a patrol car to take your temperature, rectally. Of course *his* favorites could call in sick from Las Vegas collect, or snatch an afternoon off to score a chick. Good old Mario let him run this dump like a plantation. He enjoyed everybody hating everybody else; no one had time to hate him."

"You going to the funeral?"

"I wouldn't have pissed on his head if his hair was on fire."

"Anybody here hate him enough to kill him?"

"Almost everybody."

They walked from the bathroom to the muster room and sat on the Universal bench. Jack rolled dumbbells on the floor beneath pictures of softball teams and fishing trips, good-guy trophies and plaques. Sirens wailed as the ambulances roared off to different hospitals.

"What about his personal life?" Jack asked. "Booze, broads, drugs."

"Heavy gambler, moderate drinker and not at all above dipping the wick here and there. He might have lanced the wrong old lady. Or he might have gotten in deep to the shys. I really couldn't tell you. We never hung out."

"Who did he hang out with?"

"Domminich Gaglio, before they locked him up DWI. Joey Bagadonuts. Bobby Sellers could tell you more specifics. Him and Backman worked together on the side sometimes, roofing. And of course the Dicktop was his rabbi." Tommy shook his head and grinned. "Artie sure did get to enjoy his retirement, didn't he? One fucking weekend. Is fate a bitch, or what?"

6

MRS. BACKMAN?" Claire Williamson knocked again on the screen door, her shield hanging from her blazer breast pocket.

"Yes? Who's there?"

"Detective Williamson, ma'am. I need to ask you a couple of questions."

Eloise Backman unlocked the door and let Claire into the kitchen. She wore a purple flowered housedress and slippers, no makeup. Her face was drawn with fatigue, her posture stooped. Her hands shook when she lit her cigarette.

"What's happened?" she said, blowing the smoke away from her. "Have you got any news?"

"Nothing yet, Mrs. Backman. Everything that can be done is being done, I assure you."

"I know. It's just . . . hard, not knowing who, or why." She offered Claire a seat at the table, a cup of fresh-brewed coffee.

Claire set out her clipboard, her walkie-talkie, and made herself comfortable in Artie's old chair at the head of the table. She heard a shower running upstairs. Eloise told her that her son had come to stay with her.

"That's nice," said Claire. "I'm glad there's someone here for you. Did Arthur have a very large family?"

"So-so. They weren't real close, but I expect they'll show up now to eat me out of house and home." She laughed nervously and looked at her watch.

"Did Artie have many enemies?" Claire said.

Mrs. Backman did not look stunned, nor did she take offense. She simply nodded her head up and down, then side to side in sorrow.

"He was very insecure," she said. "He also had a very short temper."

"Any ideas about who might have killed him?"

"Not really. He kept his life to himself, I'm afraid."

Claire tapped her pen on the clipboard. "Was yours a happy marriage, Mrs. Backman?"

"We lived together twenty-eight—no, twenty-nine years."

"I understand . . . but that's not what I asked you."

Mrs. Backman stubbed out her cigarette and lit another. Her brow was furrowed, her expression bleak. "Maybe he was happy, having me around to cook and clean. You couldn't say I was all that thrilled."

"May I ask what the problem was?"

"Look," she said. "I was the wife of a cop. I know you have to ask me these things. You'd make it easier on us both if you'd stop looking so serious."

"I'm sorry," said Claire. "It is serious."

Mrs. Backman lowered her head, then wiped her cheeks with her fingertips.

"Hey," Claire said. "When my grandfather died, my grandmother was absolutely devastated, and they never got along either."

"That's supposed to cheer me up?"

Claire mimicked a smile.

"Artie screwed around, honey. Just like all the other cops. Especially when he was new on the job. He made a fool of me, time after time, never once said he was sorry. I took his bullshit because of Michael, but I never forgave him. We stayed together because we weren't done fighting."

"Were you aware of any recent . . . relationships?"

"No," she said. "None recently. His hormones stopped raging quite a while ago, although his character didn't improve. Sometimes I think he lied to me just to see if he could pull it off. What else can I tell you? He gambled on everything, and I suppose you could say he was a nasty drunk. Everyone else did. We never got invited anywhere twice."

The thought crossed Claire's mind that she and Jack were wasting their time, that the world was obviously much better off without Artie Backman, and whoever did it should get a reward.

"You've got a tough case," Eloise Backman said, smiling oddly at her. "Anyone could have done it."

Claire gazed between the bamboo curtains out the window, then above Mrs. Backman's head, at the brown cork message board, the notes to return phone calls, the invitation to attend an upcoming police conference dinner, a memo about a doctor's appointment.

"Did Artie mention anyone threatening him, or any ongoing problems with any particular people?"

"No one in particular. I told you, his problems were with everyone." This seemed to amuse her, to mitigate guilt for the tone she was taking. Her wistful smile was understandable; she was one of many who had been duped.

"Mrs. Backman, were you aware of a savings account at the Franklin Square Citibank, from which Artie withdrew five hundred dollars on the day he was killed?"

"I thought we did all our banking at National Westminister."

"Can I ask you a personal question?"

"This other stuff wasn't personal?"

"This is more personal."

"Go ahead."

"Do you want us to find Artie's killer?"

She looked down at her rough red hands. "I don't honestly know," she said, her chest rising for air. "Isn't that horrible?"

"No, ma'am," said Claire. "Not if it means that you're afraid of getting hurt. Of learning things you'd rather not. It's human, very normal."

She nodded, tight-lipped, a beaten woman, but not a killer. Claire couldn't imagine her doing it, or even arranging it: the phone calls, the down payment, sitting by the radio, listening for the news. Claire usually tried to keep an open mind until all the evidence was in hand; even so, she scratched Eloise Backman from her list of primary suspects.

She could check her out in an afternoon, with one or two phone calls—progress, of a sort. Claire heard footsteps.

A man's voice called, "Mommy?"

Michael Backman entered the kitchen wearing a white summer suit and mustard tie. His hair was wet, slicked back. His mother introduced them, then hugged her son and called him "all she had left."

"Okay if we take a ride?" he said, looking over his mother's head.

"Whatever makes you comfortable."

They excused themselves and went outside. Michael's new Mazda four-door was parked in the driveway, behind his mother's car. They got in without speaking. Michael backed out into the street and they cruised the working-class neighborhood of small brick houses where he had grown up. He was careful to signal for each turn and came fully to a halt at each stop sign.

"It's funny," he said finally. "You're exactly the kind of cop my father despised—I mean a woman, which is neither here nor there, except that now you're working his case."

"What can I do for you, Michael?"

"I wanted to ask you to go easy on my mother. The old man croaking like this was more than she can take. The embarrassment alone . . ."

"I know that," said Claire. "And I feel for her. Still, she does seem rather ambivalent. Under certain circumstances she might even be considered a suspect."

"Come on."

"It happens all the time."

"I was wrong," said Michael, shaking his head. "You cops are all alike."

Claire was not a world-class martial artist, nor was she quick to fly off the handle, but she was good enough not to have to take guff from guys who used extra-hold mousse. "Listen, my man—"

"You listen, lady detective. This morning we gave your buddies samples of our hair, we gave depositions regarding the day the crime took place. We both have ironclad alibis. The phone records will match what we told you. Mom didn't do it, and I didn't do it. My father was killed by a criminal because he was a cop; I think that's where your focus belongs."

"What makes you say that?"

"Because I know for a fact that we didn't do it, so who else could it have been?"

Claire looked across at him. "Interesting logic. What are you, a lawyer?"

"As a matter of fact."

"Big shot? Little shot? Memberships in all the right clubs?"

"As a matter of fact. Yeah. Rockville Links here and Southampton out east—you know, for weekends. Part of the package. You really never heard of me?"

"I'm a Suffolk County detective, temporarily assigned."

"I work for a prominent firm in Nassau, a firm known for its close ties to the Republican Party. Nassau cops know who I am."

"Ever take your dad to play?"

"Get real."

Michael Backman drove past his mother's house

once again, seemed tempted to stop, but continued down the block. He looked like a man with a weight on his chest.

"My father was a small man with a small life. He never went to a Broadway play, he never went to a museum or a church, he never owned stock. He read *Police Chief,* the "Letters" section of *Penthouse,* and the *Racing Form.* He thought the world began and ended with the Nassau County Police Department. Everything else was unnecessary static, including his family. Everyone else was scum. His killer must be someone from his past, maybe someone he arrested."

"That's pretty rare," said Claire. "The manner of your father's death seems to indicate a more personal motive."

"Such as?"

"Such as revenge."

Michael Backman shook his head. "For a pretty girl you got a very suspicious mind."

"Mike, I'm looking at everybody and everything. Please don't take it personal."

"I take it personally when my mother is upset. That man made her suffer enough when he was alive."

"How about you?" asked Claire. "Did he break your balls growing up?"

"Oh, yeah," said Michael, snorting. "Every chance he got. The neighbors can tell you. My mother can tell you. But I was smarter than him, and then I was richer than him, and in the end I had him kissing my ass."

"How touching," she said.

* * *

"Hi, Daddy," said Jenny Mills, lugging her sports bag into her mother's kitchen. "Are you gonna make me play golf again?" She was wearing a pink swimming suit and loose white shorts, her hair neat and trim, back from the face that looked like his.

"Whatever you want."

"Hoops," she said.

"You got it."

Outside it was sunny and warm, the wind blowing inland. She popped a Sinead O'Connor tape into his Volkswagen Rabbit cassette player and made him listen to her favorite new song twice during the ride back to his house. They picked up their ten-speed bikes and rode over to Merrick Park, next to the closed town landfill. The court was empty. At her request, Jack gave Jenny a refresher course in basketball basics. She had try-outs coming up, and wanted to leave nothing to chance.

"Stay balanced on defense, Jen, feet on the ground. Coach K at Duke has his guards touch the floor on each trip to remind them to stay low."

Jack watched Jenny bend her knees and touch the court, then shuffle her feet side to side while he dribbled the ball around the perimeter. He looked one way, then the other, rocked back and swished a soft fall-away shot.

"Don't go for head fakes, Jen. There's always time to react if you don't get fooled."

On the hot blacktop court Jenny picked up the ball and drove left, using her weak hand, kept going under the basket and threw in a reverse lay-up while Jack hung in the air on the wrong side off the rim.

Jack clapped and whooped. "Doesn't matter what size you are when you move around the hoop like that. Manute Bol couldn't block it. Now try the drop step."

Later they splashed about in the surf at Lido Beach, then Jack tried to sleep on the beach while Jenny read aloud the first five chapters of the latest Nancy Drew mystery and pestered him to solve it as the clues were revealed: "You're supposed to be a detective. You oughta be able to outsmart a girl."

"Some feminist you've turned out to be." He got up and began gathering their things.

"Look who gave me lessons. Talk to Katy lately?"

Jack shook his head no. "Her mom says forget about it."

Jenny brushed sand from her knees and helped him shake the blanket. "Do you miss her, Dad?"

Jack shrugged. Katy was rigid and moody, with a list of complaints: His job sucked, he wouldn't get married, he still liked Babe and spent too much time with Jenny, their rented house was so much smaller than Babe's. He was better off without her.

After a visit to the dentist and a couple of milk shakes, he dropped Jenny at home and drove back to Merrick. The day's mail consisted of three bills.

Jack did his push-ups and sit-ups and showered again, then drove down to the Jones Beach Theater to see Little Feat play under the stars. He met his high school buddies, who had ordered the tickets in advance, and told the boys he was solo again. Stack and Berezuk made him feel better right away. They kidded him about his posters, reminded him of his excellent track record.

Berezuk wrapped an arm around him and said, "There's always beer, Jack. Don't forget that. It never minds if you bring a different beer home. It's okay to have more than two. It never talks back and you don't have to wash it to make it taste good."

The sun set red, and the smell of the beach made him ache for his youth. He sold Katy's ticket at the gate for face value.

7

JACK STOPPED at a deli to pick up his morning coffee and a copy of the newspaper. Alone at his gray metal desk in the murky blue bullpen, he read the lurid accounts of Arthur Backman's murder, the "no comment" quotes from the high command, the attribution of grief and bereavement to the widow and the son, and endorsements by rich men of capital punishment.

To the uninitiated, Arthur Backman was a beloved hero with twelve decorations, a man who had earned a long and happy retirement. A guy who would be missed by friends and loved ones. A prince of a cop. Jack pulled the ace of hearts from the evidence bag and wondered if one of the numbers scrawled on it would produce someone who would actually miss the late Captain Backman.

Flipping the card in his fingers, Jack remembered his own secret life years ago, the lies and the tension, dressing his bimbos in high heels and garters, the marriage ultimatums, his eventual disgrace. He remembered Babe's comment when she found a greeting card in his glove compartment: "I know there've been others, Jack, but this one's got me worried." That was Dana Something-or-other. He hadn't loved her. He would not have wanted her notified of his demise.

The first number he dialed—a Brooklyn exchange—was answered by a male with a gruff voice and limited education. "Yeah," he said. "What'll it be?"

"I'm calling regarding a man named Arthur Backman." Jack logged the time on the telephone interview form.

"Artie Backman's dead."

"I know that. My name is Detective Jack Mills. I'm investigating the case for the Nassau County Police Department."

"Jack Mills, eh? Not the lacrosse player?"

"A long time ago, my friend."

"Oh, yeah? Far out. I saw you guys lose at Hofstra."

"And who might you be?"

"I was Artie's tout," said the voice. "I picked his winners."

"Oh yeah? How was he doing?"

"He died two hundred bucks in the hole—to me. So figure it out."

"Sorry to hear that. If you want to give me your name and address, I'll have the PBA send you a check."

"Yeah, right."

"Who else did Artie owe?" asked Jack.

"I'd love to name names, Detective Mills, believe me. Maybe thin out the field, so to speak. But that would be foolish, from the safety point of view."

"The bookmaking field?"

"Say what?"

Bookmakers were rough customers, but they didn't murder clients for hundreds or even thousands of dollars, not where a shattered kneecap would suffice.

Jack doodled on the margin of the form. "What kind of player was the dearly departed?"

"A hoople, like all the others. He bet too much when he was wrong and too little when he wasn't. He was sloppy, too—always calling me from the station house to save a frigging quarter. I'd say he laid out three, four hundred a month on action, maybe a little more—unless he was bragging. Now and then he said he fronted bigger bets for a friend at headquarters."

"Do you know the friend's name?"

"Nope."

Jack made a note of this. "You sure you don't want to give me your name and address?"

"Not really."

"I could find out."

"Not before I could change it."

"Why go to all that trouble? I'm Nassau Homicide, not New York Vice. I couldn't care less about horses."

"Sports," said the voice, offended. "Baseball, football, college hoops and like that. No ponies. Off-track betting killed the great horse books."

"Right. Sorry."

Jack got himself another cup of coffee. When he returned to his desk, Sergeant Quickstop Izzy Goldman, Richard Mazzarella's personal stooge, was sitting in his chair, reading through his case jacket, and examining the ace of hearts.

"Hi, Izzy. What can I do for you?"

"Nothing, kid. I was on my way to heave a Havana but it was standing room only in the john. Ah ha! I see an opening. Later, kid."

Jack sat down and picked up his phone. He spoke to Arthur Backman's brother-in-law in Utica, who knew about the murder; his wife was on her way down.

He spoke to Backman's life insurance agent, who had just today been informed of the untimely passing of his valued client.

"A modest policy," he lamented. "How many times did I warn him?"

"I don't know," Jack said. "How many?" But the phone had gone dead.

He dialed another number from the ace of hearts, spoke to the cashier at the Spartacus Diner on Main Street in downtown Belmont. Then the bartender at Blotto's Pub. A woman who said she dated Backman three years ago, another woman who thought he was single. Jack made notes and gnawed his nails. Around him, in the bullpen, other detectives worked other cases, or chatted on the phone with their friends. Rodney Lomack left his office twice, both times glancing apprehensively at Jack, neither time stopping to peer over his shoulder or ask for an update. Across the hall in a conference room, a half-drunk clam digger from Seaford was confessing on videotape to the hammer murder of his wife. The phones rang constantly.

Jack got two more no-answers, a porno-personal answering machine, a wire room—and then the law offices of Benz, Tisch, Hamilton, upon whom he hung up.

The next one a woman answered, her voice sharp, annoyed, maybe sleepy, even at three-thirty in the afternoon. Jack paid no mind to her petulance, just rattled off his name, his case, the fact that her telephone number had been found in Arthur Backman's wallet.

"That's impossible," she said. "Artie Backman was a married man. Why would he have my number?"

"Look, lady, I didn't say you were sleeping with him, I just said your number was found in his wallet. I'd like you to give me your name and address so that I can arrange an interview. No big deal. We do this all the time—talk to friends of the victim."

"You wanna talk to me, you call my lawyer."

"Fine. What's his name?"

The line clicked dead.

Jack redialed. Busy. He made another note on his pad: BITCH—check reverse directory.

"How's it going, Jack?" asked Lomack, as he walked past Jack's desk yet again.

"Just ducky. You want to know what I know?"

"Come into my office," said Lomack. "I got five minutes before I walk that poor bay rat through his photo opportunity."

"Not another one, Sarge. Have you considered the risks of over-exposure?"

One of Rodney Lomack's personal affirmative-action tactics was to make himself available for reporters and photographers whenever a collar went down. The average *Newsday* reader saw him four or five times a month, his face solemn, shoulders squared, leading manacled killers to justice.

"Consider it a public service," Lomack said, and closed the door behind them. "Think of how good it must make all our white friends feel to see a spade like me hauling in the slime."

"Yeah," said Jack. "And think how bad it makes the Dicktop feel."

"Screw him," said Lomack. "He's already called me twice today to see how 'Barbie and Ken' were doing. He thinks I'm nuts to leave the case in your hands."

"My rabbi, turning on me."

"They don't call him the Dicktop for nothing."

"He could help. It's not like we don't have legwork coming out the ass."

"If it comes to that, I'll help, or get you help, but we ain't rolling over for that scumbag guinea fuck. Do I make myself clear?"

"Don't you always?"

"Court Liaison called before. Backman didn't have any cases pending. No arrests in the last seven years. I got a call in to Parole to see if any of his collars have been recently released."

"Thanks."

"The medical examiner's toxicological report concluded that Artie had a buzz on when he died, but only booze, and not so much he didn't know what was happening."

Jack shuddered, imagining the smell of earth, the

absence of light and air. "Claire says his wife didn't know about the bank account. That must have been his mad money."

Lomack nodded. "Find out how much."

"We will."

"Possible big picture?"

"Everybody did it."

"Okay, Jack, you're out of here. I got a date with the Mineola press corps."

"Give 'em a big white smile for me, sir."

Lomack threw on his suit jacket and left. Jack made another cup of coffee in the squad-room kitchen and returned to his cluttered desk. A note was taped to his telephone. Detective Claire Williamson, SCPD Homicide, desired a call.

She answered on the first ring.

"Hey," he said. "Jack Mills here."

"Hi. How ya doing?"

"Progress," he said. "Tremendous progress."

"Nothing, huh?"

"The sharks in my office are already swimming around me."

"I know the feeling," she said.

"That's one of the drawbacks, I suppose, of being such a hot tuna."

Claire did not laugh. "Fax me everything we got, Jack. On second thought, meet me at the Roadside Diner in Hauppauge with the whole damn file."

Like Hauppauge, the Roadside Diner on Nesconset Highway had successfully made the transition from small-town crummy to corporate cool. Once aluminum-sided, then stucco and tiled, the diner was now polished steel and gray formica, the curtains mauve, with smoked glass partitions between booths. But the waitress who brought their coffee wore a tight black miniskirt, which is what waitresses wore back when the diner was aluminum.

Jack and Claire faced each other over paperwork, taking turns reading upside down. When Jack had digested her notes on Michael Backman, he asked Claire if she considered him a possible.

"I consider him a pompous little ass. He actually acted indignant that I didn't know he was a suckass political lawyer, a job his daddy probably got for him."

"I don't get you. You're the daughter of a boss, you've got yourself a nice gig, and yet you say you don't like politics?"

"My brother is the son of a boss. See what that got him?"

"So what's the catch?"

Claire sipped her coffee and lit a cigarette.

"Well?" asked Jack.

"I made homicide for one and only one reason. I killed a perp in the line of duty."

Jack sat up straight. "I didn't know that."

"It wasn't on the sports page."

"Tell me what happened."

Claire smiled. "I'll tell you if you'll tell me why you're wearing the same shirt you had on two days ago."

Jack looked at his white button-down shirt. "What gave me away?"

"The tomato stains on the pocket. And the khaki suit has seen better weeks."

"My girlfriend walked. I'm running out of

clothes and food at a frightening rate. Can you imagine?"

"Of course I can imagine. You've been on scholarship since the sixth grade. Coaches, trainers, tutors. You're helpless. Why would anyone want to make Jack do something for himself? He scores all those goals . . . and all those chicks. Don't think they did you any favors."

He shrugged. She didn't know what it was like, how much fun he had had, how special those people had made him feel.

"Laundry's simple, Mills. You wash first and dry second. Do you want her back?"

"Hell no."

"Let me tell you how I got here, okay?"

"To teach me a lesson?"

"We had this crack addict working Wyandanch when I was on foot patrol there. He liked to ambush telephone linemen when they were alone, up on the poles. Point a gun at them and make them throw down their wallets. He scored twice before he lost his cool and shot one of them. I'll never forget what that poor guy looked like, hanging upside down from the pole, head covered with blood. So I got pissed and staked out the area on my own the next night. Tucked my hair into a cap, put on my vest and my raincoat and climbed a pole. Set up my video camera to film straight down. Not twenty minutes later Derrick Cody came by. 'Yo, bro,' he says. 'Chuck down the bread.' I tossed him a wallet with twenty dollars in it. 'Thanks,' he said."

Claire fell silent.

"I get the picture," Jack said.

She shook her head. "He pointed his gun up at

me and said, 'Here's something to help you forget what I look like.' From there it was easy. I put one in his forehead and two in his shoulder. He was dead before I could climb down. They showed the film to the shooting review board and I won a combat medal and a promotion to detective." She did not so much as glance away. "Even my dad had never killed anyone."

Jack wanted to slide around to her side of the booth and hold her. He wanted to punch up a couple of love songs on the jukebox and have her dissolve in tears on his chest. He wanted her to know he understood: You can be proud of yourself and sorry as hell, all at the same time. It was what manhood was all about.

"So you've got your game films too," was what he said.

She tossed her head, shaking off her mood. "I don't haul them out and watch them much. I don't know why I did it now." She sipped the dead coffee, then said, "What's the drill tomorrow?"

"You take the list of precinct co-workers. I'll do his hangouts."

"Let me get this straight," Claire said. "You think I should spend the day breaking down departmental and sexual barriers to get a few simple questions answered while you tour the bars of Franklin Square?"

"That's not *exactly* how I'd put it."

"I didn't say anything the other day when you tried to pull this bullshit because I didn't want to embarrass you in front of your boss, but when it comes to dividing the work around here, I think you should at least ask my opinion."

"Fine," Jack said. "You think I should do the cops?"

"Yes."

"And you should canvass the bars?"

"Yes."

"Meet back here at the end of the day?"

"You're catching on," said Claire.

"Any way we could do this together?"

Claire arched her eyebrows. "Whatever for?"

8

YOU WANT to know what Artie Backman was really like? You want to know if I know of anyone who wanted to do him?"

"In a nutshell," said Jack, peering through the screen into the dingy kitchen of the L-shaped cottage in Freeport. It was early afternoon. The south shore was socked in by fog and the smell of dead fish and diesel fuel.

Bobby Sellers, retired street cop, now a bronzed and grizzled roofer, opened the door and let him in. Jack sat down at the small wooden table, which was littered with unopened mail and magazines. A mountain of dirty dishes rose from the sink. Something somewhere was spoiling quickly.

"You want a beer?"

"No thanks. You go ahead, though."

"It's after noon, right?"

"The drinking lamp is lit," said Jack.

Sellers opened his refrigerator, cracked a Bud. "Artie Backman—DOA. Man, you just never know."

"I'm hearing from some of the other guys that he might have deserved it."

Sellers pursed his lips to indicate deep thought or pain. "I don't know about that. He was okay with me, but then I was his boss when he wanted some side work. I wouldn't have put up with him the other way around. I paid him real good money and he worked for me like a son of a bitch. Then, nine times out of ten, he pissed it away at the track or chasing pussy. We used to go hunting, when we both worked in uniform. He used to pretend the deer were old girlfriends."

"Any ideas who might have whacked him?"

"Not really. I've been thinking about it, though. I knew you guys would get around to me eventually."

"Sergeant Lomack kinda wondered why you didn't call us."

"Oh he did, did he?"

"Not that he thought you'd be holding something back."

Bobby Sellers snorted. "You tell your sergeant I still got mouths to feed that don't live with me, that being retired from the job is just the start of a whole new bag of problems, my precious pension notwithstanding. I call the desk these days to run a plate and they put me on hold. They don't even forward mail. So I'm supposed to drop everything and volunteer my time? Fuck that. You know the story: When you're out, you're out. The pension's your fucking alimony."

Sellers lit a cigarette. His fingers were stained by nicotine, toughened by physical labor. "Artie was cheap, he was mean, he gambled and he fucked around. But when he worked for me, he worked. So fuck it. I kept him on the payroll."

"Cheap is one I haven't heard."

"He fucking squeaked, God rest his soul. His favorite expression was, 'Cops and crime don't pay.' When we were new on the job, he used to bring winos home to do his yardwork. He'd buy them a jug and then dole it out like a slave boss, until his lawn was raked and his hedges trimmed. Never gave a flying fuck what the neighbors thought, carting in riffraff like that. When they were done, he'd pile them into his car and drive them back to the Hempstead bus station."

Jack savored the image of Arthur Backman ladling wine into his work force rather than paying them wages, then returning them to their full-time jobs as eyesores.

"Stab you in the back in a heartbeat too. He hated other cops."

"I've heard that all over."

"Most guys with something on the ball get out of the job as soon as they can. God knows, I did. The lifers hang on 'cause they've never been off the tit. They're afraid of the outside world and actually having to work for a living."

"But you said Backman didn't mind working."

"Artie was there to get even with everyone who thought he was a dipshit. He had something too good to give up—fucking power," Sellers said. "Anyone talk to Angela yet?"

"Angela who?"

"Angela Cortelli . . . Artie's main smash."

That name in the cross-directory. "No. I haven't gotten to her yet."

"I'm surprised," Sellers said. "I figured half the job was already up her shorts."

"Say again?"

"She's a punchboard for the One-Three—skinny blond waitress with some mileage, works at the Spartacus Diner."

Jack racked his memory. He had been known to seek solace at the Spartacus from time to time early in his career. And if he hadn't had her, maybe his first partner, Ronnie Johnson, had.

"She's got handcuffs tattooed on her ass, from what I hear."

That rang a bell.

"Ah, yes," said Jack. "I believe I have heard of her."

"Artie the asshole knocked her up, but I think she had an abortion. He was bitching last month about how much more it costs these days."

Jack grinned and shook his head in perverse admiration: Artie Backman had been a goddamn gangster of love.

"You gonna miss him?" asked Jack.

Sellers scratched his head. "He was good for a laugh. And the prick could sure hump shingles."

After two unproductive interviews with alleged friends of Arthur Backman, Jack Mills returned to headquarters, where a note was Scotch-taped to his phone: See me. Forthwith.

He found Rodney Lomack in his office, on the phone to Chief of Detectives David Barone. "We're looking into it, Chief. We're looking into many things. I too would love to avoid a scandal. Yes, sir. Right away, sir . . . Goodbye." Lomack hung up and grimaced.

"Now what? Is the Dicktop breaking *his* balls?"

"You could say that."

"What the fuck is with that guy?"

"He's mad for publicity, of course, since he's so obviously lacking in talent. What's worse is the dopey fuck is now hanging his hat on a shithouse scenario Inspector Mario Cullen developed, saying we should have been on it like a couple of cats."

"Mario's back to work already?"

"A real go-getter, that one."

Jack sat down in the visitor's chair. "What did I miss?"

"Mad Mario now believes Artie Backman was scamming the job for a connected tow-truck operator named Louie Allesi, steering wrecks to him and other crooked shit. Says that when Backman retired, Allesi lost his ties to the department. His entrée. If there was ever an audit, he didn't want no one left around to testify against him. The Dicktop's making out like it's the first thing we should have looked at. The goddamned 'smoking gun,' he called it."

"So I'll check it out," says Jack. "But icing somebody over a towing scam—it sure sounds like typical Mario bullshit."

Sergeant Lomack gave Jack the clenched-fist salute. "That's what I like about you, Jack. You're such a self-starter."

"What else is going on?" asked Jack. "What have you been doing?"

"Palace politicking. Gathering data. Thinking all the time. How about you?"

"I got the name of a steady girlfriend from Bobby Sellers."

"Good. Where's Claire?"

"Checking the local bars, trying to reconstruct his last hours."

"Anything like a theory taking shape?"

Jack stared at the pin map on the wall and counted homicides haphazardly. Even a glimmer was days away.

Lomack raised his eyebrows. "You don't think we're gonna strike out?"

"We still got people to see, so the good news is we haven't run out of leads."

"You need more help?" asked Lomack.

"We're okay for now."

If Jack had limitless help, he was afraid he would find it hard to keep them all busy, even harder to keep his mind on the case and off the fact that instead of two cops spinning their wheels there was now a squad.

"You sure you just don't want Claire all to yourself?"

Jack smiled. "She is hot, isn't she?"

"Blinding, maybe."

"Message received," said Jack.

Rodney Lomack laced his hands behind his head and put his chukka boots on the desk. He looked like a college professor considering the gravity of murder in safe suburban landscapes. "What's still bothering me is why do it immediately after his retirement. I think of guys who know the difference between killing a cop and murdering a civilian. I've asked the organized crime guys to run down their lists for me."

"I guess I'll go back to the One-Three and see

what Cullen has to say . . . a colossal waste of time
if ever there was one."

"Try to avoid the dueling heart attacks. I need
you on the street, not making guest appearances in
front of the Workman's Compensation Board."

"How you feeling, sir?"

Mario Cullen said, "Much better, thanks. Turns
out it was just a little gas."

Jack said, "That's terrific. We were worried as
hell."

Cullen made a pissy face and sat down behind
his big desk. He repeated his suspicions regarding
Louie Allesi for Jack in a tone suggesting he was
passing on the secrets of life.

"It's an interesting story, sir, but we're having a
hard time buying it as a motive for murder."

Inspector Mario Cullen stood up, his hands on
his hips. "Young man, you are turning your nose up
at very important evidence. Allow me to remind
you that I possess a wealth of police experience, on
the street and off."

Jack looked out the window of the ground-floor
office and sighed. It was sunny outside. Trucks
rolled by. Buses. Taxi cabs. All around him people
with real jobs were working, making things, solving
problems, nobody getting terribly rich. And yet
inside this office lurked a man earning $75,000 a
year—not counting benefits—to play with himself
in public.

"So what if Captain Backman made the street
cops call for Louie Allesi first? So what if Backman
didn't always wait the required time before strip-

ping impounds and crushing them? What were they splitting up—hubcaps and alternators? Guys don't execute one another for bullshit, sir."

Cullen shook his head emphatically. "Louie Allesi knew Backman's replacement would find them out. I'm sure of it, Mills. In fact, I can prove it. Come with me."

Jack followed Inspector Cullen outside to the precinct parking lot and climbed into the passenger seat of an unmarked black Buick. The inspector drove off, slowly navigating through the downtrodden precinct to a public park on a dead-end street, directly opposite the Mount Olive Baptist Church. On one side of the park were basketball courts with bent rims and a memorial for Robert Kennedy. On the other side were what used to be tennis courts, now piled high with a hundred automobiles in various stages of disrepair, some with their noses poking through gaping holes in the chain-link fence. Inspector Cullen slipped the car into park and lowered his electric window.

"All Louie's," he said. "Rent-free. Louie Allesi says Backman told him it was okay because 'Boogies don't play tennis.'"

"That sounds like something Backman would say. But it don't mean Louie killed him, Inspector. One and one don't equal eleven."

Cullen shook his head sadly. "Think how this must look when they come out of church."

"It probably looks like shit, sir. So you should give Louie summonses, yank his permit, tell the guys not to use him, tow these damn cars away, then apologize to the people around here for fucking up their park."

"But Captain Mazzarella said—"

"That's another thing, Inspector," Jack approximated a smile. "Rodney Lomack is running this case, not Mazzarella. Not anybody else. You got something you think we can use, you give us a call. Otherwise . . ."

"But—"

"I'll interview Louie, okay? If I find something shitty I'll run it down. If it turns out to be important, I'll see you get the credit."

Cullen stared at the ceiling of the car in the manner of an overly patient parent. He was alone in his fight against corruption, the last honest man.

Jack sighed. "You want me to give him parking tickets, too?"

"No," said Cullen. "I'll be happy if you talk to him."

Angela Cortelli lived in an apartment on the fourth floor of a building in the clogged heart of downtown Belmont, not far from the famous racetrack. That much Mills got from the reverse directory.

Rather than make an appointment, he decided to call on her unannounced, to catch her in her natural state. Driving to her apartment, he tried to recall what Ronnie Johnson might have said about her seven years ago, other than mentioning the handcuff tattoo, but nothing useful came to mind. These girls blend together, he knew. His and everybody else's.

Jack parked next to the fire hydrant in front of Angela Cortelli's apartment building, then timed his entrance to pass the security lock on the coattails of a black woman of about his age, loaded down with groceries and infant twins.

The lobby reeked of disinfectant, it was stripped of all but the bare essentials. No plants, no pictures, no occasional furniture. The wide-angle mirror in the elevator was broken.

He offered to carry the woman's bags, but she declined, preferring to lean against the wall, breathing heavily. The look-alike babies in the stroller cried.

"It's okay," he said. "I'm a cop. We help people."

"You wanna help me?" she asked. "Make Angela turn her fucking stereo down at night. My grandchildren can't sleep, and I live one floor up and three doors over."

"What makes you think I'm here to see Angela?"

"You're a cop. What else would you be here for?"

The elevator doors slid open to reveal a pumpkin orange hallway and kelly green carpet. The grandmother of twins did not move.

Jack stepped out, found Angela's door and knocked on it lightly.

"Who is it?"

He stood in front of the spyhole. "Jack Mills, Ronnie Johnson's old partner."

"Oh, yeah," she said. "Ronnie. Right."

Chains clanked and the deadbolt tumbled. The door opened six inches. "What do you want?" Angela asked. Her head was wrapped in a towel. She had probably just washed hair that would match what they had found in Backman's car.

"I want to talk to you."

"Is that so?" she said. "Do you know you're the third cop I've talked to today offering to fill 'the void,' as one guy put it. How cold can you bastards get? I mean, let's get Artie in the ground before you guys get me. Okay? Come see me in a month."

"I didn't come over to ask for a date," said Jack. "I caught the squeal on Artie's case. I'm a homicide detective."

"Oh," she said. "This visit is official."

"Sorry," said Jack. "We need to talk."

She opened the door the rest of the way. She was barefoot, wearing red Bermuda shorts and a pink tank top that revealed the outline of her nipples. Her face was prettier than he had expected. "Come on in. You can ask me what you gotta ask me. Just promise to keep me out of the papers. I never met his wife and I don't want to now."

"I gathered that when you hung up on me."

"That was you?"

Jack nodded.

"Sorry."

"You were his girlfriend?"

"His main squeeze, as he put it."

"You were going steady?"

"I was," she said, lighting a cigarette. "I'm not so sure about him."

Jack made a note on his clipboard.

Angela walked into the kitchenette, asking over her shoulder if he wanted something to drink. "I got everything," she said. "Booze, wine, beer."

"No thanks."

While she was gone, Mills looked around the well-kept living room. Angela's furniture was modern, modular. There were gooseneck lamps and hanging plants, magazines and romance novels neatly stacked on her floor-to-ceiling bookshelves.

On the long wall next to a tapestry hung the LeRoy Neiman recruiting poster done from Jack's photograph: COP A GREAT LIFE. JOIN THE NASSAU COUNTY POLICE DEPARTMENT. A dozen roses crowned her cocktail table.

It seemed Angela had lived here a long time.

"Going to the funeral?" Jack said when she returned with a glass of beer for herself.

"I don't think so. Family day, you know."

"I understand. And when did you last see Artie alive?"

She sat on the couch, facing him, holding her beer with both hands. "The Saturday before he disappeared. He met me here, like he always did, around ten, ten-thirty in the morning. He stayed about an hour an' a half."

"Did he seem worried about anything?"

She laughed. "Artie? He never worried about nothin'. He always had everything covered."

Jack said, "He was quite a bit older than you."

"Yeah," she said, nodding. "So what?"

"Almost nineteen years."

Angela drew her finger around the rim of the glass, then tapped her red fingernails on the top. She seemed to be remembering a desolate past, perhaps an unpalatable truth. Jack felt sorry for her, regret for having to ask her tough questions. Maybe her father had abandoned her, maybe cops helped her cope with that. There was something sadly girlish about her, despite the bleached blond hair. Maybe, he thought, she's lived here all her life.

"It's not important," he said.

"He wasn't a total drunk and he didn't slap me

around, like some of your other buddies. For a while I was in love with him."

"I understand that you're carrying his child."

Her eyes flashed and her cheeks colored. "You've been getting lousy information, Sherlock. I had an abortion the night that Artie disappeared. He was supposed to meet me that afternoon, with the money. He was gonna do the right thing."

"But he never showed."

She looked at her fingernails. "He never showed. I took a cab to the clinic—in case you're wondering where I was and how I got there."

"I'm sorry," said Jack.

"Me too. If I'd a known he was gonna die, I mighta kept the kid."

"If it's any consolation, it's my professional opinion that he was coming over. He stopped at a bank and withdrew five hundred bucks not long before he disappeared."

Angela smiled. "That's nice to know."

"Hey," said Jack. "Whatever."

"You sure you don't want a drink or something else? I seem to remember Ronnie was fond of cocktails."

"Honest . . . nothing."

"So what else can I do for you?"

"Any guess who might have killed him?"

"No," she said. "But he was not what you'd call well liked. He hated his job and his wife was a pain. The same old story."

"Did he ever mention his son?"

"Not really."

"Or a cop named Bobby Sellers?"

"He used Bobby as an excuse to get out of the house sometimes, but mostly we met on his lunch hours."

"Mind giving me a lock of your hair?"

She smiled demurely for a moment, then realized Jack was gathering evidence. "I'll give you some of mine if you'll give me some of yours."

Jack smiled: Angela went into the bathroom for scissors, returned with a small lock of hair.

"Thanks."

"Sure."

There were other questions, other answers, but Jack found that he wanted only to leave this woman's company, almost as if he had slept with her himself. She was so bleak, so lonely, a human black hole. He felt his energy sucked in her direction. He collected his clipboard and walkie-talkie and stood up.

"You're a little flaky, aren't you, Angela?"

"That's one way of putting it."

On her tenth try, at Clancy's Kerry Pub, Claire struck pay dirt. The middle-aged mick bartender in jeans and an apron closed his *Daily News* and said, "That's the guy they found out in Suffolk. Jeez, I read the story, but I never put two and two together. I mean, it's weird that he was here, and then he left and got killed."

"What time did he leave?" asked Claire as she opened a bag of beer nuts.

"Three-thirty, quarter to four. I'd say he got here around one-thirty, two. He drank dollar drafts and ate beer nuts. Sat all by himself at the end there.

Left a dollar on the bar, I believe, which for this dump ain't bad."

"He make any phone calls?"

"Not that I recall. A captain of police . . . would you fancy that. I thought he was a laborer myself."

"Ever see him before that Monday?"

"Now and then. Yeah. But like I say, I didn't know he was a cop. He always looked like somebody killing time, you know. Like waiting for somebody who never came."

The bartender gave a brief deposition to Claire and signed on the dotted line. He offered Claire a complimentary cocktail, and of course lunch was on him.

Claire patted her hip. "No thanks. Watching my figure."

The bartender smiled. "Now that's what I was hoping to do."

9

J ACK STOPPED at the Nassau County rec center for a sauna and a swim on the way in to work the following morning. He felt clean again afterward, alive and awake, not tired and dirty, the way the frequent exposure to death made him feel.

Little kids were the worst. Fires were bad, their victims charred and shriveled like insects. He would cringe and mumble prayers, step lightly around the bodies, transfixed in horror but not despair. Dead kids wiped him out.

He remembered the young black family crossing Belmont Avenue—father, mother and three-year-old daughter, on their way home from getting ice cream at Carvel. Jack was fresh from the academy, still a superhero raring to go. A white Cadillac with Jersey plates picked the mother and daughter off clean, yanking them from the father's hand, then sped off in the direction of New York City, never found. Jack recalled the mother's head filling the street with blood, her body wrapped protectively around the child, who was facedown in a crimson pool. No bubbles, Jack remembered. He cleaned her tiny mouth and blew his breath into her lungs, kneeling on the hard street, the child in his arms. No back-pressure. Just a broken, flaccid doll. Too stunned to cry, he held her in his lap in the back of the ambulance on the way to the hospital, where he handed her over to an old white nurse.

While doctors worked on the mother in a separate trauma room and Red Cross social workers consoled the father, the nurse bathed the child's body and dressed her in a clean white gown. The squad detective arrived drunk, breathing garlic on Jack, alternately silly and arrogant, cursing incompetent nigger security guards from Third-World countries until he realized his victims were niggers too. The old nurse suggested Jack check the detective's front bumper for damage. The maternal grandfather identified the child's body in a voice wracked with woe. "That's the only grandchild I'm ever gonna have."

His daughter had died in the room next door.

The drunk detective wept.

When Jack got off duty that night he ran ten miles through the dark streets of Belmont, then downed ten shots of Scotch. He would have tried to screw ten girls if there had been any left at the bar when he got there. He never mentioned it at home, to Babe, though he thought about that night for years after it happened. Why? he often wondered. Why blitz a family like that? What kind of pleasure did God get out of a fucked-up stunt like that?

Sergeant Lomack was waiting for him that morning, his arms piled high with reports.

"Hey, boss," said Jack. "What you got there?"

"The full lab reports on Backman's car, the hair analysis. Interesting shit, all in all. Care to hear it?"

"My mind is clear. I've recovered from my workout."

"Well, that's wonderful. When it comes time for my quarterly review, I can tell Captain Mazzarella and Captain Tomlinson that my guys don't get much work done, but, Lord knows, they're well-conditioned motherfuckers."

Jack sat down and began to flip through the lab reports.

"Before you get into those, I think you should know what that moonshot Doctor Rensallin said to me."

Dr. Alan Rensallin ran the psych-profile computer and was the man who entered the circumstances and conditions of all crimes into a data bank designed by the FBI. Every now and then Dr. Rensallin emerged from his lab with a portrait of a killer that later matched quite closely the suspect arrested. Sometimes he was ludicrously wrong. On H-11-89 the computer had said Jilted Lover because of the bruises on the face—what any cop with five minutes in the street would have said right off.

Jack folded his arms across his well-defined chest and awaited the good doctor's computer's input.

"The computer thinks the date of death is significant," Lomack said.

"I don't get it."

"Maybe the killer waited for Captain Backman to retire to avoid the extra penalties for killing a policeman. Anyway, a cop getting killed two days after he retires is statistically—psychologically—

meaningful, according to the Doc. Take it from there."

Jack placed the lab reports on his messy desk and sat back, thinking that the world was huge and he was a flyspeck.

Lomack said, "The phone company records arrived for the Backman residence, confirming the calls between Michael and Mrs. Backman. At five-fifteen on the Monday Artie disappeared, Mrs. Backman said she took a call from a woman who claimed she worked for the department, in personnel. I checked it out. No one from personnel made that call."

Jack chuckled. "Mrs. Backman was obviously unaware of the overtime cutbacks in clerical. At five that office is a ghost town."

Lomack paced the detectives' cubicle. "We found hair in the car from three knowns and two unknowns. We got Mrs. Backman, we got Artie, we got son Michael. On the two unknowns we got profiles. So maybe we got a killer and a parts thief."

"Chill a second," said Jack. He took a pad from Eats's immaculate desk. "Shoot."

"Subject number one: male, white; blood type, O-negative; from whom we collected hair and possibly beard, some dark brown, some gray. Subject number two: female, white; blood type, AB-negative. She was a brunet, but the hair is dyed blond. Mrs. Backman said she didn't know any bleached-blond bimbos. Ditto for Michael. Both again insisted Arthur's cheating days were over. Michael actually told me that his father couldn't get laid in a woman's prison."

Jack put his pen down, glad for once to have an

answer, happy to stop the drain on his limited reputation. "That hair belongs to Angela Cortelli."

"I agree. Once a snake, always a snake."

Jack did not argue the point. He gave Lomack the high points of his interview with Angela Cortelli.

"Figures," said Lomack, then resumed: "The grease on the backseat is from a chain of some kind, either a bicycle or a power tool. What's interesting is that the grease contained particles of soil from the scene around the grave . . . where we found Backman's body."

Wrinkles creased Jack's brow. He picked up his pen and started writing again. "Inside the car?"

"Inside the grease inside the car."

"And what do we make of that?"

"I don't know," said Lomack. "Maybe from the guy who stripped the car. Maybe the killer planned on hacking Artie to bits with a chain saw. Maybe he couldn't get the damn thing started. I can never get mine started."

"So then where is it?" Jack said, scribbling rapidly.

"How do I know? Maybe he ditched it. Maybe he just slung it over his shoulder like Paul fucking Bunyan and eased on down the road." Lomack put his foot on Eats's chair and stared into dark blue space.

"Maybe," said Jack. "Maybe it's still out there in those woods. And then even if the killer wore gloves for the crime, there could be prints somewhere on that chain saw."

"Arrange for Suffolk to take a look."

"I'll put Eats on it."

Lomack frowned at Jack, looked at the other

desk, empty but for the nameplate. "You on drugs?"

"I can't do it this afternoon. We got the funeral."

Lomack said, "That's right, that's right. Plan on driving me. I think it makes for a better lead-in shot when a white man opens the door for a black."

"You would."

"They're gonna be asking me questions, Jack. Got any idea yet what I ought to say to our friends in the media?"

Jack smiled. "You could wax poetic and report that Arthur Backman died of his entire life. You could say he stomped on people until someone said, 'Enough!' You could——"

"How about I just say we're making progress."

"You're the boss," said Jack. "You think our bad guy will come to the show?"

"My guess is he wouldn't miss it for the world."

Jack Mills drove Sergeant Lomack to St. Stephen's in West Hempstead, but did not jump out to open the door for him.

There was no need. The Mineola press corps opened it for him, jamming cameras in their faces, screaming questions. "Please," said Lomack, holding up a hand. "After I have paid my respects."

They grumbled, but they let him go.

Along the sidewalk in front of the cathedral, for as far as Jack could see, there were cops dressed in summer blues. Gangs of them still arriving on buses from New York, Trenton, Boston, Hartford, Philadelphia, points west, swelling the ranks, showing solidarity with the dead and the mourners.

"Good turnout," Jack said. "We're lucky they didn't know him personally. I'll bet half are here to make sure he's really dead."

Jack followed Lomack into the dark church, where one seat had been saved by the hack from the commissioner's office who was in charge of such things, a seat next to Captain Richard Mazzarella.

Jack insisted Lomack take it, then walked to the side aisle and along the wall to the sacristy. He scanned faces in the crowd while the police chaplain elaborated on the Resurrection and the Life.

In the pew closest to the flag-draped coffin, Eloise Backman was leaning on her son Michael's shoulder. Behind the family, guys from other departments were crying. Mills could not help noticing the dry eyes among the delegation from the Thirteenth Precinct.

Blue-haired sisters and cousins and neighbors were up front, stoic clean-shaven cops to the rear. There were no beards in the church, Jack noted, at least no brown ones going to gray, and precious little bleached-blond hair.

"A good man," the monsignor intoned. "A father, a brother, a husband . . . a cop. He was a child of God, my friends. A man of his community. He leaves behind a treasury of memories, a legacy of compassion and love for his fellow man. . . ."

Jack was cringing in his penny loafers, waiting for someone in the crowd to cry out, "Bullshit!" knowing as he did how prone cops are to such spontaneous displays of affection. But the blue line held; the hand-picked officers allowed inside the church sat without complaint through one boring speech after another, comforted by the knowledge that they were on the clock.

The commissioner was the first of the official delegation to walk to the altar to receive communion, followed closely by Chief Inspector McCarthy, then Deputy Chief Roosevelt Gleason, Chief Barone, Inspector Cuellar, Inspector Irving Saperstein, Mad Mario Cullen, Izzy Goldman, Captain Cohen, Dicktop Mazzarella.

Jack Mills, former member of the Holy Name Society and lapsed Catholic, stayed where he was and considered his sins, a visitor in his own house.

At Commissioner Foley's invitation, Detective Mills and Sergeant Lomack joined the bigshots for cocktails and chili at Leo's Midway in Garden City. It was there, while Jack sipped a bottle of Beck's in the corner near the kitchen, that Captain Mazzarella laid into him with a vengeance: "It's going on five fucking days now. And whaddayagot? Ya got nothing. Zilch. You're making me look like shit, kid."

The Dicktop was making himself look bombed. He held a beer mug in his hand and bobbed and weaved. Quickstop Izzy Goldman stood behind him, ready to catch or fetch.

Jack said, "We've known about it for a couple of days, Cap, not five."

"And one of those days you took off."

"I spent an afternoon with my child, just like a normal person."

"Who said cops were supposed to be normal?"

"This one is."

Mazzarella smirked. "That's what's wrong with you. You treat the job like a job."

"And you treat it like a religious order."

When it came to professional diligence, Mazzarella talked a good game, but the Dicktop picked the county's pocket as much as the next man. He had no call to jump in Jack's face.

"Boy, did I make a mistake helping you. If I had Artie's case, I wouldn't take the time to wipe my butt until I had my bad guy. You'd see nothing but assholes and elbows, my friend. I'm telling you. A cop goes down and you're not out there breaking heads? What the fuck is that? Of course, I didn't play my way into the bureau like you did."

Jack was not exactly sure how the Dicktop had made his bones in the job. But he doubted it had been through hard work or by risking his rear end. It was widely known that Mazzarella was close to the county executive, that he was a marvel at getting the hometown infirm and aged to vote.

Mazzarella set his glass down, bent over and rolled up one pant leg. He hopped on one foot and raised his leg. A jagged old wound creased the back of his pale white calf. "You gotta give a piece of yourself to this job, Mills. You got to have the guts."

"When did you shoot yourself in the leg?" said Jack.

Mazzarella straightened up. "What did you say?"

"Tell me again how you won the war, Daddy."

"Your career just ended, son."

"Bar talk," Jack said. "You're just pissed that Photo Cop spends more time on TV than your boy Izzy spends on the bowl."

"That's not true," said Izzy Goldman. "And as for my bathroom habits—"

Mazzarella scowled. "Photo Cop? You mean the Negative?"

Jack looked Mazzarella in the eye. "That wasn't by any chance a racial slur?"

"Got any witnesses?"

Mills glanced at Izzy. "None that are credible."

Mazzarella said, "Just how many years do you have left with us, Mills?"

"I got about a decade more to fuck around with you, Cap, give or take a couple of weeks."

Mazzarella narrowed his eyes and smiled. "I made you, kid. I can break you."

Jack looked over his head, around the smoke-filled barroom. Rodney Lomack was by the window, leaning on the Nintendo machine, getting his ear chewed by a local politician who was obviously pleased to be seen conversing with a black man. Eats O'Day, who had come to work just in time to slap on the feed bag for Artie, was back on the buffet line.

"No one will help you," said Mazzarella. "Lomack's got his own agenda, the skirt will wilt on you at the end of the month and your useless partner thinks the job is welfare with honor."

"Excuse me, Captain. I gotta run."

Mazzarella blocked his path, slopped beer on the arm of his khaki suit. "This ain't bar talk, Mills. This is business. You're laying down on a brother's case. I'm telling you that to your face. You want me to shout it out, I'll shout it out."

Jack stiffened. He considered the long-term ramifications of knocking the Dicktop's block off—whether he might successfully chalk it up to job-related stress or grief, and draw no more than a verbal reprimand. But it was not the time or the place. Jack would hang, Jenny would starve.

"We're at a funeral, eh? Lighten up," Jack said.

Mazzarella sneered. "Your boss can't cover you forever. In fact, I'd say by Wednesday, the latest, I'll be running this show from the top, the way it ought to be run. You'll be bringing us coffee."

"Maybe," said Jack.

"Write it down, Airhead. You heard it here."

10

At 11:30 Monday morning, Jack walked into the Mineola dry-cleaning store owned by Sanjay Behnti, a discount establishment referred to by the headquarters cops as Mahatma Coat Mapants. It was hazy and hot outside and the beer on his sleeve was ripe. Without a word to the dark, slender owner, Jack pulled off his tie. Then he stepped behind the counter and hid among the cellophane-shrouded suits. He removed his jacket and pants and handed them to Sanjay.

"Under an hour?" asked Jack.

Sanjay smiled. "I will do the best I can, my friend."

Jack sat down on a stool in the back and picked up Sanjay's newspaper. The air smelled of solvents and sweat, Sanjay's curried lunch.

"You must be very proud to have a son follow you into the department. My father so wanted me to learn his trade."

Jack said, "What do you mean?"

"Is that not his picture I have seen everywhere lately?"

"That's me," said Jack. "Many moons ago."

"Forgive me," said Sanjay. "I did not mean to offend."

Jack waved off his apology. He knew he had aged, probably more than the county executive. There was gray at his temples now, lines etched on his face. A visible lack of confidence?

"Did you hear the joke about the lottery in Bombay?" asked Sanjay.

"No."

"You scratch a card, and if the dot on the card matches the dot on your head you win a 7 Eleven in America."

"I heard it was Baghdad, and a gas station," said Jack.

"Perhaps," said Sanjay.

"Would you do me a favor?"

"Anything," said Sanjay.

Jack told Sanjay what he wanted him to do. They rehearsed Sanjay's part several times. Then Jack dialed Captain Richard Mazzarella's extension at headquarters.

"Homicide. Captain Mazzarella's line."

Sanjay said, "This is Marco Caldisa, from *Newsday*. I would like to set up an interview with Captain Mazzarella regarding his upcoming transfer to Highway Safety."

"Excuse me," said the secretary. "I don't know anything about any transfer and I'm sure the captain doesn't either. He's more than happy in homicide."

"But I was told—"

"Hold on. Let me check with him."

"Maybe this call is premature. I will call back tomorrow after further verification."

Sanjay hung up.

Jack said, "An Oscar."

The timing was perfect. With noon fast approaching, Mazzarella would not be able to reach his rabbis until after they had returned from their two-hour lunches. He could run the empty halls from office to office without surcease. He would leave his underlings alone.

Thirty minutes later Jack sat down on the hot front seat of his car, whistling. His khaki suit was clean and Dicktop had something to worry about besides Jack's progress on the case. Quite a morning, all in all.

Jack and Claire met a uniformed sergeant and three patrol cops at the Mobil station on Route 112 at Horse Block Road that afternoon. The men joked with Claire good-naturedly for a while, then followed her instructions for setting up the canvass.

Flares were lit on each side of the busy north-south road, directing passing autos to checkpoints, where the patrol cops asked them if they had traveled this route the proceeding week at this particular time, and if so, what they might have seen that was unusual.

"A policeman was murdered in those woods," they said. "We need your help. It was sunny last Monday. Windy. The day before all that rain last week."

Those who might have witnessed something useful were shunted into the gas station, where Jack and Claire held brief interrogations.

Marcia Higgenbothom of Patchogue reported observing a black man wearing a windbreaker pushing a shopping cart into the woods. David Reynolds agreed.

Tony Rizzo of Sayville couldn't be sure, but he thought he saw a woman riding a big tricycle in the vicinity that day. He said she flew the Jolly Roger from one of those big safety antennae all the old folks use in Florida. The interior of the guy's Trans Am reeked of marijuana, so Mills gave his story little credence.

At six-thirty Claire Williamson called a halt to the operation and the cops dismantled the road-block. She sat down in the front seat of Mills's car and lit a cigarette, taking care to blow the smoke away from him. The Mobile sign had flashed on and more customers—mostly men in suits—were stopping for eggs than gasoline.

"I'll have my people look around for the shopper and the old biker chick. Other than that, I guess it's time to head back to the barn."

"Thanks," said Jack. "I appreciate the help."

"Sorry about the chain saw. Even I went out and looked."

"All we can do is try."

"You getting anywhere at all on your end?"

Jack smiled and shrugged. "Into my rabbi's doghouse. Backman was a gumba of his, so of course I can't do enough. But our problem is that although nobody liked Artie Backman, except the Dicktop, I haven't run across anyone I think would be up to killing him. I'll bet he was into something shitty that went boom."

"Maybe."

"Since we're here anyway," he said, "let's take a look at the scene."

She nodded slowly, thoughtfully. "Might as well."

As the shadows of the pine trees lengthened and the western sky grew bright, Jack drove down the company road where Arthur Backman's body was discovered. He parked just off the dirt road, got out of the car and watched his loafers disappear in the mud.

"Yuck," he said. "Hold it. I parked us next to a bog."

"Don't worry. I won't melt." Claire turned her back and slipped off her high heels, then reached up under the sides of her black silk dress, hooked her thumbs in the waistband of her pantyhose and rolled them down. When she looked over at Jack, he pretended to unbuckle his belt.

"Real cute, Jack."

He held his hands aloft. "Just kidding. Honest."

They walked barefoot to the edge of the shallow grave. Jack took Polaroid shots of the scene, then compared past and present. The rusted engine block was still where it had been. The same bags of leaves still covered the construction debris: shingles, pallets, broken cement. Since the murder someone had dropped off a washing machine and a tire the size of a kiddie pool.

"As an environmentalist," said Claire, "I am deeply offended. The Island's turning into a pigsty."

"Horrible," Jack said, turning the lens on her, "simply horrible."

She crossed her arms, her face defiant. "Go ahead, sexually harass me. I'm used to it."

Jack took her picture and stuffed the still-developing print into the pocket of his suit jacket. "You want one of me?"

"Really, Jack, that's all I've ever wanted."

"Why are you so hard on me?"

"You don't know what hard is."

"You like me, don't you? I'll bet that scares the crap out of you."

Claire squinted, as if she had not understood. He put his hands on her waist and kissed her, was amazed that she let him, a kiss that smelled of perfume and smoke.

Claire stepped back and looked at her muddy feet.

"What's the matter?" Jack asked.

"I need a drink."

He took her back into his arms. "Yeah," he said. "All this glamorous detective work is making me thirsty too."

She looked up at him as she eased her way to freedom. "I haven't decided anything."

"I know," he said. "Me neither."

"Yeah, right."

"Honest."

"Maybe it's safer to take a walk on the beach?" said Claire.

"You're the boss."

They drove east fast, Claire at the wheel. Her car. Out along Sunrise Highway to Montauk Highway, through the fabulous Hamptons to the very end of Long Island's south fork. She said she wanted to show him her thinking spot, the place she ran to when she needed a brighter perspective than she could get at the end of a bar.

"They call it The Last Five Miles. A greenbelt trail from Ditch Plains to Montauk Point itself. My dad used to bring us here. We can make it by dark."

"We talking a disco or a simple country inn?"

"We're talking moonscapes, Jack. Spooky moors and cliffs and dunes. Rock formations that house animals running from the pollution, making their last stand. You can sit there and look back with a sense of equanimity. My problems always seem smaller."

When it came to beaches, Jack was used to crowds at the Lido Beach pavilion. Radio-free zones. Alcohol-free zones. Lifeguard stands. Tar balls. Bifocaled Health Department lookouts in orange windbreakers watching the surf for medical waste.

They parked the car off the road and made their way to The Last Five Miles trail down one of the few paths through the dunes. Side by side, almost leaning on each other, they walked east in the fluffy sand. The sun dipped below the hills behind them, the Atlantic stretched out before them, a lovely green. Claire carried a disposable blanket under her arm and led Jack over a mile of rugged terrain to a stretch of clean sand between two molten rocks.

"Here." She spread out the blanket and sat down chastely, her legs underneath her. Her head tipped back in rapture, she inhaled the unspoiled ocean wind and embraced the approach of night.

Jack remained on his feet, circling the blanket,

looking over his shoulder, making sure they were alone, aware of a tension in his gut he had not previously noticed.

"Sit down," she said. "It's okay. Only lovers come this far, and they have more important things on their minds."

"It's just that I'd hate to get my suit dirty."

Claire laughed. "Aw, Jack. Did I forget to compliment you on your clean clothes? I'm sorry. You see there *is* hope for the domestically disabled."

Jack rolled his eyes. "Why do men even try?"

"Another stupid question. Sit down."

Jack remained on his feet while Claire told him the story of the wreck of the *John Milton,* out of New Bedford, which ran aground four miles to the east, in February 1858, during a snowstorm. The bodies of twenty-one sailors washed up on the beach, frozen in cakes of ice, she said. "Out on the rocks, the doomed ship's bell rang all day long."

Jack saw H-11-89 in her own block of ice. He asked Claire if she believed in ghosts. She said yes. He sat down next to her, put his arm around her, nuzzled her neck. A seaplane droned overhead, the undersides of its wings glinting orange.

She smiled and kissed him hard. He kissed her back softly, put his hand on the back of her neck and pulled her closer. They struggled for a moment, mouths locked, then she wrestled him onto his back and wrapped them in the blanket. Her long brown hair fell forward, concealing her face. She leaned over for her pocketbook, snapped it open, the handle of her weapon within reach.

"Is that in case I'm no damn good at this?" he said.

11

He woke up with Claire on his mind. Lounging happily in bed, he compiled a list of things to do for her, things to tell her about himself that would make her fall in love with him.

All things considered, he was not an unattractive specimen.

She had been quiet driving them back to his car, smiling at him now and then, shaking her head and laughing, admitting that she had thought her days for romps in the dunes had passed. Never, he had said. They're only over if you want them to be over.

Claire had actually allowed as how he might be right. There was a single letter in his mailbox that morning, political junk mail he discarded, on the way to his unmarked car. By the time he pulled out, he had dialed.

"Any luck finding my witnesses?" he asked Claire on the car phone.

"As a matter of fact, one of the Sixth Precinct cops out here found the old lady on the oversized tricycle. He took her name and address and made her promise to come see me. The cop said she was a little bit screwy, but not totally incoherent, so we might get something from her we can use."

Jack made a note on a leads sheet. "Where you gonna meet her?" he said. "Maybe I'll ride out."

"My office," said Claire. "Tomorrow. She told the cop she didn't want anyone coming to her house, said it might cause her trouble with the landlord."

"Fair enough."

"What are you gonna do?"

"I'm gonna go back and see my bad boys at the One-Three."

"That ought to be fun. You're a bad boy too."

"Sure I am, but the question is, do you miss me?"

Click. Nothing but static rush.

Jack drove west on crowded Hempstead Turnpike to the Thirteenth Precinct in Belmont. Outside the station house a crowd of black people was assembled, complaining loudly about the arrest of several popular neighborhood kids for the kidnapping, rape and murder of a white woman who made the wrong turn off the Southern State Parkway. The perpetrators were chained to bars in the separate process rooms Jack looked into; Al Trankina and Rocky Greenberg were scrambling from room to room, trying to catch discrepancies in the rambling explanations each suspect was giving of his activities on the day in question.

Trankina looked at Jack. "You here to help?"

"Negative. I'm working Backman."

"Too bad."

Jack looked at one of the suspects, a skinny kid in the latest high-tech sneakers—white leather numbers that promised to launch their owners into the sky. The kid made eye contact, smirked, then spit on the floor. Jack wished for a sole malfunction, imagined nuclear shoes launching the asshole headfirst into the plaster ceiling.

"Have fun," he said to Trankina.

"Fuck me up the ass."

Jack was given the use of a spare basement office for interviews he did not want to conduct. Five minutes later a sheepish young patrolman appeared at the door, holding his hat in his hand. He was not wearing a wedding band or any other jewelry. A black shroud covered his shield number.

"I'm McKay," he said. "What did I do?"

"Jack Mills, Homicide. Come in and close the door."

A crooked smile crossed Billy McKay's face. "Should I have a lawyer with me?"

"Not unless you've killed someone lately."

McKay nodded and closed the door.

"I want to talk about Angela Cortelli," said Jack.

"You guys think Angie offed Backman?"

"I don't know. What do you think?"

"I think that's crazy," said McKay. "Angela loves cops."

"So I hear. Now one of them is dead."

McKay whistled and rolled his eyes at the ceiling. Jack watched the young cop try to imagine Angela a murderer.

"When was the last time you hit the sheets with her?"

McKay colored slightly and grinned uneasily. "Bout a year ago. Before I moved in with my current girlfriend, if anybody asks. She cruised my footpost about two in the morning. I gave her one for old time's sake."

"She any good?"

"She's fucking terrific."

"Any weird stuff? Pain or bondage? Water sports? Drugs?"

"Not with me. Just backseat blowdinis and a good solid roll in the hay up at her place."

"And you don't think she's the kind of broad to have Artie Backman blown away? Even if she was knocked up and he wouldn't do the right thing?"

"No way. She's a pussycat. Angie knows ain't no one gonna marry her, at least nobody working here."

Jack asked, "Why'd you stop seeing her?"

McKay laughed. "She wanted to get married."

"See what I'm saying? She's got her hopes. You could have saved her life. Backman could have."

"Hey, besides she's about ten years older than me, I didn't want the mother of my kids to have a tatoo on her ass. Pussycat or not, that chick has seen miles of pecker. Most of it hanging off guys I work with."

"Which guys?" asked Jack. "I need their names."

McKay stepped back and looked at his feet. "Ah, man. Not this."

"Oh, yeah," said Jack. "This."

"Are we all jammed up?"

Jack remembered the rampant paranoia at the Thirteenth, the feeling that at any minute Internal Affairs would arrive with indictments and a paddy wagon. "Nobody's in trouble. I'm simply trying to rule her out as a suspect is all."

"You want to know all the guys who fucked her, or just the guys she dated on a regular basis?"

"Everybody, Billy. Sorry."

"God, I hate this fucking job."

Jack took down the names, listing for each the amount of time Billy figured they had spent with her. In spite of her reputation, the total was only four steadies and eight one-night stands, including Ronnie Johnson—twelve men in a twenty-year career. Nowhere near the totals Jack had racked up. He decided to think better of her.

McKay said, "There may have been others. These are just the guys who kissed and told."

"Thanks, Billy. You did the right thing."

"Nobody whose name I gave up is gonna think so."

Jack looked at the list after McKay left the office. Of the three other known steady boyfriends, one was dead by his own hand, one was on his regularly scheduled day off and one had retired.

Jack picked up the phone.

Officer Blaney could be questioned the day after tomorrow, he was told by the desk officer. Two of Angela's one-nighters were working, Myron Belton and Duane Meenan. Jack called them in together.

"Belton and Meenan, reporting as ordered," said Duane Meenan. "Under protest." Meenan was sallow and skinny. There was dandruff on his collar and epaulets.

They were wary, keeping their distance from the desk that held their service records, a salt-and-pepper team of seasoned veterans. They could not have failed to be guilty of something. Jack smiled and told them to relax.

123

Officer Myron Belton, an overweight, balding black man with a chest full of medals, laughed and said, "Yeah, right. When you gonna read us our rights?"

"And why would I read you your rights?"

"No offense, my man, but fuck you, my man," said Belton. "I ain't telling you nothing. He'll vouch for me and I'll vouch for him. Just like always." Officers Belton and Meenan hugged each other and growled like bears.

"Yo, fellas—"

"Will there be anything else, sir?" asked Meenan, turning to leave.

Jack shook his head as if he was confused. "Who do you guys think you're talking to?"

Belton said, "Nobody, man. A tit-sucking headquarters snitch."

Jack stood up, incredulous. "What did you call me?"

"Sit down, pretty boy."

"Fuck you, fat ass."

Belton stuck his jaw out. "Why don't you just call me a nigger?"

"Cause I noticed your fat ass first."

Myron Belton shoved Jack in the chest with a finger as thick as a nightstick.

Jack shoved Myron Belton.

Then Jack's face exploded and the lights went out.

Jack woke up on his back in a private stall off the emergency room at South Nassau Hospital. Hovering over him were the concerned faces of Police Officers Myron Belton and Duane Meenan from the Thirteenth Precinct. Jack could not breathe through his nose, and his formerly clean suit was spattered with blood.

"What happened?" he asked.

"You slipped," said Belton.

"You smacked your nose on the edge of the desk," said Meenan. "Doc said it's broken."

Jack examined his face gingerly with his fingertips.

Where his nose had once been, a gauze-covered boot had been installed, toes pointing down.

"Jesus," said Jack, "is that what happened?"

"Yeah," the cops said in unison.

Jack looked at Meenan closely. "Bullshit. You sucker-punched me, didn't you?"

"Worse," said Meenan, shaking his head. "I jacked you."

Jack closed his eyes. A wave of nausea washed over him.

"I'm sorry, man. I lost it for a minute, when you shoved Myron. I just flashed red and gold and suddenly the jack was out of my pocket and . . ."

Jack remembered, got angry again. "And of course I can report this assault, which would qualify me for lots of line-of-duty benefits, and you'd both get fired and probably arrested too."

"I guess that's up to you," said Belton.

"See," said Meenan, "I don't know if you ever had a partner, but me and Myron been together in this sewer for six years now, and I just can't tolerate no one shoving him around."

"I've had partners," said Jack.

"But you ain't been stuck in no sewer," said Belton.

Jack looked up at the ceiling, wondering what good could come of revenge, imagining the office ridicule he would endure if it was known that suspects, however ancillary, were free to knock the snot out of him. What would Claire do? Stupid question.

"Please don't make us beg," said Meenan.

Jack closed his eyes. "Don't shit your pants, boys. I can take a joke."

"You mean . . . ?" said Meenan.

"We'll stick to your version."

Meenan thanked him, kissed his hands, offered to have his baby. Jack laughed and the center of his face stung with pain.

"I never thought so before," said Belton, "but you a stand-up dude, Mills. We owe you. Anything you want."

"Tell me everything you know about Angela Cortelli. And get me a mirror."

"Aw, no," said Meenan. "Fuck the mirror. You might change your mind."

"That bad?" asked Jack. "Really?"

"Well," said Belton, "you know what an elephant looks like, right?"

Jack got out of bed and walked to the bathroom. He took one look at his ruined face in the mirror and ralphed.

Jack removed the bandages in his bathroom at home the following morning. He studied his reflection, the faint purple rings around his eyes, the hilly dogleg left in place of his once straight nose. A Gerry Cooney nose he had now. The hard-bitten face of a tough guy. He considered plastic surgery (an ambitious second-year resident had clipped his business card to Jack's follow-up care manual). He practiced speaking, trying to disguise the packed nasal whine.

Claire called to remind him of their interview with an eyewitness.

"I'm sick," he said. "I need you to come over and take care of me."

"Bullshit."

"I fell and broke my nose."

"That's not sick. Get tough."

"Line-of-duty accident, Claire."

"Noon," she said. "Be there. Aloha."

12

SUFFOLK COUNTY Police Headquarters was located in the rural hamlet of Yaphank, just down the street from a quaint little business district one might discover on Cape Cod. Crafts shops, churches and country florists dotted the shady streets, with none of the atmosphere of political-industrial complexity that blanketed Mineola. There was what looked like a NASA tracking installation on the roof of headquarters, radio equipment required to communicate with the far-flung outposts. A police cadet at the front door logged Jack present and escorted him to homicide.

Claire's desk was neat and orderly. It sat in the corner of the well-lit bullpen, by a window. Potted plants surrounded her; a radio on the windowsill played rock. Jack doubted that her duty sergeant made a habit of describing his bowel movements to her.

She wore a green plaid skirt and light gray tennis sweater.

Seated across the desk from her was a white woman in her sixties, he guessed, in a dirty black sweatsuit, her sneakers fashionably unlaced. She had red-gray hair done up in cornrows, and a lifeguard tan, weathered and spotted. She was drinking coffee with both hands on the mug.

"Hello, Jack," said Claire, looking up. "Hey, nice snot locker."

Jack felt the sore bridge of his nose. "Thanks, Claire. I needed that."

"Don't be a baby. It'll heal."

He began to make a sarcastic face at her but the pain stopped him cold.

"Meet Lucy Lallos, our infamous woman on the bike. Lucy, this once very handsome man is Jack Mills, the detective from Nassau County I told you about . . . the one who didn't call or have the decency to send flowers."

Lucy Lallos nodded shyly and said hello with a bit of a brogue, showing Jack her rotten teeth and spacious gums.

"Lucy might have seen something that could help us, isn't that right?" said Claire.

"I seen the man on the bike, if that's what you mean, coming out of the cut-through."

"What man?" asked Jack.

"The guy with the helmet on, crying his eyes out when he whizzed on by me. Not for nothing, sir, but I remember him 'cause he was riding on the wrong side of the road, damn near knocked me over."

"What time was this?" asked Jack.

"'Bout six-thirty, last Monday. That's when I usually start my evening run."

"What run is that?" asked Jack, pulling up a chair from the vacant desk next to Claire's.

"Well I call it resource recovery, but you might call it scavenging junk. To supplement my SSI . . . now that Mr. Lallos has passed over."

Claire said, "Lucy is widowed. She lives in a rooming house in Gordon Heights. Half the time the crack fiends swipe her check."

"And when the chocolate drops don't rip me off, what the government sends ain't enough to properly feed a cat."

"I'm sorry for your troubles," said Jack.

"I get by with the help of the Lord Jesus Christ."

"What'd this guy on the bike look like?"

"Maybe your age," she said. "White or I-talian or A-rab, sometimes it's hard to tell. He had nasty eyes and a very dark beard, and he was riding a brand-new silver Fuji."

"How do you know that?"

"My bike is my life, sir. Without it I can't do my work. Before I spent all my money to buy it, I made sure to hang around the bike store, learning what I needed to know. I picked things up. Those Fujis are really loverly machines."

"I understand."

"I got a second look at him whilst I was cursing him, God forgive me. He shoulda had his seat set higher."

"Excuse me?" said Claire.

"His seat was too low," said Lucy. "His knees were bent at the bottom of his stroke . . . He was tall, I suspect, like you."

"Or maybe it wasn't his bike?" said Jack.

Lucy nodded. "Which means maybe he stole it."

Jack got the feeling Lucy thought bike theft ought to be a hanging offense. "How tall do you figure?"

"Six feet," she said, "give or take. Maybe two hundred pounds."

"That's very good," said Jack. "You're very observant."

Lucy brightened at the compliment, leaned forward and asked, "Can you spare another cup of coffee? And maybe one of them buns I saw on the table, as long as no one else looks like they're eatin' 'em."

"Sure," said Claire. "I'm sorry. I should have offered them to you with the coffee."

"Don't think nothing of it. How was you supposed to know I was hungry?"

"Six feet," said Jack. "About my height?"

"Give or take."

"Would you know him if you saw him again?"

Lucy considered this carefully, wrinkling her brow and tugging on the end of a tiny gray braid. "Maybe with his helmet on, I might. Like I said, he was sobbing like a maniac."

"Did you notice if he was wearing gloves?"

"No," said Lucy. "I mean I didn't notice. I'm sorry."

"No need to be," said Jack. "You've done a bang-up job for us, maybe given us the break we needed."

Lucy sat up straighter in her chair, bold enough to rest her elbow on the desk. Claire returned with a buttered bagel and another cup of coffee. "Eat," she said, rubbing Lucy's back. "We can talk more later."

"How good is your artist?" Jack asked Claire.

"Generally terrific. I've seen him do guys better than their mug shots."

"Can we get him?"

"If he's around." Claire picked up her phone and dialed the sketch man's extension. "Vince?" she said. "It's that girl who still won't pose for you. I need a little favor."

"To Lucy," said Jack, raising his wineglass in the late-afternoon sunlight, savoring the Pindar chardonnay, world-class homegrown from the north fork of Long Island.

"And to little old me," said Claire, "a girl, a skirt, who made this moment possible."

She clinked her glass against his and took a sip of Kir. Their eyes met, then broke away, both gazing out at the Great South Bay from the deck of Richardson's Seaside Pub. The bay was becalmed in the late summer doldrums, sun-soaked by a particularly persistent Bermuda high. On the table in front of them were copies of the sketch Detective Vincent Shulthiess had assembled at Lucy's direction.

"Yes, to you," said Jack. "My goddess of law enforcement."

Claire placed her index finger down her throat and pretended to throw up on the table.

Jack said, "Of course, you know as well as I do that any good defense attorney will make Lucy look like a lunatic in court. And that's if we can find this guy . . . and if he had something to do with the murder."

"Why?" asked Claire. "Because she's poor and alone?"

"Because she's fifty-nine years old and looks sixty-nine, because she calls black boys chocolate drops, because she differentiates between whites and I-talians, and because her principal method of transportation is a tricycle flying the goddamn Jolly Roger."

"This could make for an interesting trial."

After the sketch was done, they had walked Lucy Lallos to her tricycle. Chained to a light pole, the army green monster boasted, in addition to the biggest basket Mills had ever seen, a skull and bones pennant on an eight-foot-long antenna. "One of the gang kids give it to me," she told them, "so cars could see me in traffic, and wouldn't nobody mess around with me if I flew their colors."

In the distance a Fire Island ferry blew its whistle. Claire lit a cigarette and took another sip of her drink. "You think this guy is our killer?"

"He's got more going for him now than anybody else. Remember the fibers in the car included beard from a male white, dark brown hair."

"What if the guy was John Q. Citizen out for a ride, and he saw the doggies eating Backman's face and it freaked him?"

"Then someday he'll make a wonderful witness," said Jack. "But why hasn't he come forward?"

"Maybe he's scared. Maybe he rode up on a gang-style execution and it blew him away."

Jack did not think so. The sketch of a man seen fleeing the scene under emotional duress was not a Murder 2 conviction, but this might move the investigation one step closer to resolution. Sergeant Lomack would certainly be pleased. He might even share news of the progress, if not the actual information, with Aaron Delany from *Newsday*. For the moment, the guy on the bike was their boy.

"Does that explain the grease on the seat of the car?" asked Claire.

"It could, if it wasn't from the car-stripper. The bad guy coulda kidnapped Backman, stuffed him in the trunk of his own car, put a bike in the backseat, driven him out here, killed him, then ridden away on his bike to a car he had stashed or a train station. Maybe he had an accomplice. We should show these sketches to the railroad guys."

"And then he did what? Ditched the bike?"

"I don't know. It could be hanging on a wall in his garage. Maybe he sold it. Maybe he put it in a shop to be repainted. Jesus H," said Jack. "The legwork on this case could be phenomenal."

Claire told Jack not to make himself hysterical. It was just as likely someone would recognize the man from his sketch and drop a quarter in the phone.

"Look on the bright side," she said. "We might have this wrapped by tomorrow."

That did not seem like the bright side to Jack.

He dreamed instead of a permanent assignment in Suffolk, a crash pad at the Sheraton, working with Claire every day, every night, running down leads and doing lunch. Next time he would remember to send her flowers.

"What about the sand they found in the grease?" she asked.

"That's simple, I think."

"Oh yeah?"

"He scouted the area beforehand, on his bike. He did his homework."

"Which means he lives near the scene."

Jack explained that a good rider could comfortably cover fifty miles, never mind the extra adrenaline pumping through his body. "What it means," said Jack, "is that our boy could live absolutely anywhere."

Claire spun around to flag the waitress and ordered more wine. Jack checked his reflection in the window, saw a man in lust, with pleasure boats gliding on the bay behind him, their sails the size of his nose.

"So why'd he leave the victim's car there?" she said. "It was dry the night of the murder; those rear wheels weren't buried; if he'd wanted to, he could have dumped the car in Speonk or Brooklyn. But he didn't, and right away that raised the odds we'd find the body. And anyone who knows the score knows some physical evidence is worse than none."

"Unless it's left behind to confuse us, to play games with us. Maybe that's part of the satisfaction."

"Games, eh?" Claire gracefully waved smoke from over the table. "Pick a possible player."

"I don't know: someone close to the victim. Hey, how do you like Dicktop Mazzarella?"

"If nothing else, Jack, you've got balls."

Where do we find such women? he wondered. Why are we never married to them? "Want to know something else? I'm falling for you hard."

"That's only because we're new to each other. Put me in the Nassau bullpen and you'd never even notice me."

He shook his head. "I can't imagine you in our bullpen."

"Sure you can," she said. "I'm one of the boys.

You'd be a drinking buddy. We'd all go out at night for some serious bonding."

He thought not. "Why do you do it, Claire?"

"What—police work?"

"I mean, you must have had countless proposals."

"I wasn't ready to hit the sweats and chase babies, at least not for some benevolent despot. When the right guy shows up, I'll do the right thing."

That her remark struck home was impossible to keep from his face. He shrugged sheepishly, hoping to convey the message that he was not like all the other brutes.

"Don't try that schoolboy look on me, Jack. I've been hustled by the best of them. We're talking guys with something to offer. Not a grunt without bucks."

"So what are you, a gold digger?"

"Right now I'm a cop," she said, "with a gold shield that I didn't get in a Cracker Jacks box . . . and you don't have the sense God gave a crowbar."

They were closing the county recreation center when Jack arrived. The security supervisor knew Jack from the department's summer basketball leagues and didn't mind letting him lock up. It was not the first time the detective had grabbed a late-night workout after a long day. "Y'all get a good pump. I'll catch you on the rebound. And hey, homey," the supervisor said, "who clipped your jib?"

"I fell."

"Un huh."

Alone in the pungent locker room, Jack changed into his shorts and sneakers, tossed his clothes on top of his gun and shield, left the locker closed but unlocked. He jogged down the semidarkened hallway to the weight room. Jack went once around the stations on the Universal Gym, warming up, forcing blood to his muscles, then added weight for the second rotation. For twenty minutes he grunted under the clank of iron plates, pushing himself until his breath ran short, burning air and alcohol. Then he flexed his muscles in the mirror, impressed—the lat spread, double biceps, which way to the beach?—until the sensation struck him that someone was watching him. He dropped his arms and spun to face the door.

Nobody.

In the sauna he turned on all the lights and stretched out naked on the bench, eyes closed, thinking of Claire, hoping that she was home alone, thinking of him. He sweated as much as he could without fainting, then went to the pool and lowered his body into the second lane. He turned lap after lap as his penance for self-abuse. He thought of the silence of underwater death in frozen waters, his gun in an open locker, there to be snatched by an enemy or a thief. He was five feet from the wall when the lights went out, plunging the pool into darkness. His wrist and forehead cracked on the tiled concrete.

"Jesus fucking Christ!" he cried, then swam a frantic backstroke to the center of the pool, waiting for a bullet, possibly from his own gun, the way Artie Backman bought it.

Emergency lights over the doors snapped on.

Jack could see well enough to know he was alone. He breaststroked slowly to the ladder and climbed out, crossed the cold tile floor to the locker room. The clock over the door said 10:01.

13

THE SKETCH ran in Wednesday's late editions, so Jack spent Thursday morning at his desk, facing the wall, fielding calls from every whack-job in the New York tri-state area who knew someone who looked like the man on the bike. Three guys on loan from the vice squad were called upon to help. They logged forty-two calls in four and a half hours, seventeen of which were judged rational. A list of look-alikes was compiled. Jack instructed his new assistants to find these guys and take pictures of them surreptitiously. He would then show them to Lucy Lallos, for a possible photo-pack identification.

The vice cops divided the work and left.

Jack made himself a cup of coffee, then took out his MCI card, punched fifteen numbers into his phone and spoke to his parents in Florida, told them everything was going great.

"How is the weather up there?" his father asked.

"Ninety-two degrees today, Dad. My pants are riding up my crotch."

"Ha—it's cooler here. Say hello to Jennifer."

Quickstop Izzy Goldman came out of his office, told Jack that Captain Mazzarella had asked after him and continued on his way to the john, to "lob a log." Jack thought about taking a ride to Carvel, but mostly he thought about Claire.

"Mills!" Lomack shouted from his door.

"Yes sir?"

"Get into my office!"

Jack followed his leader. Lomack closed the door and sat down behind his desk.

"What's the matter with you, boy?"

"Sir?"

"Answer me this: How come your chick splits and you gain weight? How come you look like you been hit by a truck? And where's the answer to this fucking case?"

Jack studied his wingtips.

"Is it just an act, or are you all fucked up and won't admit it? Because I'm getting the feeling that folks around here are hoping you'll fail. Half is they didn't like Backman, and half is they know you didn't earn this job. They'd like to see you fall on your face, which it looks like you already have."

"I'm okay," said Jack.

Lomack massaged his eyes. "Tell me about Backman's son. Is he a possible? If not, why not?"

"Still working on it," said Jack.

"Tell me everything you know about Louie Allesi."

"Besides that he thinks blacks don't play tennis?"

"Yeah," said Lomack. "What'd he say when you talked to him?"

"I . . . ah, I got Louie on my back burner."

"Your stove is getting awfully fucking crowded."

"I'm just getting started, boss. It's early in the game."

"No, it's not, Jack. If I lost my pen I wouldn't ask you to look for it. You're O-for-forever."

Jack returned to his desk and buried his swollen face in his arms. Lomack was right. He didn't measure up. This job called for brains and talent. The poster pose was not enough. And if the guys resented his previous soft parade, what were they saying now about his slipshod investigation of a brother cop's murder? Nothing good, he wagered.

Two hundred fans filled the bleachers that night to watch the charity game through a chain-link fence, a happy crowd dotted with local celebrities: Jimmy Breslin, Doctor J, Bob Buchmann and Tracy Burgess.

They brought with them Igloo coolers and sacks of Big Macs, ice cream and soda pop, blankets and children. The lights were on, the diamond raked and freshly lined. Jack Mills stood on the sideline and watched the mostly overweight ball players in form-fitting polyester uniforms snap the ball around the diamond before the game, aping Yanks and Mets. He turned down the PBA manager's offer to suit up and play.

"Thanks, but no thanks," he said, pointing to his nose. "Every fucking step hurts."

"No sweat," said the manager. "Just stay close in case this turns into a brawl."

Friends of his from past assignments stopped by

and caught up, commiserated with him on catching the Backman squeal, laughed at his nose and offered to pinch-hit for him in bed with his girlfriend if the job was taking all his time. One old buddy from the Thirteenth confessed to having his wife on the PBA side of the field and his bimbo sitting with the scribes.

So maybe everybody *didn't* hate him.

Tommy Bledsoe, wearing baggy blue jeans and a Catholic Big Brothers T-shirt, inquired of the managers if the charity game needed an umpire. He was certified, he said.

Jack watched the organizers say no, thank you, and send him to the next diamond over, where a girl's CYO game was about to begin. Tommy was rapidly recruited. Jack stood behind the backstop as Tommy crouched behind the catcher in perfect mimicry of a major-league umpire.

"Batter up," he shouted.

The pony-tailed ten-year-old adjusted her batting helmet and stepped up to the plate.

The pitcher delivered.

Tommy yelled, "Ball!" on the first pitch with an enthusiasm rarely seen at CYO games. A called third strike sent him one step away from the catcher, pumping his right arm like he was stabbing a rabid dog. "Yer out of there!" he cried, which made the batter's face screw up in tears.

Several fathers came down from the stands to confer with the managers. Tommy was asked to tone down his act.

"Yeah, yeah," he said. "You want kid gloves. I got it."

Jack chuckled, then strolled to the *Newsday* bench, to say hi to old hands, to put a good face on things. Aaron Delany spotted him, gave a half-hearted wave, approached.

"Hiya, Jack," said Delany. "Who kicked your ass?"

"That's my face, Aaron. And I got hurt fighting someone who called you a hack."

"You here to watch us slaughter your buddies?"

"Yeah," said Jack. "Please—go easy on us."

"I'm serious," said Delany, pounding his fist into the pocket of his baseball glove. "This year we got us a pitcher, a girl from circulation. She's all-league down at the beach for the last five or six years."

"Your secret weapon is a girl?"

"Isn't yours?"

"What do you mean?"

"You're hot copy around town these days. I suggest you suppress your libido."

"The story's wrong."

Delany cocked his head to one side, stopped pounding his mitt. "Katy here tonight?"

Jack shook his head no.

"How's the Babe?"

"I get your point, Aaron."

The police chaplain was calling for the crowd's attention with a bullhorn from home plate. He wore his clerical collar and a big blue chest protector, the umpire with whom no one was likely to argue calls. The monsignor thanked everyone for coming out to support the Heart Association, he thanked the ball players for the fine show he knew they would provide, he thanked the Lord for the gorgeous summer night, and Billy Joel sang the "Star-Spangled Banner."

Jack wished Delany good luck, said he would talk to him later, then sat in the bleachers on the PBA side of the field and drank beer from a Styrofoam cup.

The PBA All-Stars took the field to loud applause, and sent the News Crew down in order.

The News Crew took the field. Jack recognized Aaron Delany's pudgy body in the catcher's gear as he attempted to squat behind the plate. He didn't know the pretty blond pitcher, but he felt sorry for her working to Delany. He rarely caught her underhand tosses, which meant he had to struggle to an upright position, step around the chaplain and retrieve the ball from the ground near the backstop. His return throws were wildly inaccurate, pulling her off the mound, making her lose her spot, her rhythm. "Sorry, Lisa," Aaron kept saying. "Sorry."

The PBA scored twice in the bottom of the first, on four base hits. The PBA crowd cheered lustily as each run crossed the plate. Jack poured himself more beer, and refrained from adding his voice to the celebration. He wanted the cops to win, but he didn't think a blowout would be terribly smart politics. Unfortunately, the boys on the PBA bench gave not one whit about politics. They wanted to bust some ass. One yelled across the field, "Hey, *Newsday,* how's your damn morale?"

There was no further scoring until the top of the fourth inning. Both sides made good plays. The girl could pitch. And Delany's throws found the mound with more regularity.

The News Crew got a man on first with two out in

the fourth, and then their cleanup man smoked the tying run over the fence.

The *Newsday* crowd roared their approval. The celebrities departed. The police fans poured fresh beers and pretended nothing to worry about had happened.

The next three cops to bat grounded sharply to second base for easy putouts.

Jack stood up to stretch, watched flies swarm the floodlights in the parking lot, kids sitting on cars, Tommy Bledsoe walking over from the girls' game. On the other diamond, one of the fathers was working home plate.

H-11-89 probably played in games like this, he thought. Probably stood around in the outfield, dreading her next appearance at the plate, wondering why her parents were making her participate.

"Batter up!"

Aaron Delany led off the fifth by striking out— caught looking. The next batter homered to right.

Once again, in the bottom of the fifth, the blonde kept the cops off base.

Three up, three down in the top of the sixth, and the cops ran into the dugout.

"Last licks, guys."

"I won't be able to face my kids."

"Stop watching the broad and start watching the fucking ball. We owe these motherfuckers."

The leadoff man, a wiry young motorcycle cop, stroked a solid single to left. The next batter hit behind him, advancing the runner to third. The PBA crowd stood up and chanted, "We're gonna kick your butts, hey! We're gonna kick your butts, hey!"

The next two batters fell for sucker pitches and hit sky-high pop-ups to the mound. Lisa snapped them arrogantly out of the air. Fans on both sides stood, cheering their favorites, with so much more than the game on the line.

The pitcher prowled the mound, flipping the ball into her mitt as Demeulenare, a well-muscled robbery dick, stepped into the batter's box. His jaw was clenched, his eyes beady, tendons taut in the forearms.

"No pressure, Mark baby," someone called from the PBA dugout. "It's not like our manhood or anything is hanging in the balance."

Demeulenare smiled grimly and took a deep breath.

Lisa toed the rubber. Leaned forward.

Demeulenare hit the first pitch on the screws, a laser shot at the pitcher's pretty head. She twirled, somehow knocked the ball down with the back of her glove. The runner on third broke for home.

Aaron Delany struggled out of his crouch, tossed his mask, stepped in front of the plate, his mitt held low to the ground. The ball rolled sideways off the pitcher's mound, toward third.

The runner passed the point of no return.

Lisa recovered her balance, pounced on the ball, whirled and fired an underhand strike. The ball arrived in Delany's mitt, as did the runner, sliding hard, spikes high, knocking Delany on the seat of his pants. The ball popped loose, rolled to the backstop. The runners advanced to second and third.

The chaplain called time and checked Delany for

visible wounds. Some of the *Newsday* crowd booed the aggression of the slide, called the base runner names as he trotted to the dugout. The PBA crowd booed the *Newsday* crowd.

The motorcycle cop came back out of the dugout and held up the middle finger on his right hand. "Go play your fag, writer buddies in the Hamptons."

"That's it," Lisa announced, walking in from the mound. "The boys want to fight. I'm sorry, Father. It has nothing to do with you."

"Not a problem. I've half a mind to go with you." Delany put his arm around her shoulders. "Where are you going, Lisa?" he asked. "The score is tied. We can beat these sons of bitches."

"You love these sons of bitches, Aaron. Why would you want to beat them?"

"Because they need a beating, that's why."

"Sorry, Aaron. I can still pitch the second game at Jones Beach if I hurry. We only play for money there."

"But—"

She picked up her windbreaker and aluminum bat, slung her pocketbook over her shoulder, then set out for the parking lot, walking more like a woman with each step from the field. As she wiggled into a red Camaro, you could almost hear hearts breaking.

Everybody got up quietly and left then, without finishing the game, without their trophies, without cleaning up, walking slowly to their cars in grumbling clusters, feeling bad.

Jack hung back, then herded Aaron Delany to his

own car and talked the veteran newsman into a late snack. "No hard feelings, right?"

"You fucking guys suck."

Aaron Delany was only too happy to eat dinner on the arm with a member of the Homicide Squad. He was a bachelor, a man who lived on processed meats and microwave prefabs. Jack trusted him, also felt a bond with him, a sudden similarity in living conditions. They met up at Chez Liz, near Jack's house in Merrick, where the highest point of elevation was the town of Hempstead Landfill. Jack asked for a table in the back and made sure in advance that he would be given the bill.

Delany still wore his softball uniform and loafers. His frizzy hair circled his head like a halo. The scraggly beard was streaked with gray. He was forty-something, an old hippie without a college degree, a street reporter for almost twenty years. He ordered Jack Daniels on the rocks and lit a Camel cigarette.

"How do you feel?" asked Jack, raising his beer in toast.

Delany frowned, said in his gravelly voice, "Bruised and betrayed—how I usually feel after dealing with you guys."

"Sometimes we don't work and play well with others."

"No shit."

"I need to ask you a question, Aaron, if we're back to being friends."

"You need to ask me a question? Ain't that a fucking switch. And here I was, thinking you were gonna give me the Backman exclusive."

"Maybe I will, when I have it."

Delany turned his head and glanced sideways at Jack. "Save the butter and buy me whiskey. If I'm being stroked, I want to enjoy it."

Jack looked around the room, ignored a glancing pass from a woman sharing her table with a loaf of bread. He explained where he was with the case: "Stuck dead in the mud."

"That's a shame. Why tell me?"

"I don't know. Get you to help?"

Delany laughed, and knocked back the rest of his drink. "Is this on the record or off, I can't remember."

"I'm not laughing," said Jack.

"No," said Delany. "I can see that. Rod Lomack on you hard?"

Jack shrugged. "It could be worse. Mazzarella could have the case."

"Ah, yes," said Delany. "The hard-on with ears. How are Dicktop and Quickstop?"

"They suck, same as always."

Delany lit another cigarette and sat back, shaking his head. "So you need help. What kind?"

"Who would have the balls to tell me what was going wrong in Backman's precinct?"

"Someone who knows you and has nothing to lose. Someone who hates their guts."

"Yeah."

"You know Tommy Bledsoe?"

"Yeah, sure."

"He told me tonight he's retiring. Said working for Mad Mario made him feel like ten pounds of shit in a five-pound bag. You should maybe go say good-bye."

14

 SUNDAY, THE homicide bullpen was staffed by a skeleton crew, men collectively hoping murderers goofed off on the Sabbath.

Lomack was off. Captain Richard Mazzarella was off. Quickstop Izzy Goldman had run to the men's room to "pinch another loaf" over an hour ago and Chief Barone was in Atlantic City at a three-day seminar on Maximum Efficiency for Minimal Expenditures: Getting Everything out of the Cop on the Street. Detectives Mills, Trankina, Donleavy and Schultz sat around the office with their ties down and their collars open, agreeing that it was too hot to go outside and too fucking boring doing nothing.

Jack had tried to catch up with Tommy Bledsoe on his day off to no avail, and Louie Allesi's shop was closed for the weekend. Claire was off, she said having dinner at her parents'. Jenny and the Babe were at Babe's sister's house in Hampton Bays.

Someone suggested taking turns at a nearby saloon. Too risky, said someone else. Captain Mazzarella might pull another surprise inspection, as he had the week before and the week before that. "And you know the mood he's been in lately," Trankina said.

Jack's phone rang. "Detective Mills."

"How ya doing, guy. Allen Cipriot, Jersey State Troopers. That's C-I-P-R-I-O-T."

"What can I do for you?"

"I'm out in Morristown, looking at a picture of an unidentified dead girl in a swimming pool. My computer tells me you're working a similar case."

"That's right," said Jack. "A case that's dead in the water. No pun intended."

"My girl looks about twenty years old. She was nude, in about four feet of very funky water. A pool service crew found her, getting the place ready for a closing. The owners of the house say they don't know nothin'."

"This is a nice place?"

"Nice enough. Maybe six hundred, seven hundred thousand."

Jack said, "Mine was even ritzier. Got a pen?" He filled in Trooper Cipriot on the high points of H-11-89. "I'll send you what I got. Let's bang our heads together. Maybe we'll start a fire," he said, though he doubted it. This was the fourth such call he'd gotten in the last three months. They never amounted to anything but they helped lend the appearance of progress, or motion anyway.

"I appreciate it, Mills," said the trooper. "Send it to the Trenton Barracks overnight Federal Express. I'd like to have it on my desk tomorrow morning."

"Okay," said Jack. "No sweat. This could help me too."

"So other than that, how's it going? You in on that big cop killing?"

"It's mine."

"You're made if you crack it."

"And doomed if I don't."

"Anything to go on so far?"

"Squat."

"Keep the faith, guy."

When he was off the phone, staring into the empty space behind Eats O'Day's desk, Al Trankina lifted his head above his glass divider. "Downstairs called. Dicktop's in the building."

Captain Mazzarella had indeed been rather cranky the last few days and Jack did not relish seeing His Eminence.

Jack grabbed his radio and briefcase and slipped out the back.

He spent the next two hours parked in the loading zone outside Angela Cortelli's apartment building, mulling her over again as a suspect and imagining himself banging the balls off her, chauvinist pig that he was. Poor folks came and went, no one Jack recognized. What a waste of time. He turned on the AM radio. The Mets were losing in Chicago, and the Yanks had already lost in the Bronx, exacerbating the rotten mood he was in. He was just about to pack it in when a florist's delivery truck pulled behind him and honked.

Jack fished his shield out of his pocket and held it out the window.

An old black man limped down from the driver's side and came to Jack's window.

"I need the zone," he said. "S'posed to be for

workingmen's trucks. Otherwise I get a ticket for double parking."

"Why don't you park around back," said Jack. "I'm busy right now."

"Why don't I just chuck my deliveries off a bridge and set the truck on fire."

Jack relaxed and laughed. "Okay, I get the picture. Is it really that bad around here now?"

"Crack," the man said, "changed everything."

"I hear ya. Who's the lucky lady?" Jack asked, nodding at the building.

"Same as always. Woman named Angela Cortelli."

Claire Williamson entered the Citibank branch in Franklin Square at the appointed time on Monday morning. Twenty-three-year-old Assistant Manager Richard Kinard III, recently of Rutgers University, had her wait ten minutes on a couch perpendicular to his office. When he finally opened his door, he tossed a file to his secretary. He did not even glance at her. A busy man, with violet suspenders and a Hamptons haircut. He was headed back into his office.

Claire stood up.

"Uh . . . Detective?"

"Claire Williamson. Thank you for taking the time—"

"I'm sorry to keep you waiting. Would you care for a cup of coffee?"

"Why thank you, Mr. Kinard."

He led her into his mauve office and closed the door, apologizing again for the wait, the banking crisis, the sorry state of law and order. He pulled the visitor's chair around next to his, so they could read together "to facilitate my explanation of banking codes."

"Thank you," she said. "How thoughtful."

While Richard Kinard showed Claire the records pertaining to Arthur Backman's money market savings account, he made sure to brush his thigh against hers. "Four grand and change," he said. "Not a whole hell of a lot, I'm afraid."

"I don't believe this was his principal investment," she said.

Mr. Kinard patted her black-stockinged knee once, one mover and shaker to another. "Ke-rect."

Claire smiled, an older woman glad for the attention. "I meant this was his private mad money. He had other accounts that his wife was aware of."

Kinard leaned close enough for her to smell his cologne. "And a couple more that she wasn't."

"Oh, really?" Claire raised an eyebrow.

"Really."

"Where?"

"Your copy's on that table." An anonymous manila file rested on the laminated surface of the conference table.

"But I don't have permission for that—yet."

Kinard leaned closer. "Maybe I can give it to you . . . without all that legal crap." He gently took her hand.

"Do you think that's possible? You aren't frightened of taking such a chance?"

"I have a confession to make, Detective." He

smiled, thinking he was witty and charming. "I find you incredibly attractive. I think I could handle dating a cop."

Claire smiled coyly. "So many men wilt when they think about what I do. The gun I carry. The handcuffs."

"Not a problem, I assure you."

"I have your number," she said, and plucked his suspender like a harp string.

"Please use it."

Claire stood up and straightened her dress. She picked up her pocketbook and the other Backman file.

Walking out of the bank she thought of her father, and wondered whether he would be proud of her at that moment. In spite of her career she was still his little girl, but fast becoming the spinster daughter, Aunt Claire, charged with emergency babysitting duties and remembering birthdays and other people's anniversaries. No one thought she would marry. Maybe they wrote her off as gay. At the last Friday night dinner, her father had asked skeptically after "Durwood."

"That's Drew," she had reminded him.

"I'm sorry. And he's a flight attendant?"

"You can stop with the Drew jokes. I'm not seeing anyone now."

"Good," he had said.

In her car she opened the file and read down a long list of figures, until she got to the bottom line. Certificates of Deposit in Arthur Backman's name totaled $237,000. The first deposit had been made almost seven years prior, around the time, if memory served, that Arthur Backman took over the administration of the Thirteenth Precinct. Backman's side job?

"What a lot of roof shingles," she said.

"You were lucky the bank was so forthcoming." Rod Lomack was hunched over Eats's desk, examining the figures. "They only had to give us what we asked for."

"It wasn't luck," said Claire. She was leaning on the glass partition, smiling broadly.

"No?" said Jack. "What was it? Your superior technique?"

"No. But it could have been."

Lomack laughed. "You offered him immunity, right?"

"I offered him sex."

"Hey," said Jack, tossing his pen aside.

"Nice work," Lomack said. "Now what do we do with it?"

Jack sat back and scratched his head, squinted, decided to risk it. "I got an idea."

Claire feigned astonishment, as if witnessing a miracle.

"A guy I know at the Thirteenth is packing it in. Maybe he hates management enough to talk to us."

"Not bad," Lomack said. "Keep trying."

"That's it," said Jack. "They come to me one at a time."

"We know," said Claire.

Jack drove Claire to Tommy Bledsoe's Syosset address in wounded silence. Since he had been intimate just once with Claire, small problems had grown larger and new ones had appeared. The girl was tough. He kept his mouth shut and sulked. Claire looked out her window when they were moving, read a newspaper at the lights.

They found Tommy Bledsoe in the driveway of a large red ranch-style house. He was loading baggage into his black Jeep Cherokee.

"Hey, Jack. How ya doing? Ma'am."

"Fine, Tommy, fine. This is Detective Williamson from Suffolk."

Tommy bowed. "Charmed."

Jack said, "I heard you got a notion to pack it in."

Tommy said that was true, that he'd been thinking about it for quite some time. "I've had it up to here with their Mickey Mouse bullshit. Mad Mario was the last straw. Twenty years is more than enough of my life to piss away. I'm out there hauling battered old ladies to the hospital while the titless wonders at headquarters are checking price fluctuations with their brokers. And if I say something, I'm the one who's disloyal, the honky they stick on steady midnights."

"Where you headed?"

"Vegas for a while, probably. The wife don't mind. Too many old cops in Florida, sitting around gabbing about capers no one else remembers."

Tommy slammed the tailgate shut.

"Did you know Artie Backman had a lot of money hidden away?

Tommy looked at Jack, surprised, suddenly aware that this house call was for more than wishing him well. "Hidden? Hell, he bragged about it."

"How'd he get it?"

"Probably stole it. Everybody was busy getting theirs." He snorted disdainfully, then turned on his heel for the garage. Jack followed him at a distance while Claire petted his Jeep. Tommy handed Jack a fishing rod. "Make yourself useful," he said. "Goes on top."

"How'd he do it?" asked Jack.

Tommy shrugged, walked slowly to the driver's door, flipping his keys. "Goddamn, I knew this was gonna happen."

"What?"

"Do me a favor, Jack. Let me rest in peace."

Jack looked up and down the block. "We really need to know."

"But—"

"Hey!" said Claire. "You gotta help. You'll be sitting in Vegas at Christmas, saying you wished you had. We're talking about a cop-killer here."

Tommy Bledsoe turned a disturbing shade of chalk.

"She's right," said Jack.

"Goddamn," he said. "If you'da come ten minutes later, I would've been gone."

"Just point me in the right direction," Jack said softly.

Tommy nodded, led only Jack back to the garage where he rolled out his Lawn-Boy and tugged on the cord. The engine turned over immediately, filling the air with blue smoke and noise enough to ruin any audio recording.

He leaned into Jack's ear: "He had a car scam going. Something about condemning the rear ends of good patrol cars and then sneaking them out as parts."

"And putting them back together?"

"Yeah. And then probably Louie Allesi gave them a fresh coat of paint. He could get them registered in Jersey because the DMV there is so screwed up they run a six-month backlog."

"You found this information . . ."

"Going over motorpool paperwork. Too many bad universal joints in a row."

"Artie had in excess of two hundred grand stashed away. That's an awful lot of broken patrol cars."

Tommy Bledsoe smiled. "Over too many beers once, Artie told me him and Captain Mazzarella had done a couple of favors, setting up a goon squad for landlords in Long Beach that wanted to go condo and couldn't get their renters out. They moved a gang of wino crackheads into the vacant apartments and let nature take its course. Maybe it was bar talk, maybe they really did it. Fucking Artie could always lay his hands on willing workers."

"For who?" asked Jack.

Tommy shrugged. "Probably his smut buddy, Louie. They were real tight. Backman even used to get invited to Louie's private Christmas parties. He'd hire broads to gang-bang his business pals in the wrecked cars, right at the shop, like some kind of Fellini movie—until his wife's Uncle Joey found out and had him beaten up with a baseball bat."

Jack hit the stop button on the Lawn-Boy and straightened up. "Have a nice life, Tommy."

When they were back in the squad car, Claire asked Jack what Bledsoe had said. He told her, almost word for word.

"Your job is worse than mine," she said. "Fucking crooks."

"I know, I know," said Jack. "All Nassau cops are scum. That's probably why you've already dumped me. Or is it my fucked-up nose?"

"What?"

"I mean, we make love on the beach and now it's like it never even happened."

Claire scoffed: "Listen to you."

"You think I don't have feelings?"

She looked out her window. "Of course you do, but they're getting in the way of the case."

"Okay. What if the case was solved?"

Claire looked at him and said, "I don't know, Jack. What exactly are you asking for?"

15

THE INVESTIGATION jumped the tracks that day.

Jack and Claire returned to headquarters and began a secret file on a brand-new suspect.

Claire felt Nassau cops would speak more openly if she was not present, so Jack roamed the halls alone.

That afternoon a disgruntled cop in Records told Jack what he already knew—that Captain Mazzarella was tight with the Republican Party and the brothers Otto. He had made his climb up the ranks of the Nassau County Police Department with all possible political assistance. The Records cop said, "The greasy bastard would stab himself in the back, if one of the bigshots suggested it."

An old pal, now the deputy commander of Internal Affairs, said Mazzarella was a rat, an open mike among the troops, and had been since his first day on the job. Fifteen years back, maybe more, during a difficult contract negotiation, Mazzarella had given the name of the PBA president's married girlfriend to the negotiator for the county. Immediately afterward, important language was changed in the contract regarding overtime benefits and sick leave. The union caved.

The deputy commander slipped Jack memoranda regarding Mazzarella's connections. The files revealed that Mazzarella had received a verbal reprimand for "associating with persons of questionable character, to the detriment of the Nassau County Police Department." Mazzarella, the deputy commander explained, had been filmed by the FBI while serving as chauffeur and occasional bodyguard to Joey Buscemi, the president of Scaramouche Real Estate and Construction Corporation. Mazzarella also allegedly lined up off-duty cops through Captain Arthur Backman of the Thirteenth Precinct, NCPD, to drive uninspected, uninsured, unregistered taxi cabs from New York City to auctions in Pennsylvania for Scaramouche Motors, Inc.

At the departmental hearing the previous year, in his own defense, Mazzarella had maintained that Joseph Buscemi of Harbor Point Bluffs was a respected member of the community. He was involved in charity work and Republican fund-raising, a deeply religious man. A wing at the medical center bore his name. Mazzarella's lawyer offered to parade the cream of Nassau County politicos through the hearing room to establish just these relevant facts.

Tribunal eyebrows rose. Throats cleared. Then somebody called timeout. The board huddled. Calls were made. Oaths muttered. Orders given. Mazzarella made his deal for the slap on the wrist.

Jack also discovered, in an addendum to the original complaint, that leading citizen Joey Buscemi was currently under investigation by the district attorney's office for renting lavish suites of offices at cut-rate prices to businesses with ties to the Republican Party, such as Scaramouche Travel, Agnew and Agnew Printers, the law offices of the venerable Mr. Wallace Wilson Benz. In return, it was alleged, Joey Buscemi, Louie Allesi and others got seventy-five-year leases from the county at incredibly favorable rates on commercial property at Switchel Field. The lawyer who negotiated the leases was Wallace Wilson Benz. His junior partner, Michael Backman.

None of this was terribly good news to a floundering detective whose career had been built on his popularity with the powers-that-be. In Nassau County, one did not bite the hands that fed.

"Captain Mazzarella is about the last fucking guy I wanted to interview," Jack said as he drove back from a late lunch in heavy traffic on Jericho Turnpike.

Claire blew smoke out the car window. "Don't matter what you want. Your captain's got himself a little problem."

Jack stopped at the traffic light on Glen Cove Road and rested his head on his forearm against the wheel. It was almost five o'clock in the afternoon, and the normally busy commercial strip in Mineola was clogged with roadwork every half a mile. The labor crews were from Scaramouche Construction Company, the materials from Scaramouche Cement.

"You don't understand," said Jack. "The Dicktop made me. Never mind that he's turned on me."

"Cut it out."

"He's a jock-sniffer. He used to like me, from the Boys' Club and the Police Olympics. We used to bend the elbow on the rubber-chicken circuit. My money was no good. One night at a retirement party I told him I was frustrated. 'Back in a flash,' he says. He went to the bar, bought the right guy a fresh drink, and the next day I had my promotion to homicide. How am I gonna ask him about goon squads?"

Claire stubbed her cigarette out in the ashtray and said nothing.

Jack gestured helplessly. "He was with me when you guys found the body."

"Where was he when Backman disappeared?"

"He's a cop."

"You have to roust him," she said. "And I have to be there, to cover your ass. Probably Lomack too. Mazzarella's a hard case. When he knows we're onto him, he could get really pissy."

"Oh, God," said Jack, "is this gonna suck."

Rodney Lomack was gone for the day when they got to headquarters. The duty chart showed him back to work the following morning. The duty chart also showed that Captain Mazzarella had pre-signed on his meal period for the last hour of his tour. He'd be taking his dinner break from six to seven. It was 5:20, and he was gone like a big bald eagle. Jack was relieved; he hoped Claire could not tell.

Claire said, "He's not on lunch till six. Call radio and have him get back here."

"This is a captain we're talking about, you know."

"Say his input is needed."

"You're sure?"

"Absolutely. Yeah. And the more I think about it, the more I think we should leave Lomack out of the loop. Mazzarella would probably appreciate the discretion."

That made sense to Jack. He called radio and paged Captain Mazzarella. Waited fifteen minutes. Tried again. Nothing.

"He's got his radio off," Jack said. "Which means he's probably got his pants off too."

"Maybe somebody called him. Maybe he's huddled with his lawyer. Or buckling in for the flight to the Cayman Islands."

"I'm gonna have radio put out word to have the patrol cars scout the immediate area for the captain's car. What the fuck? Could be he went to dinner."

"Get him in here, Jack. Don't fuck around with this. It's our asses on the line now too, you know."

"Okay, okay," said Jack. "I'm making the call. See—I'm dialing."

Captain Richard Mazzarella finished off his little snack at B. K. Sweeney's: three Rusty Nails, a deluxe shrimp cocktail and a rare filet mignon. Tonight was his card night, the game close by at a full inspector's house in Carle Place. No point in going all the way home to Island Park, which he rarely did anyway when work or play could keep him away. He thanked the maître d' for so graciously picking up his tab, then left by the back door, well fed and satisfied, a properly appreciated servant of the masses.

The beat cop watched him nervously from across the street, trying not to show it. He had been waiting by the captain's car, nodding and smiling at rich Garden City commuters: young women with attaché cases and Reebok pumps, men in club ties and tasseled loafers, squash rackets under their arms. They were glad to see him. He could tell that they thought he worked for them, personally.

Mazzarella waved to him as he walked to his car. He had his car keys in his hand, an important man in a very big hurry. "How ya doing, guy?"

"Good, Cap. How 'bout you?"

"Good. Can't complain."

"I've been waiting for you, Cap."

Mazzarella squinted at the face. "Look, I'm running late. Do you have some business with me?"

"'Fraid I do."

Mazzarella looked angrily from the name tag to the shield, dissected by a mourning band in honor of Arthur Backman. He slid behind the wheel and hit the ignition.

"Captain?"

Something was up, Mazzarella sensed. The engine turned over and revved; the radio came on, repeating the call-in request for Captain Mazzarella. The beat cop bent forward to peer into the car window.

Mazzarella's attention was divided between the

radio and the cop. Probably wanted a favor, some kind of boost off his foot post.

"Helpless assholes," Mazzarella said, grabbing the handset. "Can't live without me for ten fucking minutes."

The gun barrel floated up next to his earlobe.

16

THE FOLLOWING morning, Jack Mills sat in a daze at his desk, watching the swarm of activity around him. Reporters arrived at Lomack's door, uniformed brass. Lomack was in and out of the office, unavailable to anyone under the rank of captain. Claire was in Suffolk County court, on a prior case come to trial. He ate lunch with Al Trankina at the Jack-in-the-Box on Jericho Turnpike.

At 2 P.M. they brought the family in—Mrs. Mazzarella and her teenage sons. The pretty woman broke down and wailed like a banshee. The police chaplains responded, the trauma counselors. Doors were closed and voices lowered. The rumor flew about the building: mob hit, mob hit, like a mantra.

At the 3 P.M. staff meeting, after a lengthy update, Lomack told the rapidly assembled task force about a disturbing departmental phenomenon: a spate of threatening phone calls to superior officers, telling them they were next. Lomack glanced around the room.

"Apparently some of our own guys think this shit

is funny. One brazen motherfucker told the commissioner's secretary that a deputy inspector was next on the list, then an inspector, and so on up the ladder."

"You got one too," said Trankina. "Guy sounded loopy."

The men did their best not to giggle.

"We can't let our guys be kidnapped out of their patrol cars," said Lomack. "It looks like hell on the nightly news."

The vacuum created by the disappearance of Detective Captain Richard Mazzarella had sucked Sergeant Lomack to the top of the Homicide squad. With Captain Tomlinson on loan to the Federal Narcotics Strike Force, and Quickstop Izzy Goldman battling his spastic bowels, Chief Barone knew Lomack was the only man capable of directing the Mazzarella task force.

Lomack used that leverage to negotiate for himself the use of six full-time homicide detectives and three more men from Vice. He was promised flash money, unlimited travel if necessary. Barone threw in the use of a conference room, extra phones, a copier, a computer and a coffee maker.

Lomack gathered what information he had and gave a press conference from the stage in the headquarters auditorium. In his opening statement, Lomack told the reporters that the blood next to Mazzarella's car was undoubtedly the captain's, present in sufficient quantity to suggest serious injury. Tracks on the pavement indicated the captain had been dragged to another vehicle. Kidnap or kidnap and murder? At this time there were no witnesses, no suspects. All possibilities were being considered. Nothing was being ruled out.

"Any questions?" said Lomack, hands on the lectern, ready to propel himself from the spotlight at the first opportunity.

A tall thin white man with long gray hair stood up. "Will Clarke, the *Village Voice*. Would you care to comment on last year's rumors and allegations concerning Captain Mazzarella's connections to organized crime?"

"No, I would not, other than to state that the charges were dismissed."

"For insufficient evidence?" asked Will Clarke.

"That is correct."

"Which means the rumors weren't necessarily untrue."

"Next question," said Lomack.

"What about the condoms in the glove compartment of Captain Mazzarella's car?" Clarke said.

"Mr. Clarke, I'm getting a little tired of you hogging the spotlight. I'll move on to someone else."

"Aaron Delany, from *Newsday*."

Lomack said, "No kidding."

"Could Mazzarella's disappearance be some sort of an elaborate hoax?"

"To what end?"

"To cover his tracks."

"Why?" said Lomack.

"In case he had reason to want to disappear."

Lomack smiled paternally at the faces behind the lights. "I think we're getting a bit silly here, don't you? Doesn't it seem more likely the captain was attacked in connection with his duties for this police department? It shouldn't come as a surprise to you that cops make themselves many enemies. I'd venture to say Captain Mazzarella has personally placed behind bars five hundred felons during the course of his career. All of these felons have family and friends. Some nurse grudges."

Delany raised a pencil. "What if Mazzarella thought someone was closing in on him? No way he goes to jail, right? So he spreads a little blood around his car and takes a walk. He knows the cops never look among the living for a man they think is dead."

Lomack sighed and looked at the ceiling tiles. Aaron Delany had a mind that constructed conspiracies. Lomack had found him sympathetic and helpful on occasion. Not this time.

"As I said before, nothing, and I mean nothing—not even the most farfetched scenario—has been ruled out. You will excuse me then, people? I've got an awful lot to do."

Lomack walked off the stage and made his way to the conference room next to the Homicide bullpen, where his task force was gathered, drinking coffee and smoking cigarettes, watching the chick from Channel 12 News express her fears for the safety of all policemen everywhere.

"How'd I look?" Lomack asked Jack.

"A cross between Judge Thomas and Jesse Jackson."

"Maybe that'll buy us time."

Chief Barone sat in the back of the room while Lomack laid out a strategy on the blackboard for gathering background data. Each man was told what he would be doing, why he would be doing it and what was the ultimate point of it all. One man would follow the physical evidence, the lab tests on the results of the search of the car. One man would work the organized-crime angle. One, the personnel files. One, the captain's family and friends. Izzy Goldman would study Mazzarella's open cases, since he was already familiar with most of them.

Chief Barone stood up and cleared his throat. All heads turned his way. "I don't have to tell you how important I consider this. A brother is missing."

"Yes, sir," said Lomack. "The men understand."

The chief slipped out as the task force packed up and dispersed, leaving Jack alone with Lomack.

"Well?" said Lomack, closing the door. "What the fuck is going on here? In a month, we lose two unpopular bosses. Is there a connection inside the job? Why do I have this creepy feeling?"

"If I didn't know before who killed Artie Backman," said Jack, "losing Captain Mazzarella hasn't made it any clearer."

"In your opinion," said Lomack, "is it in any way possible the same guy did them both?"

"Who the fuck knows? I was starting to wonder if Mazzarella waxed Artie."

"Oh, yeah? Like a chain letter? You sound like Delany."

Jack told Rod Lomack what Tommy Bledsoe had told him about the car racket and the eviction service. "I had the guys out looking for him," said Jack. "That's what I was trying to tell you last night."

"Go check Allesi," Lomack said. "The cops who worked for him. Check the mistress. Check fucking everybody. I want alibis, ironclad. I want phone records. And then I want my hands around the neck of this scumbag." He looked at Jack with a hardness Jack had not seen in the man before. "Do everything—now."

Officer Charlie Blaney of the Thirteenth Precinct sat in Jack Mills's squad car parked at the curb while Jack laid it out for him: The guys upstairs need help. What did he know? What did he think?

Blaney looked past Jack to his tiny house, a basic white Levittown ranch nearly overgrown with shrubbery. All of his neighbors' yards had been landscaped, the houses expanded in one way or another, then cedar-shingled or aluminum-sided. Their owners must have considered Blaney a loser, Jack thought, the occupant of the neighborhood eyesore. There were sleep lines on his cheek; he said he was working midnights.

Throughout the interview, Charlie Blaney sat balled up in the front seat, whining in a high-pitched voice that Jack was gonna ruin his life. He had a nosy wife, nosy neighbors. Nobody trusted him as it was.

"Bottom line: Is Angela a viable suspect?" asked Jack.

"Not to my mind, but maybe you know something I don't."

"Nice girl?" said Jack.

"A royal pain in the ass. I poured a month into her and then ran for my fucking life. Then I got phone calls and heavy breathing for the next six months. I'm still not so sure she didn't talk to my wife." Blaney bit the fingernail on his thumb. "I paid, Mills. You can believe that. Six months without sleep, afraid the bride'd blow my brains out. Now I don't go nowhere without her. Not even to the bowling alley. I'm lucky she lets me go to work."

"How long ago was this minor marital transgression committed?" asked Jack.

"Three years, maybe."

"Any ideas who might have offed Backman?"

"Sorry. Any word on Captain Mazzarella?"

"Nope."

Jack drove east on the tree-lined Northern State Parkway to the Long Island Expressway, out to Exit 62, Nicolls Road. Retired police officer Anthony Zendt lived on Blue Point Road in Farmingville, and Jack needed to speak to him to close out his inquiry among the legion of Angela Cortelli's swains. So he'd have something to tell his boss at least. *The Lovers of Angela Cortelli,* he thought, a Thirteenth Precinct Production.

Tony Zendt's neat gray ranch with red doors and trim was on a fenced rectangle in a wooded hollow near the highest point of Blue Point Road, where it crested the Ronkonkoma Moraine. From Zendt's paved driveway Jack could see the Great South Bay, Fire Island, the silver Atlantic. And yet the neighborhood was shoddy, the surrounding bungalows in various states of disrepair.

Jack knocked on the front door. No one answered.

He looked through the letters in the mailbox, found a Long Island Lighting Company bill bearing

Zendt's name. A letter from the Nassau County Patrolmen's Benevolent Association. Credit card offers. A contest announcement from Ed McMahon.

Jack took a stroll around the grounds. In the well-kept backyard he saw a small vegetable garden. A hammock. A redwood picnic table shoved flush against the house under the dining-room window. No benches. No nothing.

"Shit."

He left his card in the mailbox, with a request that Zendt call him as soon as possible, then got back in his car and made the long drive back to Mineola.

Sergeant Lomack was waiting for him, and not in the best of moods. "Well?" he said when Jack walked in.

Jack shook his head.

"Hey, honky," said Lomack, "people are starting to forget my beautiful face. Can you dig it? I had to wait fifteen minutes for a table at Dion's this afternoon, and I'm fairly certain I heard the N word used by someone at the bar. That shit don't happen when I'm dragging in bad guys on *Jive at Five.*"

"Sorry, Sarge. I'm doing my best." He mentioned the miles he had covered that day.

Rodney Lomack looked at the ceiling grimly.

"Make copies of your logs for me. I want to be able to document effort and diligence. Maybe our perp really did think of everything and this ain't our goddamn fault."

"Effort we got. It's results that are looking thin."

"Stick with it, Jack."

Jack threw him a clenched-fist salute and sat down to type up his notes. The telephone on his desk rang, the sound of a reprieve.

"Homicide," he said tonelessly.

"Detective Mills?" said a man's voice.

"Speaking."

"Tony Zendt. You want to tell me what were you doing snooping around my house today? My neighbor down the block thought you were one of those bastards from the retirement board, trying to catch me cutting my lawn. Then I saw 'homicide' on your card."

"I wanted to talk to you about Angela Cortelli."

"So you call, you make an appointment. I'm not a hard guy to find."

"You're right, I should have called. But I was on my way back to the barn so I figured I'd give you a shot. Sorry to worry your neighbor."

"You don't know the shit they've pulled," said Zendt. "I got out on three-quarters a while ago, and twice now the slimy fucks on the pension board have tried to say I faked a bad back to do it. Even gave me four flats one day, hoping I'd run out and change them myself. I finally got myself a hooked-up lawyer and the fucking bullshit stopped. Do yourself a favor, guy. Never get hurt on this job."

"I'm hip," said Jack. "I know I'm just a number."

"Cocksuckers."

"How are you fixed for time these days? I'd like to meet with you for an hour or so next week. I hope you can give me some insight into Angela's

176

character. Her name has come up repeatedly in the Backman investigation."

"Name it," said Zendt. "My time is my own. And I don't mind driving in to see you."

"Please," said Jack. "Any chance I get to skip town I take. I'm sure you remember the feeling."

Scaramouche Body and Fender did business out of a cinder-block three-bay garage on Main Street in Belmont. Jack counted five workers and a big brown German shepherd. The air was filled with the dusty haze of paint and the air-jack sound of automotive repair.

The little office was paneled, the green-checked linoleum floor streaked with grease. A pretty girl in a black T-shirt sat behind the desk, talking on the phone. Her tits were huge, encased in a bra with girders and struts. A hospital mask was hanging from her neck. The hand-lettered sign on the wall behind her said: LABOR RATES: $50.00 PER HOUR. IN-SURANCE ESTIMATES GIVEN GLADLY. The radio played "Money for Nothing."

She looked at Jack Mills, rolled her eyes, and said into the phone, "Ya got three more days, for which I'm charging you storage. Then Louie's selling your car for whatever he can get. Now goodbye."

She hung up without emotion. "Hi," she said. "What can I do for you?"

Jack showed her his badge. "I'm looking for Louie."

"In the back, with his head up the ass of the Camaro. Tell him I said his mother called too."

Jack found Louie Allesi at the back of the shop, talking on a wall phone, smoking a cigarette. In his

midforties, Allesi wore dark brown coveralls and a
New York Yankees baseball cap, cocked ninety
degrees to the side like a street kid. From the chain
around his neck hung what looked like a golden
sperm cell.

Louie Allesi hung up the phone. "Good afternoon, Detective. What can I do you out of?"

"Did she tell you to call your mother too?"

Louie grinned. "Ya gotta call your mom."

"Any place we can talk?"

"Out back. Where we don't have to breathe no
enamel."

Jack followed Louie out the side door and
around to the storage lot that was packed with cars.
They sat on rusty aluminum chairs, facing each
other, leaning forward like tired ball players. Louie
puffed on his cigarette. "You wearing a wire?"

"No."

"Mind if I check?"

"I'll submit to the indignity of a search if it
means you'll be straight with me."

Louie looked Jack over, then nodded. Jack stood
up and allowed himself to be frisked.

"So, okay. What do you want to know? My silent
partners, right? They're dropping like flies."

"It looks real bad for you, Louie."

Louie removed his cap and ran his hand through
his dark brown hair. Cleaned up, in a silk suit and
pointy shoes, he was probably handsome. Jack
wondered if he was doing the girl in the office.

"Whaddaya talking about, bad for me?"

"It looks like some funky shit 'bout to hit the fan.
People are saying the meanest things about you
guys."

Louie took a drag on his cigarette, then flicked it into the weeds. "Uncle Joey ain't gonna like that."

"Uncle Joey can kiss my ass."

"I'll forget you said that—save us all a lot of trouble."

"Suit yourself. All I mean is, two cops you've done business with ain't doing so good anymore. People start to wonder what the fuck is going on."

"Look," said Louie, "my thing with the cops was always strictly legal. We bought some buildings together. We made a couple of bucks. Is this America or what?"

"What buildings? Where?"

"Freeport, Belmont, Hempstead, Long Beach. We diversified."

"You bought tenements," said Jack. "You rented to welfare."

"Someone's got to, right?"

"Who?"

Louie sighed dramatically. Jack got the message: The act of naming names was painful.

Painful but sometimes necessary. "Richie Mazzarella, Artie Backman and me . . . we put together a buying coalition and split the profits when we had 'em. Even paid our taxes, you could check it out. The company's called Allesi Management Corp. The phone rings here."

"What'd you need cops for?" asked Jack.

"Good help is hard to find."

"What do you mean?"

"What do I mean. Like here, these guys that paint cars, they ain't no good for fucking nothing. This one dumb fuck I had to fire, every day at lunch he's smoking hash oil. Then he's real surprised when the Vette he's got on the lift comes tumbling down on its side. Didn't think it was possible he could forget to set the locks."

"Again," said Jack, "why cops?"

Louie shrugged and showed Jack his palms. "Who don't need a cop now and then? I don't have Uncle Joey with me in this, so I looked for an edge of my own, a fallback position. Maybe one day Uncle Joey goes away, or the fucking Democrats get in, and then who's gonna look out for Louie? Louie's gonna look out for Louie, that's who."

"How much cash did they invest?"

"Ten grand apiece at the start, to buy our first building and get it fixed up. More after that. Artie Backman always put in a little less, but he swung the hammer."

"How much money did you make?"

"We took a freaking bath on paper, but to tell the truth, each of us was pulling in fifty, fifty-five a year last time I looked. It isn't one of my major investments."

"Who's your lawyer, in case I want to check out your paperwork?"

"W. W. Benz."

"You know a chick named Angela Cortelli?"

"No."

"You're a wise man, Louie. A wise man ought to be more careful than to get wrapped up in a homicide investigation. You got too many fronts to defend."

Louie slapped his forehead with the palm of his hand. "What am I thinking about? That was you put the bug in Mario Cullen's ear, on that tennis-court thing."

"Nope," said Jack. "That was Richie Mazzarella, your former gumba."

"That Dicktop motherfucker!"

"So you see how things are looking bad for you? Besides repainting those patrol cars for Backman."

Louie dug around in his jumpsuit, then lit another cigarette, inhaled deeply, hissing the smoke through his teeth. His fingernails were black. A nude was tattooed on the back of his hand.

Jack frowned. "Louie?"

"Look, Mills. I never in my life killed nobody. I don't even think my Uncle Joey has. We do business. We have friends. You know how these things go."

"So what happened to my cops?"

Louie Allesi shrugged. "I'm starting to wish I knew."

"Put your ear to the ground," said Jack. "It's in your own best interests."

"Like any other law-abiding citizen, I am always happy to cooperate with the police." Louie started to offer his greasy hand, then stopped and laughed, tucked it in his pocket. "Kinda ironic, ain't it? I do business with nine thousand wise guys and never hear boo. I do one square deal with cops and here comes the bullshit."

"Call your mother, Louie."

17

Louis Allesi thought this was it. His last link to those stupid, crooked cops. One last fucking Dodge. Louie parked at the deserted curb and let himself into his darkened body shop at five minutes to midnight, then stood by the slightly open door until midnight to make sure there was no one following him. His shepherd nuzzled his leg, then sat by his feet, waiting for food and water. Louie ignored the dog. He went out back and jock-eyed cars around the rear lot, until a seemingly new canary yellow Dodge stood idling by the fence gate.

"Come on, Champ," he called, and the dog ran out of the shop and jumped into the front seat of the Dodge.

Louie hung a transporter plate on the back bumper and slid behind the wheel. Louie loved transporter plates almost as much as he loved dummy corporations. It was warm, raining lightly. The car idled smoothly. Louie smoked a cigarette and listened to a late ball game from the coast that he had action on; the dog went to sleep.

Between innings Louie remembered the days

before he had access to the best of the tools of the trade, the winter he drove a stolen Lincoln with dirty snow packed on the wanted license plates. On the side he'd sold speed to niggers and called it coke. Made a gang of bread. Louie believed he had always had the balls to go big time, and now he had the connections.

Maybe too many connections.

When the moment felt right and the street was deserted, Louie pulled out onto Main Street and turned west. The blacktop was slick with oil and Louie drove carefully, a strict observer of traffic regulations. The ball game ended, with Louie a five-hundred-dollar winner. He tuned the radio to some old-time rock and roll and settled back. A snap, he figured. No need for all this agitation.

He drove north, crossed the Throgs Neck Bridge, and rode the crumbling, pockmarked Cross Bronx Expressway to the George Washington Bridge under city-lit skies that glowed amber and rose. He made the first turn south in Jersey to Fort Lee. On the Palisades he entered the parking garage of a skyscraper that overlooked upper Manhattan. He parked in section 2B and turned the engine off. It was 12:42 A.M. Three minutes early.

Robert Bozo Vaccaron appeared a moment later, on foot, from the elevator, in the company of a skinny black man with a shaved head. Bozo Vaccaron did not look at all the clown. His hair was black and cut short. His suit was dark. Vaccaron was called Bozo because once, while strangling a man to death, he had begun laughing uncontrollably, to the point of making even his hardened accomplices nervous.

"Louie, my man," said Bozo. "Right on time."

Louie got out of the car. "Yeah."

"Same as the others?" said Bozo, jerking a thumb at the yellow Dodge.

"Yeah. Like we said. Sixty-five hundred. And the tank is even full."

"She's pretty," said Bozo. "I might give it to my youngest daughter."

"In that case make it a flat six."

"Yeah?"

"She rides nice," said Louie.

"I'll bet she does. Check her out, bro."

The black man leaned into the car and popped the hood, checked the belts, the hoses, the radiator and the transmission. "The dog cool?" he asked Louie.

"A sweetheart."

The black man opened the door and started the car, revved her several times, filling the damp air in the garage with fumes. He shut her down and got out with the keys in his hands, knelt next to the tires, got on his back and examined the undercarriage. "Cool," he said, getting back up.

"Beautiful," said Bozo.

While Bozo counted out the money to Louie near the front of the car, the black man checked the trunk. Then he walked forward on the driver's side and shut the driver's door, locking the dog inside. "Bozo," he said. "Got a minute."

"Hanh?"

"What's the matter?" said Louie.

"You all stay right where you are, homey," he said to Louie, showing him a silver automatic.

Bozo joined the black and stared into the trunk.

"What the fuck?" said Bozo. "You setting me up, motherfucker?"

"What?" said Louie.

Bozo reached out and grabbed Louie by the back of the neck and shoved his face into the open trunk.

Louie's heart stopped cold when he saw the body wrapped in see-through plastic sheets, felt the cold barrel of a gun at the base of his skull. The shepherd barked wildly and threw itself at the window.

Bozo said to his partner, "Take another look around. Make sure this dumb fuck wasn't followed.

"Jesus, Bozo. I'm just as surprised as you are."

"Does your wife's uncle know you're here, you piece a shit?"

Louie did not answer. He continued to stare at the body, the face wrapped tight and distorted, the bald head.

"Maybe I'll tell him you've been beating him out of some bucks."

"Just shoot me now," said Louie. "It can't be no worse than what he'll do."

"I'm thinking about it," said Bozo. "Believe me." He stood Louie up and got in his face. "Who the fuck is this?"

"A cop, from the Island. A fucking homicide captain. I swear to God, I had no idea. This car's been finished and locked up in my yard for a week."

Bozo thought the situation over.

The black man returned and shook his head. "Just us chickens," he said.

Bozo thought it over some more, slow as an old computer.

"On my children's children's heads," begged Louie.

"Get in the car, Louie, and get the fuck out of here. And lose my phone number too. *Capisce?* You're bad fucking news."

"Thank you, Bozo. Oh my God, thank you. I owe you. Big."

The black man slammed the trunk shut and Louie climbed into the yellow Dodge. He was waiting for the bullet in the side of his head, sure it was coming, sure his life was ending just as he was breaking out of the pack. But Bozo and the black man were waiting by the elevator doors, not even watching him.

Louie paid the toll to return to New York on the bridge and rode back to the Island while the dog sniffed and clawed at the rear seat of the Dodge.

"Yeah?" said Louie. "Where were you when I needed ya?"

No music this trip. Only fear and every prayer he could think of under the circumstances.

He rode the dark, wet Long Island parkways for almost two hours before he found what he thought would be a suitable resting place for the late Captain Richard Mazzarella. He did not wait around and pray for the deceased, who was already wherever he was going.

Louie Allesi drove a circuitous route back to his shop, wondering who would try to frame him for the murder of a cop. He kept the overhead lights off in his shop and spent the rest of the night hard at work in the back bay, hosing out the trunk and breaking the last yellow Dodge down to its smallest salable parts.

* * *

It was raining hard the following morning, steam rising from the street. The car windows were fogged. Claire's mascara was streaked, as if she had just been rescued from the rubble of a natural disaster, and Jack's blazer was a rumpled mess. He parked underneath the railroad trestle at the Freeport station. Claire fixed her makeup in the mirror.

They interviewed Carlos Baez in the rear of the small deli where he worked. Baez was happy to tell them what life was like in the apartment building owned by Allesi Management, once the decision was made to go co-op. He wiped his hands on his apron and lit a cigarette, his face dark with hate. No one had ever wanted to hear this before, he said, not the city inspectors, not the town, not the county. Now detectives were seeking him out at his job? A strange place, America. Slow but sure.

"They turned it into a fucking shithouse, setting fires in the stairwells, turning off the water and the heat. They scared my wife and babies so much at the end I brought them here with me during the day. My boss was very kind, thank God, or they would have had no place to go. He let them play down in the basement."

"Who did this to your family?" asked Claire.

"They called him Rahjah. He sold dope from his apartment when he wasn't messing with the decent people who lived there."

"Do you know if he still lives there?" asked Jack.

Baez laughed. "They tossed him out too, last I heard, then moved in the rich people."

"Any idea where I can find him?"

"Hempstead, I think."

"Where you living now?" asked Claire.

Carlos looked at the dirty ceiling over their heads. "Two rooms, five people and a cat. I am going backwards."

The sky remained overcast but the rain had stopped. Puddles hid potholes and storm drains backed up, a bad day for axles and tires in those sections of Nassau that nobody fixed.

Jack and Claire watched Rahjah Knowles step out of the Homeboy Barbershop doorway and stroll up to their unmarked Plymouth with a knowing smile on his dark brown face. "Yo, Five-O. What it is?"

"Hop in, Kenneth. We got to talk."

Rahjah looked both ways, then got in the backseat of the car and removed his floppy hat. "Book, man, befo' anybody who's anybody sees me collaboratin'."

Jack pulled away from the curb and drove north on South Franklin Avenue. On the seat next to Claire was a mug shot of Kenneth Knowles at age thirty-two and a previous sheet, showing collars for drugs, prostitution, disorderly conduct and loitering for lewd purposes. In the glove compartment a tape recorder rolled, on the off chance incriminating remarks were freely volunteered.

"What's up?" said Rahjah. "What squadron you all fly with?"

"Nassau, Homicide—working the Artie Backman case."

"So why talk to me?"

Jack said, "We understand you did a little work

for him down in Long Beach, cleaning out a building."

"So?"

Rahjah smelled of musk and incense, marijuana on his breath.

Jack said, "You know Richard Mazzarella?"

"The Dicktop? Yeah, I worked for him too, on the side. I ain't no fuckin' snitch."

"No one said you were," said Claire.

"Word up," said Rahjah. "Where we going?"

Still northbound, they rolled past the Garden City village line, into the land of great lawns and huge houses, a route Rahjah only traveled when he was going to jail or the courthouse.

"Just cruising," said Jack. "Don't get nervous."

"It's just when all of a sudden everything gets green and pretty, I hear cell doors slamming."

"Where should we go, Kenneth? Where would you feel comfortable?"

"Ride the highways, if we gotta go somewhere. Hey, just what you want to know?"

"The deal, Rahjah. At the condo."

Rahjah Knowles considered the ethics of his situation while Jack drove east on Stewart Avenue, past the Roosevelt Field Mall, the multiplex movie theater. Mirrored office buildings reflected cars, the low gray clouds.

"What's in it for me?" said Rahjah.

"What do you need?" asked Jack.

"What does anybody need?"

"Like a hundred?"

Rahjah looked insulted.

"Hey," said Claire, "we'll just go to the next guy,

189

okay? And maybe he adds something to the story you'd have the opportunity here and now to leave out. You know what I'm saying? Asshole. We're looking for a cop-killer. We don't care about fucking misdemeanors."

Rahjah hockered up a lunger the size of a tadpole and spit it out the window. Lit another cigarette. Tough women didn't scare him.

"Time's up," said Jack.

"Okay, okay. Jesus Christ." Rajah cleared his throat and wiped his arm across his nose. "Backman and me go way back. I used to get him guys to do his lawn, shovel his driveway. Put up more than one roof with him too, before I went away."

"When was that?"

"Eighty-two. For selling reefer, which is like nothing compared to now."

"What happened in Long Beach?" asked Jack.

Rahjah tapped his hand on the seat, looked out the back window of the car, sighed. "Last summer Back-man paid me and some of my boys to move to this building and confrontate with these spics that wouldn't move out."

"How much were you paid?"

"Three thousand bucks, cash money, plus we lived rent-free on the beach till the job was done."

"What'd you and the boys do?" said Jack.

"Aw, man, all kinds of shit. We set fires in the lobby, we stole they mail. We broke the boiler. Shut off they watah whenever we fucking felt like it. People'd complain about roaches, we'd spray insecticide in the hallways, and sugar-watah in they apartments. It must have worked too, 'cause no one ever needed us to do it again." Rahjah broke into a big smile, remembering. "We had a pahty one weekend, and a lotta windows got broke, and people pissed where they shouldn't have, and dudes were droppin' they trousers on ladies and kids."

"Sounds like the last retirement party I went to," said Claire. "Anybody try to eat a light bulb?"

Rahjah looked at Jack as if she were crazy. "Naw, girl. What the fuck fo'?"

"No reason."

"Keep going," said Jack.

"We was down to three families left, right? And Back-man said the owner was breaking his balls 'cause he was losing eight grand a month. So now—dig this—one night we spread twenty pounds of chopmeat round the courtyard, in the bushes, in the garage. By dawn we had rats and squirrels and dogs, just tearing the place apart. Those last three families upped and split like you wouldn't believe. The last cab waited at the corner. My friend Darnell got bit while we was checking out."

"He shoulda filed for workman's comp," said Jack. "What happened then?"

"What happened then was that Mr. Allesi got pissed about the damage we done, and didn't want to pay us. Back-man and Mr. Benz set him straight on that. After that, I don't know. I moved back to my mom's."

"Good summer, eh?" said Jack.

"Like the Fresh Air Fund."

Jack pulled to the side of the Southern State Parkway on a wooded stretch, about a mile from the closest entrance ramp, not a sidewalk in sight.

"Out of the car, Kenneth."

"But—"

"You like fresh air," said Claire.

Jack said, "Breeze, before I confrontate your face."

The look on Rahjah's face suggested to Jack that the man had absolutely no idea why anyone would be mad at him. He was a victim, an oppressed member of society, dumped at the side of the road.

Before they were even out of sight, Kenneth had his thumb up, hailing his fellow man.

18

JACK CLIMBED out of his unmarked car in front of the open bay doors of Scaramouche Body and Fender. The dirty brown shepherd on the apron looked him over, went back to sleep. It was five o'clock, an uncommonly warm late September afternoon. Claire was at headquarters, where Rod Lomack had her coordinating the task force working the displaced tenants of Allesi Management Corporation, everyone searching for someone with the guts to pull a trigger.

Louie's crew of mechanics had gone home or out to blow their paychecks, and Jack surprised Louie and his big-chested office girl in swimsuits—hers black, a one-piece; his a Speedo banana-hammock. They were lugging a loaded Igloo cooler from the office to the street.

"Quitting time?" asked Jack.

Louie stopped short, squinted in the light. "What's it to you? You got a warrant for me?"

"Nope."

"Terrific. Suzie, keep loading the car."

"Okay, Louie."

193

"We're going fishing," Louie told Jack. He was scratching his nuts and looking around. "I'm sick of this smelly dump. You start to wonder if anybody can drive anymore, we see so many bloody wrecks."

Suzie flip-flopped across the greasy floor in rubber sandals, bent over, dragging the cooler. Jack admired her rear end.

"I love fishing," said Louie. "You guys got that down in my jacket?"

"Probably. Nice evening for it."

"So what can I do for you?" asked Louie. "The sun is going down."

Jack cocked his head after Suzie. "Uncle Joey know you're fucking her?"

Louie stepped closer and looked around for other ears. He was smelling awfully good for a man who worked in a body shop. "You tryin' to get me killed?"

"No, Louie. It's my job to prevent that sort of thing."

"Uncle Joey drops me in the river, he ever catches me cheating on his niece. Carla would mix the fucking cement."

Jack said, "I didn't think that would be a problem for a wiseguy like you."

"Years ago, maybe no. The modern wife is different. And blood is blood. You know what I'm saying? Why we let 'em out of the kitchen, I'll never know. It ain't like I don't send her diamonds and roses on her birthday."

Jack grinned. "What kind of boat you got?"

"A cigarette."

"Nice?"

"Oh, yeah. We should hang out, you and me. I'll take you for a ride someday."

"Not funny, Louie."

"I didn't mean it like that."

"I know."

"Forget I mentioned it, Mills. You'd probably cause me problems too."

"Right."

"So that's it? You just stopped by to say hello?"

"Just thought I'd let you know as a courtesy that we're passing our paper to the district attorney. Rahjah Knowles and some of your other boys bent a few laws down in Long Beach."

"I don't know what you're talking about." Louie scratched the hair on his belly, the inside of his thigh. "Backman and Mazzarella handled the day-to-day bullshit."

"We'll see."

Louie Allesi hit the switch on the electric garage door and they ducked out onto the sidewalk. Louie held open the door of his black Mercedes for the dog, then the girl. He gave Jack one more charming look over the hood of the car. "Forget about me, Mills. I ain't worth it."

"You underestimate yourself, Louis."

Allesi darkened. "Guys like you and guys like me, we're not big shots, so we're either on the bus or we're not on the bus. *Capisce?* You should maybe think about that."

Jack had been thinking about it all his life. "Enjoy yourself, Louie. There won't be many more nice days like this."

Jack sat in his car for five minutes after the Mercedes had driven away. Several things were bothering him. Louie Allesi was the only merchant in crime-ridden Belmont without an alarm system. And hardly any locks. And he took the dog with him. Jack had never seen a shop dog leave the shop. Which told him Louie didn't give a fuck about the shop.

Why not?

He obviously kept his real business records at home, or at his lawyer's office, where they would enjoy the highest level of constitutional protection. But if his wife was straight and without a sexy sense of humor, where did he keep his widely revered collection of smut? And if he had a safe place for his smut, why not keep his records there too?

They were here, thought Mills. At the shop. In one hell of a hiding place.

He looked up and down the deserted commercial street, thinking that glass was easy; dogs were hard. Then he went around back and slipped through the weeds, broke a small pane of glass on the window near the door and was inside the dusty shop in a minute, searching for a safe or a false floor, some place big enough to hide files. He checked in the bathrooms, behind the lockers, under the lifts, inside the toolboxes. He found a bottle of wine and a hundred-dollar bill on the front desk with a note: "Take it and get the fuck out of here."

Jack walked back to the rear of the shop and sat on the trunk of the same Camaro Louie'd been working on the last time he was here, N.Y. Lou-69.

Then he smiled like you do when the goalie falls down.

The keys were in the ignition. He opened the

trunk. Saw nothing but dirty rags. Jack smiled again and raised the hood. Inside he found an old leather suitcase where the engine should have been. Inside that were manila folders marked BLACK, WHITE, BLUE, HARD, HARDER, SNUFF. A storage box of videotapes, similarly labeled.

Jack looked the collection over, starting with the SNUFF box, nine nasty snap shots through the window of hell, girls dead or dying for the momentary pleasure of freaks. On the backs were the prices Louie had paid for each, and the names of the dealers in Bolivia, Mexico, Cincinnati, Guam. None of H-11-89 or the other lost girls he knew. Two snuff videotapes had titles: *Cutting up Candy* and *Giving Head*. They were marked with five-hundred-dollar price tags.

Jack opened the BLUE box and saw Angela Cortelli. She was on her hands and knees on the hood of a red Cadillac, her face a mask of indifference, taking it dogstyle.

"Louie, Louie," said Jack, "it's not nice to lie to the police."

Claire's county car was in his driveway when he got home that evening. He found her in his dining room, in his robe, a glass of champagne in her hand, reading mail he had left open.

"Make yourself at home," he said as he pulled off his blazer.

She looked up, smiling. "You didn't really place a personal, did you?"

"For a roommate."

"Yeah, sure."

"How desperate do I look?"

"Pretty desperate."

"Maybe you ought to get going," he said.

She bared one shoulder and cocked her head to the side. "Really?"

"Claire."

"What?"

"Don't play with me."

She stood up and wrapped her arms around his neck. "I'm not. I've simply decided to separate your performance as a detective from your performance as a man."

"Well isn't that big of you," he said.

"You'll pay for that," she said, and attacked.

It went on for hours. Just as he was about to peak, she'd bump his nose with a knuckle or rake his privates with a nail. When she finally finished him off, he was a wreck—totalled.

"Why so glum?" asked Claire. "Didn't I make you happy?" She was stretched out next to him in his platform bed, now and then scratching his hairy shin with her toenail. He kept dodging her big toe, trying to protect his nose.

His bedroom lights were on low. The white walls were plastered with action photographs of him in his playing days, an orange Syracuse banner, ancient wooden lacrosse sticks crossed like swords over a phony cardboard fireplace. An undergraduate's room. Home away from home.

"I'm a failure," he said.

"Yeah, maybe a little," she said, "but now you're competing with pilots and lawyers and that cute young doctor—"

"Fuck you, okay?"

"But sweetie, you just did." Claire kissed his cheek and began to run her fingers along his thigh. "Wonderfully."

Jack rolled over. "Could you please keep your mind on the case."

"Isn't this a switch?" she said.

"Yeah. Maybe."

"Tell me the truth, Jack. What the hell are you doing in homicide?"

Jack recalled his days at community relations, the sense that he was a cheerleader rather than a player, where the celebrity was nice but the thrill was gone. His days as an imposter. A fake. He had missed the excitement of risk and the swagger that went with winning, the honest sweat of dirty work, the gritty satisfaction of being a valued member of a team.

"Do you even like homicide? I mean, it takes a while to get into it. You'll know you're getting good at it when you can go to a grisly scene and focus on your work, not everything else that rushes through your soul, like terror or disgust. Or what your next-door neighbor or your kindergarten teacher would think of all the blood. Your last vacation. Your next vacation. Vomiting."

"I think homicide sucks, to tell you the truth. Not at all what I'd bargained for. I might feel different if I ever solve a case."

She wrapped her arm around his waist and squeezed him. "You will," she said. "You'll solve this one."

"If I don't wind up in jail first."

"My, my, we are depressed."

Jack shook his head. "I wasn't gonna tell you—I went a little crazy tonight."

"Meaning?"

"I broke into Louie Allesi's body shop."

Claire blinked and tilted her head. "You committed a burglary?"

"More like a criminal mischief."

"Oh, Christ."

"Besides a disgusting stash of snuff photographs and tapes, he had a picture of Angela Cortelli, probably taken at one of his Christmas parties. She was nude, on her hands and knees, getting porked in the buns. Scumbag Louie told me he didn't know any Angela Cortelli."

"Hot damn," said Claire, shaking his shoulders and wrestling him onto his back. "I like it."

"I liked it too, for a while. Then I started thinking maybe Louie was telling the truth. Maybe she was Monique that night, or Crystal. Who the hell knows hookers' real names?"

Claire grabbed his hair and playfully shook his head. "No, no, no. You've got to stop making excuses for people. Assume everyone is lying, hiding a secret. It's the best tool a detective can have. A built-in bullshit detector."

"Yes, my mentor."

"What made you do something so rash?"

"Because I'm getting my nuts kicked in playing it straight. A fucking freak like Louie Allesi can laugh in my face."

"Not forever."

"One on one, a level playing field, I eat his lunch."

"No such thing on this crooked island."

Jack shrugged "So now what? I keep asking myself: What can we do with what we know?"

"Put a tail on Louie, for one, using the extra guys we got hanging around the office. Or maybe get Barbara Fisher from my job. Louie's never seen her, and she's the best damn tracker. Gorgeous face. Fits in anywhere. Sometimes the FBI puts her on mob wives or mistresses. Maybe Louie leads us where we want to go, maybe he makes a mistake. Maybe he does something else we can pop him for. We sure can't get any warrants with the 'fruits of an illegal search.' "

"I know," said Jack.

"What did you do with the picture of Angela?"

"Put it back."

Claire thought about this for a moment. "Just as well."

"That's what I figured. I took a hundred bucks he had stashed there and we just drank his bottle of wine."

Claire laughed, shook her hair from her face. "Did Angela make you hot?"

Jack smiled to himself in the dark, then rolled over to face her. "You asking me does."

·"Oh, yeah?" She nibbled his chest. "You like naughty girls?"

"Who doesn't?"

She kissed his belly button. "And you won't think less of me in the morning?"

19

BY SATURDAY morning Jack's cupboard was finally bare. Nothing in the refrigerator but olives and beer and grapes that were turning into raisins. He called out from the kitchen to his daughter, "Jenny!"

"Yes, Dad."

"I need you."

"Well, of course you do. Isn't that nice. What's for breakfast?"

She walked into the kitchen in time to see him shaking the dust from a corn flakes box.

"Did you know," she asked, "that girls take shop now and boys take home economics?"

"I had a course like that at college," he said. "Me and some football players. I got an A minus, not that I ever went to it."

"Did *you* put one over on *them.*"

Jenny also pointed out that the grass in the front yard was over ten inches long, that she could understand confusion in the kitchen, but any fool could mow a lawn.

"Anything less than forty acres is woman's work," said Jack.

Jenny started to make a shopping list while they drove to King Kullen, then tore it up and said, "Forget it. You need everything."

"It's just that I've been so busy."

"You haven't heard from Katy?"

"No."

"You getting used to living alone?"

"I'm not good enough at it to be used to it. I'm able to sleep."

"Mom says you've never been without a woman to pick up after you. She thinks this will be a learning experience."

"Mom has a big mouth."

Jenny laughed. "I'm telling her you said that."

The King Kullen parking lot was full, as Jenny had said it would be. He might have known. Jack found grocery shopping as complicated as registering for classes at college. There were fliers and coupons to be considered, ounces and liters to be factored, lists to check off. What a moron he was. Total mopes could shop. He'd seen them. They were always in front of him at the 7 Eleven.

A pregame adrenaline surge rushed through him as the electronic doors slid open—the cold smell of vegetables and the dread of humiliation. And then he saw the salad bar.

"When did they start putting those in supermarkets?"

Jenny said, "A couple of years ago."

"Great. What kind of dressing do you want?"

"What about lunch?"

"Pizza Hut."

"Dinner?"

"I'm working."

"Daddy."

"What?"

She smiled up at him. "I don't know what kind of husband you make, but you would sure be a terrible wife."

"You think so?"

She pulled a cart from the holding pen and led him down the frozen-food aisle.

At noon Jack coached Jenny's Catholic Youth Organization basketball team in a preseason scrimmage in a tiny school gym filled with parents and friends and grandparents and siblings. The other squad's goons were shoving his kids around to make up for their lack of skill. Jenny hit the deck hard, came up holding her elbow, fighting tears. Jack called time. Gathered his girls.

"Goddamn it!" he yelled. "Don't take that kind of shit! Fight back!"

The gym fell silent. His girls stared up at him in horror.

Babe leaned into the huddle, grimacing.

"Uh, Jack?" she said. "Church league?"

He pivoted back and forth, hands on hips, aware of the shocked faces on the other parents. "Yeah. Sorry."

Jack rode slowly east in traffic on the jammed expressway with the AM radio on and the sun setting red in his rearview mirror. Mike and the Mad Dog were arguing again, this time over George Steinbrenner's latest lawsuit against major league baseball. Then Mike made fun of Mad Dog's love life and Jack was where he wanted to be. Outside the Days Inn in Medford he pulled to the side and called Claire at her home.

A man answered, a comfortable, jovial voice, the kind that gave air speeds and estimated times of arrival calmly no matter what the circumstances.

"May I please speak to Detective Williamson?" Jack said. Wind blew his hair, and the diesel roar of passing trucks made it hard to hear.

"Sure thing. Who's this?"

"Detective Mills," he shouted. "NCPD."

"Got it. Hold on. Honey . . . it's for you."

Claire came on the line. "Well, hello, Detective Mills, NCPD. What's up?"

"I'm hot on the trail of our fiend."

"Oh?" she said. "Is that why you're yelling in my ear?"

"I'm just down the road, headed for your office, or Lucy's rooming house, wherever you think it's better. I got a photo pack I want to show her of guys who look like the sketch."

"I'll go myself, first thing in the morning."

"But you don't have the photo pack."

"I will when you get to my house."

A tractor bled its air brakes loudly.

"Are you sure?"

"Sure I'm sure." She gave him directions.

"Oh, goodie," said Jack. "I can finally meet Drew."

"Who says I'm letting you in?"

Jack hung up and brushed his hair in the rear-view mirror, checked his nostrils and teeth with care.

Jesus, he thought, he was one moonstruck

motherfucker. He realized that he didn't care terribly one way or the other if Lucy picked out the murderer tonight or tomorrow morning or two weeks from next Wednesday.

Claire's county car was parked near the walkway in front of the neatly landscaped white high-ranch. He popped a stale Life Saver into his mouth and tucked his shirt into his pants. She wasn't perfect, he reminded himself. She had her opinions, a cocky swagger. She smoked cigarettes, a stupid, self-destructive habit he hated in others. Yet when Claire smoked it suggested angst, depth of feeling. She drank. Her hours were criminal. And taking your eyes off her was like parking a new Porsche behind the welfare building.

I don't need this, he thought as he rang her doorbell, head swimming in the smell of freshmown grass.

"Hey, Jack," she said, opening the door, waving thick smoke from her face. "Come on in. Never mind the smell. I burned the Buffalo wings." She was standing on the landing wearing white jeans and a man's white shirt, barefoot, her toenails painted pink. Behind her, in the smoke-filled living room, people were laughing, probably at him. He could see children playing in the rec room.

She took his arm and spun him into the crowd. "Mom, Dad, this is Jack Mills, from Nassau. He'll probably be asking you for my hand in a couple of months."

Jack's cheeks burned and his nose throbbed as he made his way around the room, meeting her brother, his wife and their two small children. Each member of this solid family was better looking than the next. For once Jack felt himself to be the least attractive person at a gathering.

Claire led him by the hand into a large white kitchen whose bright counters were bare except for an ice bucket, crystal tumblers and liquor bottles. Charred chicken wings filled the sink, still hissing.

"Nice ambush, partner," he said. "Where's Drew?"

"Come on now, Jack. You know you wanted to meet my family."

Jack blushed boyishly. "Warning would have—"

"Yeah, yeah. Give me the photo pack."

He handed her the envelope. Twenty-seven faces, some of them worthy of some good citizen's suspicion.

"Coffee or a drink?" she said, studying the photos.

"Coffee," said Jack. "I gotta drive back. Hey, your mother is gorgeous. I see where you get it."

"She's my idol, Jack. I hope to God I look that good at her age. And she does that herself. No beauty parlors. She works, she cooks, she cleans, and she's the nicest mother on earth."

"Your dad looks like Charlton Heston."

Claire nodded. "Drew said you sounded old."

Jack raised his eyebrows. "Is that right?"

"He likes to think I work with father figures."

Jack sneered, "Father figure, my ass."

Claire laughed. "That wasn't Drew. That was my dad who answered."

"Right." Jack remembered that he was also a father, that he had not made his call to Jenny yet, to check on her elbow. That if he had not been such a dog, their family would still be intact.

"Any word on Captain Mazzarella?" Claire asked.

"Not that I've heard."

"Barbara Fisher and her backup team started on Louie Allesi this afternoon."

"Good. Thank you. Your word must carry some weight."

Claire flipped through the pictures again and frowned. "I don't like this. One cop, maybe. But two—"

"Maybe we should stay together twenty-four hours a day, you know, to protect each other."

"Would you stop thinking with your dick."

Jack took a deep breath, slipped his arms around her waist and pulled her close.

She looked up at him and smiled.

Her father poked his head into the kitchen, held up his empty glass. "Mind if I come in?"

Jack and Claire stepped apart.

"Of course not, Daddy. We were talking about the case."

"That cop-killer?"

"Yeah," said Claire.

"You'll get him," he said. "Just stick with it." He turned to Jack and sized him up. "My little girl always gets her man."

"Yes, sir."

"Best damn cop in the family."

"Yes, sir."

"Make sure you watch her back."

"Oh, I do, sir."

Her father laughed and slapped Jack's shoulder. "I like this guy," he said to Claire. "Better than Durwood."

"That's Drew, Daddy."

"What's the difference?" he said, pushing past them to refill his glass.

Claire poured Jack his coffee to go. She said she would call him later, after everyone had gone home. Jack shook hands around the living room again and said good-bye, though he very much wanted to stay.

The front door closed behind him. A pizza deliveryman passed him on the walk, his tattooed arms loaded with three large pies. "Mr. Williamson?" he said.

Jack pointed over his shoulder. "Right there."

"T'anks."

Homeward bound, mesmerized by the lights of the Long Island Expressway, he imagined a pipe-dream life in Suffolk County, his every need attended to by Claire, in fishnet stockings. And yet, as he crossed the county line, he had the feeling of making an escape.

She wanted more than she was letting on, and he was falling for her, trick by silly trick. He turned the police radio on, seeking comfort in missions of mercy, the good-guy sounds of home.

Katy had not liked his cop friends, and he had thought hers were bubbleheaded bimbos. He was older and burdened with a past. During their three-year affair she had changed from loving and carefree to cold and pushy, a sullen fan disillusioned by proximity. Jack was certain that he had not changed; he had oral testimony on that point from almost everyone he knew.

It was different with Claire. She knew his faults better than he did and had fallen for him anyway.

Although she had not come out and said so, he had the feeling that she loved him, at least a little.

Angela Cortelli answered the dreaded knock on her apartment door and accepted the roses from the nice old black man without protest. She gave him a dollar tip and offered him a nice cold drink. "No, thanks" he said, just like always. "My products are dying as we speaking."

Angela added the roses to her large collection, massed from wall to wall across her living room, lending the apartment the sweet, stale air of a funeral home. Her face tired and white, hands trembling, she opened the card, moaned softly, then tossed it on the table with all the others.

> I MISS YOU SO MUCH, MOMMY.
> I AM WAITING FOR YOU.
> YOUR BABY IN HEAVEN

20

KERRI NESSBAUM'S front right tire blew out on her way home from Hofstra University. At a little after 10 P.M. she wrestled her 1987 tan Ford Taurus off the Northern State Parkway at Wolf Hill Road in Huntington and parked next to the impact attenuators, those sand-filled plastic barrels placed at the foot of the flagstone overpass. She walked to the back of her car and removed the small spare from the trunk, the jack, a set of instructions she had never read before. Something smelled, like shit. Not her catalytic converter. A dead dog, she thought, that had crawled among the weeds to die.

A New York state trooper pulled in behind her, knew the smell at once. He walked to the first plastic barrel and lifted the lid. Recoiled, his hand over his face.

Inside the barrel was the bloated, rotting body of Captain Richard Mazzarella.

Sergeant Lomack and Detective Mills reported to Chief Barone at 6 A.M., as ordered. Headquarters was bustling like noon on payday.

"Enough," said the chief, "is enough. People are starting to question my competence, never mind yours. Sergeant, you told me a week ago that if we found Mazzarella's body we could put the case together."

"Sir—"

Barone stopped Lomack with a raised palm. "Let me ask you this: Do we believe our current lines of inquiry have a chance to be productive?"

"We don't know," said Lomack. "We would be remiss not to follow them."

"Mills, you sure you like this crap? Flatline Hoskinson would love you back at relations."

Jack recalled the carefree nature of his previous assignment, the fresh air and exercise, the feeling he was skipping school. Right at the moment it was easy to forget a few brief humiliations. He looked at Lomack, who was looking out the window, watching the sun rise over Mineola.

"Can't do it, sir. I'm the brains of this outfit."

Lomack flinched, waiting for the explosion that did not come.

Barone sat back in his chair. "Listen, boys. The county executive sent a delegation of peons over here an hour ago. He is apparently livid over one of the damn recruiting posters he saw on the way in this morning. Seems he's asking you who is killing these cops, and you're smiling and telling him you haven't got a clue. He wants you back at community relations and he wants Lomack assigned to records. He wants the FBI serial-killer folks called in, and he wants Internal Affairs to carry the ball for our side."

"You got to be kidding," said Lomack. "What'd you say?"

"I asked them for a two-week reprieve."

"And?"

"The man said sink or swim. Meaning me."

That morning Aaron Delany sat in his yellow Honda in the parking lot of Cow Meadow Park, leaning his head out the window to catch a little sun on his chubby face, old editions of *Newsday* strewn all over the backseat, where he habitually pitched his office copies.

Jack parked next to him and got out. "Let's take a walk."

Jack did not wish to sit in Delany's car. Not that Aaron was the enemy. Jack knew that five or six years ago Delany had witnessed an illegal search of the home of a brutal ganglord. From his place of concealment on the roof across the street, Delany had seen the ganglord hanging from his feet out the window, howling, confessing, then being hauled inside by large white hands. Evidence suppression hearings were held. Arrogant lawyers cried foul. Delany said nothing, volunteered nothing, threw away photos that might have brought him fame. The evidence, a Colt revolver, was admitted. The case came to trial. The bad guy got twenty-five to life.

Delany was golden, as far as the cops were concerned. There was every reason in the world for Jack to trust him, except that he was learning not to trust anyone.

Delany locked his car and they walked along the

jogging path, past the busy tennis courts and empty softball diamond, around the pond into the marsh grass, and sat on a bench with a view of the Freeport River. Across the river, cars whizzed north and south on the Meadowbrook Parkway. The wind smelled of salt, mud and goose shit. They waited for a stringy octogenarian wearing headphones to shuffle by, then settled back to talk.

"A little birdie just told me Wally Willy Benz and Company was making loans from the party bank account, paying back the principal and going Dixie with the interest," said Aaron. "Mazzarella got some and so did Backman and his kid, who's in with Benz, maybe other guys on the job."

"You want to tell me where I can find this same little bird?"

"No."

"Why did he tell you this now?" asked Jack. "And why tell you, not me?"

"Said he's interested in justice."

"You trust him?"

"No reason not to."

Jack chewed on the cap of his pen. It was very possible this source so interested in justice might be merely using the investigation to further the embarrassment of political foes. Jack hoped Delany was smarter than that. He watched a charter boat slide by, waved at kids who waved at him.

"Another paw in the cookie jar," Jack said. "My job is homicide, and you're telling me about a fraud case."

"You want I should stop?"

"Where are you getting this stuff, Aaron?"

"As a member of the fourth estate I hear the cries

of agony from the downtrodden herd, the woe of the rank and file. I am honor bound to protect their confidentiality, just as I am honor bound to you."

"That was lovely."

"Hey, I'm helping you all I can. I've never given a cop a bum steer in my life."

"I didn't mean it like that."

"Two guys with ties to power get whacked. We check the power source. Shit turns up. Then more shit. We keep digging, 'cause now we got a shit mine. You need evidence to present in court. All I need is more shit."

"That it?" asked Jack.

"The tip of the iceberg, from what I hear. You *are* looking for ties between the victims?"

Jack laughed. "Was Artie Backman a prince or what?"

Delany said, "I knew Artie Backman pretty good, when he was running the paperwork down at the One-Three. A total fucking nutcase. He loved to phone in preposterous stuff you knew had really happened but couldn't use because it was so blatantly off the wall."

"When do I get the rest?"

"When you dig it up."

"Just how big is this thing?"

Aaron Delany said, "Smaller than a credit union, larger than a friend helping out his friends. Ten percent interest, tax-free, is my kind of investment; forget the influence it buys. Benz is a bullshit blowhard with greasy playmates. Shit happens. Sometimes conspiracies form, and sometimes it only looks that way. What else do you have?"

"Squat," said Jack. "We're starting over again."

"Jesus."

Two more joggers cruised by the bench, then a wheelchair athlete, his muscular shoulders shiny with sweat. Near the parkway bridge, river kids rode jet skis while they still could. Jack envied them their free time.

"You don't really think the esteemed Wallace Wilson Benz and Michael Backman had anything to do with these murders, do you?"

Aaron ran his hands through his hair, rubbed his face, smoothed his moustache. "Wouldn't it be great if they did?"

Back at headquarters the news was bad: Lucy Lallos was certain the bearded man she had seen on the Fuji near the body was not among those in the photo pack.

"A longshot's a longshot," Jack said to Claire. "Not many come in."

"So what's next?"

He said he had more interviews to conduct with cops Angela Cortelli had taken to her bed.

Claire disagreed. "I don't think she loved him enough to kill him. He was one of many; she knew there would always be more."

"Heartless wench," said Jack.

"Hey," said Claire. "I've yet to see anybody from your job with tears in their eyes."

"I heard one guy sniffle, but the pollen count was high that day."

Jack and Claire drove from headquarters to the bayside community of Island Park for a follow-up interview with Mrs. Rita Mazzarella at her home. It was 10 A.M. and she was dressed in a gray suit.

Her eyes were puffy. She gave them coffee and they sat in the living room, their voices low. Her sons were sleeping upstairs after, she explained, a very rough night. "They were hoping," she said. "So was I."

Claire held her hand and they sat in silent sorrow.

Jack remembered how Mazzarella got his nickname. There had been a grab-bag Christmas party in the office. His gift, from an anonymous donor, had been a six-foot-long full body condom. He was Dicktop by the time Santa split, and *hated* it—which was why it stuck. Jack wondered if Mazzarella had had to hustle the extra money to keep his lovely wife happy. He thought of all the beautiful chicks you see on the arms of toads wearing Rolex watches.

When Mrs. Mazzarella had composed herself, Jack brought up the name of attorney Wallace Wilson Benz.

The pretty brunet widow smiled warmly. "Oh, yes," she said. "He's a wonderful man. He calls every day now."

"Had they known each other long?"

"Richie worked on the side for him since he went on the job. Driving him and stuff. Back and forth to Atlantic City. He was a very good provider."

Claire nodded agreement. Indeed he had been a good provider. The house was lavish, inside and out, with an outdoor pool and deck, marble floors, chandeliers and mirrors.

"Your home is lovely," Claire said.

"We got a great deal on it. Otherwise . . ."

"Buy it from family?" Jack said.

"No. We bought it new."

"Builder going broke?" Jack said.

Rita Mazzarella laughed. "Uncle Sam? He's been going broke for years."

"I don't understand."

"Well," she said, "Richie never wanted me to tell anyone. He thought owning a HUD house sounded low class, you know? It doesn't bother me, though. Lots of our friends got them."

"How?" asked Jack.

"These were first come, first served."

"And you were first."

She giggled nervously, as if leaking national security. "The week before the official announcements went out, we got a phone call from a friend."

"Lucky you," said Claire.

"Yes," she said. "Lucky me."

21

LOMACK DROVE, Jack read the paper. The front page of *Newsday* heralded a reward offered by the Patrolman's Benevolent Association for information resulting in the arrest and conviction of those responsible for the murders of Arthur Backman and Richard Mazzarella. The story was written by Aaron Delany. The slant was revenge, the tone angry.

Sergeant Lomack turned into the restaurant parking lot from Post Avenue at twenty-five minutes to twelve. The young Italian valet—in tight black jeans and duck's ass hairdo—waved the unmarked Plymouth toward the board of keys near the portico. Lomack ignored him, parked at the end of a row, next to a Lincoln Town Car. In his side-view mirror, Jack saw the car-park boy make a face of high disgust. Lomack saw it too.

"Easy, boss," said Jack. "He's just a dumbass kid. Don't spoil your digestion."

Lomack walked to the front door of the restaurant, his walkie-talkie in his hand. "Hey, fuckhead," he said to the boy. "You ain't man enough to drive that car."

The boy realized his mistake and apologized, both to Lomack and to Jack.

Lomack wasn't ready to accept it. "You give that look to the wrong nigger and he'll change your life forever. You understand me?"

"Yes, sir."

Jack and Lomack went inside, where they slipped ten bucks to the maître d' and took a table in a corner of the atrium. Ten minutes later they watched Wallace Wilson Benz enter and slip the same guy folding money, then watched the maître d' explain that his guests were already seated. Benz held his hand out; the maître d' returned the money.

Wallace Wilson Benz stood over six feet five. He was bald in the manner of an old Roman senator, an eagle-faced patrician.

Wallace Wilson Benz, Esq. was a gentleman beyond reproach, who lived in a neighborhood where houses went for two-point-this to six-point-that. Not homes but woodland forts, designed to isolate and protect their inhabitants with distance, alarms and security staffs—vast manors owned by foundations, relief pitchers, scoundrels and rogues. It was whispered in town that the Benz estate had a moat. Jack had met him once or twice on the rubber-chicken circuit; he remembered most the booming goodfellowship with which the lawyer customarily spoke, even to strangers and people he didn't like. The voice he used to greet them today was somber, as if he was addressing a jury decidedly not of his peers.

Benz sat down across from Lomack; sunlight streamed across his craggy face. "Distressing business, all of this."

"Yes, it is," said Lomack.

"I was wondering," said Benz, carefully unfolding his napkin, "if our conversation might remain off the record."

"Of course not," said Lomack. "But let's be candid." He grinned, all teeth.

"That's why I called," said Benz. "Before all this goes any further, I thought it wise to place myself at your disposal. Sure, my clients have done business with a couple of cops, made loans within the limits of the law and with the knowledge of the party, not that you'll hear anyone admit it until they have to. But we've never asked for any special favors. Never needed to. And we've never hired goon squads to depopulate buildings in the process of conversion. I don't mind telling you, my partners are considering a lawsuit against the department for dragging us into this mess."

So much for keeping things quiet, not tipping their hands. Benz already knew what they had.

Lomack said, "Louie Allesi is what dragged you into this mess."

The waiter arrived and took their drink orders: Benz, a dry Beefeater martini; Jack and Lomack, mineral water. Benz laced his fingers together on the table. His watch was from Rolex; his college ring, Harvard. Jack remembered beating the pants off the Crimson in his senior year, how good it felt to score against the upper crust. Then came the chant from the Harvard fans: "That's all right, that's okay. You're gonna work for us someday."

Wallace Wilson Benz smiled quickly and said, "Perhaps you might be good enough to tell me how to extricate my clients from this Passion play."

"We'll start with a list of your loans within the police department and the status of each account."

"Alas," said Benz. "Privileged information."

"We'll subpoena," said Lomack. "And we'll get it. I'll give you two hours to save me the trouble."

Benz's mouth smiled but his eyes did not. "I think you gentlemen should remember that the elephant party never forgets."

"Yes or no?" said Lomack.

"As you wish."

Their drinks arrived. The Muzak played "Wichita Lineman." Neighboring tables filled with businessmen and ladies in pastel dresses. Jack wondered if they would be thrilled to learn they were dining in close proximity to a homicide investigation, that the black man was not the suspect.

"So who killed my brother officers, counselor?" said Lomack. "What's the smart money guessing?"

"They don't know," said Benz. "They're contending that it has nothing to do with them."

"Yeah, right," said Lomack.

Benz looked disdainful, a man who clearly believed the announced functions of government were secondary to the real function of wasting taxpayer money on patronage and favors for the friends and relatives of the party in power. "Homicide detectives," he said, "just like on television, and a former all-American to boot."

"Third team," said Jack, sucking on a breath

mint, then to Lomack, "I hope you haven't over-sold me."

Benz smiled. "I was wondering who had the bad judgment to promote you two role models."

"The commissioner, I think," Lomack said.

"But it must have been cleared with our people."

"I didn't know you clowns controlled the cops too," said Jack.

Benz threw back his head and laughed. "All you losers sing the same tune. I suppose it makes the nights at home on the K-Mart couch a little less unbearable."

Jack was stunned. He had rarely heard such unbridled honesty, such self-satisfied admission. Jack hoped there was a hell, then, remembering his own mistakes, suffered a vision of eternity stuck with guys like Wallace Wilson Benz and Michael Backman. Not engulfed in flames but a clubhouse, wearing alligators on their shirts, talking prep-school trash, waiting for the lightning outside to stop.

"Not all of us lead lives of quiet desperation, Mills. It has become somewhat more difficult to properly thank our supporters. But it is not impossible. Helping our friends is never impossible. For Rodney here, this is the best he can do. It's under-standable and of little consequence. A guy like you should know better. But you're just a go-to-hell jerk ball player who doesn't have the sense to use his advantages."

"What advantages?"

"Everybody's got their own old-boys' network. You—you're a follower . . . a pretty dummy. You settle. The point is, you don't have to. You're bright, you're handsome, recognizable. I could help a guy like you. Think for a moment. What is it you really want? If you can bring yourself to admit it."

Jack pushed from his mind visions of everlasting youth, the roar of the crowd, spring sunshine, the taste of his very first beer: things over which Benz could not exercise control. Time. Another chance not to damage Babe and Jenny. Himself. He looked at Benz and saw a pimp in better tweeds who could have used the floppy hat.

"I want to be good," said Jack. "Can you help me with that?"

"You're finished," Benz said through grinning teeth.

"Evidently."

Benz turned to Lomack. "In any case, I have every faith that you and your men will nab the culprit. And when you do, and you find he has nothing in the world to do with my clients, you might even want to apologize to us." He put his glass on the table and abruptly stood up. "Gentlemen," he said. "I'll call my office from the car and arrange delivery of the pertinent documents."

Lomack said, "We'll catch you later, counselor. Thanks for the help. Really."

They watched him walk out, giving the folks a nod here, a wink there, ever the cheerful public face.

"'Catch you later, counselor'?" Jack repeated when Benz was out the door. "That's rich."

Lomack smiled, rubbed his hands together. "Come on. Let's go find a way to stick it up his ass."

On the way back, Lomack told Jack he thought it

was time to start over on the Backman case, reinterview everyone, reread the initial reports, all the interviews, factor in Mazzarella, return to the scenes of the crimes.

"The wife and son again, the girlfriends, Louie Allesi. We're missing something obvious. Something that connects them." He pulled the Lucy Lallos sketch out of his pocket. "People know this fuck and they're not saying boo."

22

SATURDAY, SITTING at Jack's desk, flipping through the balance sheets of brother officers, Claire came across the name of a client of Wallace Wilson Benz who lived in Suffolk County, had worked for Arthur Backman, and was a friend of Angela Cortelli's.

Retired Police Officer Tony Zendt had borrowed $5,000 twenty months ago and paid it back plus interest after six months. Tony Zendt had worked with Arthur Backman at the One-Three. Maybe he had participated in after-work activities as well. Maybe he knew who hated Backman, who hated Mazzarella. Maybe, maybe, maybe. She tossed the paperwork across to Jack, working at Eats's desk. "Where's his interview?" she asked. "He's the first one to make both lists."

"I haven't seen him yet. He wasn't home the last time I was out there."

"Great."

Jack scanned the financial records and then opened the personnel file on Anthony Zendt.

He read that Zendt had joined the force in 1974,

even that. I used to do reenactments, for a couple brigades, maybe ten a year. Now I can't, 'cause of my fucked-up back."

"This stuff all real?"

"Some of it."

"Worth a lot of money?"

Zendt moved next to a mannequin dressed like Davy Crockett, who was next to a World War I doughboy. "This Kentucky rifle that Caleb here is holding is worth a grand by itself."

"What a beautiful setup."

Tony pointed at the guns. "Everything from a matchlock musket to an M-sixteen."

"Who is this?" asked Jack, pointing to a soldier in a kilt.

"My favorite," said Tony. "Monty. A member of the Forty-second Regiment, British Highlanders. The Black Watch. Wearing a horsehair sporran, Glengarry cap, nineteen fourteen spats with diced hose tops. His weapon is the three-oh-three Enfield, with a bit o' steel at the end of it."

"And this one?"

"That's Allen. A member of the Second Wisconsin, the Iron Brigade. Held the field at Gettysburg the first day. Decimated. That's an eighteen sixty-one Springfield musket, percussion cap. Hardee hat."

Jack stepped down the line, as if reviewing the troops. He stopped at another Civil War mannequin.

"Duffy. From the Fighting Sixty-ninth, the Fighting Irish. Standard Union uniform and cap, brass shoulder scales, Springfield musket."

Then a marine from Iwo Jima, with a Thompson

submachine gun. A Korean colonel. A female mannequin in black pajamas, holding a Russian automatic.

"Where'd you get the dummies?"

"Thrift shops, department stores. That's the cheap part."

Tony reset his alarm and locked up. Jack followed him back through the house to the kitchen, which was bright and modern, a testimony to taste.

"Sit down," Tony said, pulling back a chair at the kitchen table. "What can I get you?"

"Coffee, light and sweet."

"Something to eat?"

"Nah," said Jack. "I'm watching my weight."

Zendt pinched an inch on his waist and laughed. "I should be," he said, "but once you've fucked up your back, the stomach's a lost cause." He poured the coffee, sat down at the head of the table.

Jack asked, "How'd you get hurt?"

"Lifting a stretcher, believe it or not. With a kid on it. It was ridiculous: Thirteen years of wrestling baboons and nothing happens. Pick up a fifty-pound girl and I'm crippled for life. They wanted to take out two disks and hurry me back to the street. I told 'em, 'Get fucked,' and put in my papers. I'm nobody's piece of meat."

"I hear you," said Jack.

"It's a girl's job now, anyway. I really don't miss it. They don't have the same kind of kick-ass bastards we had when I first came on the job. That's why we're losing the war in the streets. Someone should tell the governor it's too late to bring back the chair, we need electric bleachers. And I'd be only too happy to throw the fucking switch."

Jack smiled. "What do you do with yourself, now that you're retired?"

"Besides jerking my mule?"

Jack grinned and shook his head. "You think I really care if you mow your own lawn?"

"I got a little side business repairing TVs and those Japanese piece-of-shit VCRs. Strictly word of mouth and off the books, you understand. Tony's Tubes. With that and the pension, I get by. The rest of the time I fuck off or fish or play with my guns."

"Your wife work?"

"I'm divorced."

"Who isn't. Tell me about Angela. When did she come into the picture in relation to your wife?"

"After," said Zendt. "Honest. I'm not the type to fuck around."

Which, Jack thought, made Zendt an atypical policeman. Jack believed the police quartermaster should pass out condoms along with the bullet-proof vests.

"I visit my kids once a week, I pay the fucking bills. The woman—I'm rooting for her brakes to fail."

"What happened with Angela?"

"We split up when I retired, more or less. She's got a thing about her men being on active duty."

Jack nodded. "I've heard that."

"She was okay," said Zendt. "I've married worse."

"You think she had Artie Backman killed?"

Zendt shook his head. "I seriously doubt it. They

were pretty much already over, from what I had heard."

"I'm not so sure about that," said Jack. "She was pregnant with his child when he died."

Zendt laughed out loud, a cynical outbreak of mirth. "I guess they reconciled then. A very pretty story."

"You hated Artie Backman, of course."

"Of course."

"I'm starting to hate him too. Did you know Mazzarella?"

"Only by reputation. You guys running out of leads?"

"I don't want to think so."

Zendt lit a cigarette, then tapped the edge of the Zippo lighter on the table. "Where'd you get that sketch I saw in the paper?"

"Some wacky old dame. It don't have nothing to do with nothing."

"Poor Artie," said Zendt.

"Fuck Artie," said Jack. "Poor Mills."

Zendt laughed again, his eyes twinkling. "You want another cup?"

"No, thanks. But I will take the name of your hooked-up lawyer, in case I want to slip on the stairs and dive out of this place a little early."

"Wallace Wilson Benz is the guy you want to see," said Tony.

"Why am I not surprised?" said Jack.

"He's a big player," said Tony.

"So I hear. Tell me about the loan program. I understand you once borrowed a couple of bucks."

Zendt frowned and cocked his head. "Benz loaned me that money to pay his fucking bill. Don't go thinking it was no fucking political favor. I never, ever, sold out to those scumbags."

"Relax," said Jack. "No one said you did."

"Come on in here a minute, Jack."

Rodney Lomack was leaning out of his office, a look of shocked exhaustion on his dark brown face. The long morning was drawing to a close, and he had been sequestered with Quickstop for the better part of an hour, curtains drawn. Maybe he wanted Jack to tell them the latest Negro joke making the rounds. Maybe he just needed air.

Jack closed his file and walked into the office. Lomack closed the door behind him. Izzy Goldman was sitting on Lomack's green vinyl couch, obviously trying to hold back tears.

Lomack stood over him. "Tell him."

"I can't," said Izzy, heaving forward, blubbering.

"Tell me what?" asked Jack.

"Quickstop here deserves his nickname for more than his spastic bowels."

"Oh, yeah?"

"Yeah." Lomack suddenly slapped Izzy hard across his face, the first time Jack had ever seen the man resort to violence. "Ain't that right, scumbag?"

Izzy took the blow without retaliating or covering up. Lomack whacked him again.

"Sarge!" cried Jack.

Lomack raised his hand. "Tell him!"

"You're enjoying this so much," said Izzy, whimpering, "you tell him."

"Fine," said Lomack. "You got it. . . . This sniveling piece of dogshit you see in front of you has been fucking Rita Mazzarella for the last six months or so. He came to me this afternoon with his hat in his hand, hoping we could keep the information 'contained.' That's the word, isn't it, Izzy? He knew we'd discover from the neighbors that his car was in Mazzarella's driveway more than the Dicktop's. You know what he said, Jack? His excuse? He said him and Rita the Putita both got tired of holding the great man's coat." Lomack drew back his hand to slap Izzy again, then refrained, dropped his hand to his side in disgust.

Jack examined the molelike sergeant from a new perspective and remained unconvinced. "No offense, Izzy, but you were really drilling that fine-looking well?"

Izzy snarled, "Looks ain't everything, Mills. I listened to her. I respected her. And at least I got hair."

Jack laughed. Most of Izzy's hair grew out of his nostrils and ears.

Izzy said, "He didn't think much of you either, Mills. He said you had the attention span of a flea, the only guy he knew who was over the hill at thirty-five."

"Hill?" said Jack. "I don't remember a hill."

"He used to say that most of your goals bounced in off your head."

Jack looked at Lomack. "Can I slap him?"

"Please do."

Jack hit Izzy so hard he fell off the couch.

"That was fun, Sarge. Can I kick his fucking balls in?"

Lomack smiled at Jack and shook his head no.

Izzy crawled back onto the couch, cowering like a dog. "No more," cried Izzy. "Please."

Lomack said, "You're on the polygraph, asshole, right now. No phone calls. No lawyer. And if that needle so much as quivers, you're going down."

"What are you gonna ask me?"

"Simple shit, Izzy. Don't worry. Like did you or she have anything to do with his murder? Are either of you holding back information the department could use? The color of her bush. How many times a night did you make her come? Does she swallow?"

"Give me a break, Rod."

"Does she like two guys at once? How about black men?"

"Please!"

"How many breaks have you given me?"

"Whenever I could. We're both minorities."

"You ain't no brother of mine, you back-stabbing worm."

"My God, I'm so sorry." Izzy covered up and resumed his crying jag.

Lomack looked at Jack and smiled. "You learn anything here, flea brain?"

"Who, me? Where?"

"Nobody is all they're cracked up to be. Not even me. Now get back to work and forget this ever happened."

Jack nodded at Izzy Goldman, who nodded back. A deal. Then Jack returned to his overflowing desk, his palm still stinging from the blow he had delivered to the face of his superior officer.

It was noon. He had plenty of time to pick up Jenny and get to the stadium by game time.

On Saturday mornings there were always plenty of empty bottles and cans by the side of the road. Lucy Lallos's practice was to get up and out early, beat the bums to the harvest. One good Saturday or Sunday was worth four weekdays; she might make twenty, thirty dollars, as she had that particular morning, enough to keep body and soul together.

It was almost noon when Lucy finished her daily slice of pizza in the window booth she chose for its uninterrupted view of her big trike. She said good-bye to the counterman, pulled on her black nylon parka and walked outside. Jean, from the beauty parlor next door, saw her and waved, mouthed the word, "Coffee?"

Lucy shook her head and mouthed "No, thank you."

It was enough they occasionally trimmed her long gray hair, charging half-price, refusing tips. Pretty girls with pretty cars, and boyfriends. They were good to her, as were many of the local merchants. Of course it worked both ways. She kept their lots clear of all but the most unsalvageable items, as regular as the U.S. Postal Service, and she never failed to offer daily prayers for them at Saint Sylvester's early mass.

Lucy climbed into the saddle and continued her journey north along the rutted shoulder of Route 112, keeping a constant eye on the rearview mirror for the frequent eighteen-wheelers and overloaded gravel trucks that caused her to wobble.

She slammed on her brakes, stopped abruptly

near the curb, found four Beck's bottles in weeds that ringed the base of a telephone pole.

Outside the bagel place, she recovered a Volkswagen hubcap and from the woods near the newly built town offices four lengths of PVC pipe. She stowed her goods in the basket and remounted. Rode back into the dwarfing wind and noise of traffic.

The parking lot of the Beverage Barn was all but deserted, a good time to make a drop at the redemption center and buy a quart of beer. Afterward, she pulled her trike around back, out of the wind, and sat against the south side of the building with the bottle of Colt .45. The sunlight warmed her wrinkled face and hands, the bitter malt washed the oily taste of pizza from her throat. She was happy to rest, to look at the sky. Compensation, she felt, for the difficulty of her life. At least the poor, she thought gratefully, have time to see the sky.

A white Jaguar pulled up, scattering gravel. Two young men in pastel golf clothes leaped out, looked at her, looked at each other, then entered the store after making some comment. It did not bother her what they thought. They came out a minute later with a case of Budweiser and drove away without a second look. Which was fine, she thought. Have mercy on them. They have much to learn and many handicaps.

She raised her bottle to her lips, quickly finished the cold brew, then knocked out three Hail Marys for her penance. With her thirst quenched and her change purse filled, Lucy got up and headed for home. She had enough for the day, enough money to make it till morning, and her legs hurt, the varicose veins, the cartilage in her knee Dr. Rodriguez always wanted to remove. There were some cookies in the house, instant coffee, discount bread that she had bought on its expiration date, a jug of wine.

As Lucy approached the intersection of 112 and Granny Road, a man on a white Ross ten-speed pulled next to her, crowding her nearer to the curb. He was clean-shaven and darkly handsome, wearing a plain gray sweatsuit and a protective helmet that she could never have afforded. She looked straight ahead, but she could feel him staring at the side of her face.

"Remember me?"

It took a moment, but she did. The eyes were the same, the coloring of the skin.

"You got a big fucking mouth, you know that?"

"Oh, my God."

"We're gonna go to your house and have a little talk about keeping our mouths shut, or I'm gonna hurt you bad. You know I can do that, don't you? You've seen my work."

Lucy's legs went weak as her heart began to flutter in her chest. It was him, come to kill her. Lucy Lallos, the only eyewitness, those stupid cops had called her.

Her home was to the right, then another right down the hill. He might not know that. He might have found her by staking out the area. He had not called her by name. But to make a left in front of him and all those whizzing cars would be suicide, and straight ahead led up a hill into a wooded stretch of road without stores. He took the choice away from her as he forced her right on Granny Road, in the direction of Gordon Heights, her rooming house, her death. So he knew, she thought. This was planned.

This day her life would end.

But not without a fight.

Lucy stood on her pedals and pumped for all she was worth, reaching speeds in excess of four miles an hour, a brave but futile gesture. There was no way to outrun his racing bike on her slow but steady tricycle, no way to outlast a man twenty years her junior. She was required to make two revolutions for each of his, on a bike that weighed twice as much. And her chances to escape harm diminished as they rolled away from civilization.

"Don't think about yelling for help," he said, not even breathing hard.

Lucy was gulping for air. With pressing motive and superior technology, he hovered on her wing.

"Please," she said. "I have to stop. I can't breathe."

To go further into the woods on Granny was dumb. The houses up ahead were sometimes a quarter-mile apart. Anyplace he wanted to, he could pull her into the tall trees shrouded with bramble bush. The orange signs posted every twenty yards prohibiting hunting, fishing, trapping and trespassing would not deter this man from taking her life. She slowed her pace and pulled to the side.

The man swooped in behind her and slapped her hard on the back of the head, causing tears to well in her eyes. He skidded to a stop in front of her.

"Move it, lady. I ain't fucking around."

"This never happened," she said. "I'll move

away, out of the state. Dear God, have mercy. Please."

"That's one option. There may be others. We'll talk."

He raised his arm and pointed east.

Perhaps he did not intend to kill her. Perhaps, she thought, he will buy my silence with as little as bus fare. He did not have a gun that she could see, or a knife. There was no point in making him mad. Lucy nodded and continued down the wooded lane. The killer coasted behind her, his face expressionless.

She turned right on Middle Island Road, across from the entrance to the All-American Air Gun Games, where on weekends grown men played at war over acres of undeveloped forest. She worked hard to make the top of the hill, then coasted down the other side, seeing the trees and blue sky as if for the first time, trying to remember them, jealous of their permanence, that they could stay and she must go.

The man on the bike dropped back fifty yards, letting out his line, maybe taunting her, making sport; or perhaps he did not wish to be remembered as riding with Lucy past the young black boys playing stickball in the street up ahead.

The batter was Ahmad Gilliam from the second floor of her building, one of the neighborhood chocolate drops. And there was Dion, his younger cousin, pitching a red rubber ball. And Gus . . .

"Help!" she screamed. "He's trying to kill me."

They stopped their game and watched her approach, puzzled.

"Help! Please!"

Lucy used the last of her strength to race flat-out for the boys.

In her mirror she saw the man stand up on his pedals, the bike sway from side to side. He was smiling, she thought, having fun. He was closing the gap with ridiculous ease.

Ten yards from the rock that marked the pitcher's mound while Lucy crossed the plate.

Five yards.

But then Ahmad, the batter, who was nothing if not a brave defender of old neighbor ladies, flipped his broom handle into the front spokes of the passing ten-speed Ross. Which suddenly had one speed, a much slower velocity than its rider, who flew head over handlebars into an evergreen.

"Whoa," said Dion. "Check it out."

"You check it out. I'm booking."

By the time the cursing white man had extricated himself from the gummy branches, the boys had disappeared. He could hear them crashing through the woods, laughing, laughing at him. And he wished he had his little .22, so he could pick one off. And make the other dig the grave.

Lucy never broke stride and never looked back, not until she was all the way home. She dropped three nickels and spun five into the pay phone in the dark lobby of her rooming house.

"Suffolk County Homicide."

"Detective Claire Williamson, please."

"I'm sorry, Ma'am. She's out of town on assignment. Would you like to speak to anyone else?"

"When will she be back? This is very important."

"I can beep her."

"Please."

Twenty-five minutes later the man got out of his car in front of the Gordon Heights rooming house. He wore a three-piece gray suit, flashed a silver badge at the women drinking wine on the stoop. "Strike Force," he said. "Official business."

Ahmad's mother, Betty, looked up from her paper cup. "Is they any other kind?"

Two minutes later he brought Lucy out of the house, handcuffed. "From now on," he said, "this woman is under the protection of the Joint Narcotics Strike Force. You and your kids better leave her alone."

He sat her next to him in the front seat. She was crying, the skin around her lips roughed up. She said nothing as they drove away from her building.

"I'll bet you thought you'd never see me again."

"That ain't true," she said.

"There's no reason for you to be afraid of me. I'm not the animal you think."

Claire walked down the rickety flight of wooden stairs from Lucy's room to the second floor and knocked on the door of the Gilliam apartment. "Police Department, Ma'am," she said. "I'd like a moment of your time."

Three keys operated three separate deadbolts, then the door opened halfway. Mrs. Betty Gilliam, still in her robe at six o'clock, asked what Luther had got himself involved in now.

"Nothing, Mrs. Gilliam, that I know of. I'm looking for Lucy Lallos."

"Really? You all ought to talk to each other more. She left here this afternoon with one of your narcs."

"Are you sure?"

"Showed us his damn badge and ev'ything."

"What did he look like?"

"White dude. In a suit."

"Did you get a good look at his face?"

"What I care what he look like? It ain't me selling drugs around here."

"Anyone else see him?"

"Couple folks. You could ask around downstairs."

Downstairs no one had seen anything. On her way out to her car, Claire was stopped by a skinny black boy in thick glasses and a Columbia University sweatshirt.

"Ma'am?"

"Yes?"

"You looking for Lucy?"

"Yes."

"I didn't see anything but I heard some of the other boys talking before. They were saying how they'd messed up some white man who was chasing Lucy on her bike." The boy gave Claire a short version of the bicycle chase through the stickball game.

"Which boys?" Claire asked.

"Ahmad Gilliam and Gus. Maybe Dion Vailes too."

"Thank you, son."

"You're welcome."

Claire went back to the second floor and knocked on Betty Gilliam's door. "I need to talk to Ahmad

Gilliam," she said. "He may have acted quite heroically."

Betty Gilliam threw her head back and laughed, showing Claire a fat, coated tongue. The air was redolent of gin and stale smoke. "You come on in, girl, and sit down anywhere. This shit I gotta hear."

Claire stepped into the tiny apartment. The landlord had obviously knocked down a wall between two small closets and listed it with Welfare as a suite, and if no one from Social Services ever checked, next year it would be carried as a woodland condominium. The kitchen belonged on a boat; its aluminum sink was the size of an ashtray. A cockroach strolled the brief length of faucet. Two stuffed chairs, two aluminum snack trays, two mattresses, separated by a bed sheet that hung from the ceiling. His clothes in a pile against one wall. Hers, seemingly, everywhere. Where, she wondered, did Ahmad do his homework?

"You want a drink?" asked Betty Gilliam. "I'm having one."

"No, thanks."

"Suit yourself." Betty Gilliam slumped in one of the chairs with her glass, her duties as hostess fulfilled.

"Do you know where Ahmad is right now?"

"You mean Luther. His name be Luther. Luther Gilliam, just like his asshole daddy. Where he got that Ahmad bullshit, I don't know. Says Luther's his slave name, I'd like to die. These older boys 'round here, some of them crazy from jail, they come home running they mouths about Africa and shit. And my boy, he think they know what's happening cause they been away. He find out when it's his turn, them fuckheads don't know shit."

"Could I speak with Luther?" asked Claire.

"Long as I won't have to be dragging his ass to court." Betty Gilliam struggled up from her chair and opened her only window. "Luth-er!" she called out.

A boy's voice from outside: "Yo."

"Mamma needs you, Luther."

"Coming."

Luther Gilliam entered the room a moment later, looked at Claire, sized up the situation, and put a scowl on his otherwise handsome face. He was twelve, maybe thirteen, skinny, with big bright eyes. "What, Mamma?" he said. "Who's she?"

"I'm Detective Williamson, Luther. I'd like to talk to you about what happened today."

Luther looked at his mother. "I been hanging out back. Mamma seen me."

"Don't ask me for no alibi, Luther. Tell the lady what you done."

"Nothing. Honest. Who said I done something?"

"I understand you helped old Lucy escape from a killer."

Relief showed on his face, then patience. "You been talking to that nerdy motherfucker out front? He always saying something wacky. Nobody round here pays him any mind. Nobody with any sense."

"She said a man was chasing her on a bicycle, and you and some friends knocked the man down and allowed her to escape. If that's the case, Luther, I think the Suffolk County Police Department is very much in your debt. There might be awards involved, maybe press coverage. The case is very important."

Luther looked at his mother, his surroundings, with an eye sufficiently worldly to know better than to seek publicity.

"You all can owe me one."

"Please, Luther."

"I'd love to help you, lady. But like I said, nothing happened."

Something had happened, and Luther had rightly guessed that to say so would be dangerous. He was not much of a liar yet. But he would be.

Claire drove to the nearest pay phone and called Jack, who could not be reached. Then she beeped Barbara Fisher and waited. The phone in the booth rang in three minutes.

"Sergeant Fisher," a voice answered.

"Hi, Barb. Where's Louie been all day?"

"Asleep in the backseat of his Mercedes in his own driveway. He came home around five A.M. from a night of Manhattan debauchery and his wife wouldn't let him into the house. He was so drunk it was actually funny. You want me to lock him up?"

"No. I want you to go home. And thanks, Barb. It was worth a shot."

"He was easy. The cocky ones always are."

Jack couldn't sleep that night, tossing and turning, thinking of Jenny and Babe and how he had neglected them and Claire and how he would not ever neglect her if given the chance. He chewed for a while on the deaths of Arthur Backman and Richard Mazzarella, the romance of Izzy Goldman and Rita Mazzarella. Louie Allesi and Angela

Cortelli. What a swamp of swingers this case had uncovered. So he was wide awake at one A.M. when the phone on his bedside table rang.

"Mills," he said.

It was Claire.

"Oh, it's you."

"Did I wake you?" she said. "Are you alone?"

"No and yes. What's up?"

In a voice filled with anger she filled him in on the kidnapping of Lucy Lallos and the large but likely unsuccessful efforts she had organized in Suffolk County to find her. "You would have known all this earlier if you bothered to stay in touch."

"I was off. I took my kid to a ball game."

"You have a bad habit of taking off at critical times."

"I want to go to sleep and never wake up," Jack said.

"That's a *stupid* thing to say!"

"Well, you're the expert. You tell *me* what the fuck is going on."

"What's going on, Jumpin' Jack, is that we're being led by the nose somewhere bad. I feel like I did when I was on that telephone pole. Alone!"

She hung up.

23

THERE WAS a Sunday-morning blood drive going on in the lobby of headquarters. Volunteers with coffee and doughnuts solicited donations. Jack respectfully declined to part with a pint of his all-American blood, for humanitarian reasons. "I have syphilis, malaria and hepatitis," he told the blood bankers.

He went upstairs to his cubicle and sat at his desk disappointedly packing a voluminous file on Louie Allesi into an interoffice envelope. Destination: Records.

In the cubicle next to him, Al Trankina was fending off two reporters who wanted the details of the suicide of a Carle Place honor student, an early admittee to Princeton who had left behind a note that said only: "Homey can't play this no more."

The reporters did not care what Jack might be up to. Trankina could serve up tragedy enough for one day's news.

Jack looked up at the missing persons poster of Lucy Lallos on the bulletin board among the

248

wanted posters, the handprinted ads for cars, boats, houses and weapons, all the commerce of cops. He looked for help in the empty space behind Eats's desk.

Jack pulled Anthony Zendt's file from his desk and stared at it, found himself wondering if the dummies ever scared Tony, startled him down there in that basement right after he flipped on the lights. Maybe that was why he named them. Maybe until he knew them personally, they oozed menace. He looked over at Lomack's office door, which was closed and presumably locked. He checked the duty charts. The sergeant would be in tomorrow, eight to four. A blessing, perhaps. There was time for him to do some double-checking.

Tony Zendt had worked with Arthur Backman at the One-Three, he had dated Angela Cortelli. He had even borrowed bread from Wallace Wilson Benz. Jack remembered Tony's tan body. Was his face paler? Perhaps he had shaved off a beard recently.

But that was not the worst of it.

With a hollow feeling in his gut, Jack recalled his mention of the wacky old dame who had provided Suffolk County with a sketch.

Jack picked up his phone and made arrangements with Emergency Services for the use of the snoop van that night, a dented white Ford Econoline with bogus Cablevision logos on the outside and state-of-the-art surveillance equipment inside.

"How long you need it?" asked the lieutenant.

"Overnight."

"How far you going?"

"Figure maybe round-trip a hundred miles."

"I'll have one of the guys gas her up."

"Thanks."

"Don't mention it. We in the basement also serve."

Then Jack put on his sport coat and did something he had not done since college: he went to the library.

The wise and mysterious smell of books reminded Jack of Mrs. Matts—his elementary-school librarian—and the sun-filled second-floor stacks from which he had withdrawn hot-rod novels, biographies of Davy Crockett and Nathan Hale, *Winning Pitcher, Shadow Over the Backcourt, Fighting Five.* It dawned on him that libraries were about the greatest places on earth. Unless one was a college student. He remembered the frustration of being forced to manufacture phony term papers on macroeconomics while seated across a long study table from one of the first women he knew to eschew her bra: the Babe. No wonder he had not voluntarily returned.

The senior reference librarian was sure he knew Jack, or had at least seen "that handsome face" before.

"Probably only two or three times a day."

"Excuse me?" He was thin and precise, perhaps British or Welsh, dressed in a houndstooth blazer with a black vest. "Are you somebody famous?"

Jack turned from the desk and pointed at the main doors, at his poster wedged between announcements of adult-education courses at Nassau

Community College and the Reggae Sunsplash concert at Bald Hill.

"My word," said the librarian. "It is you . . . almost."

"I broke my nose," said Jack.

The librarian regarded Jack's face. "So you did. I trust you were dragging some nasty lawbreaker to justice."

"In a roundabout way."

"How may I help you?"

Jack told him.

The librarian offered Jack the use of his tiny office, then scurried off to the stacks. He returned five minutes later with a book and several periodicals. "Here you go, Detective. Everything I could find on glorified coat hangers."

He closed the door and left Jack to his reading.

Over the next two hours Jack learned that mannequins have been with us since ancient times, fantasy versions of the human figure. A wooden torso was discovered in the tomb of King Tutankhamen, perhaps the world's first dress form. The making of mannequins by the fashion world reflected the values and attitudes of their eras. Marie Antoinette kept her mother and sisters in Austria apprised of the latest styles at Versailles by sending them elaborately clothed mannequins.

In the 1930s, a New York soap sculptor named Lester Gaba created an ideal woman named Cynthia. So enchanting was she that he took her riding on double-decker buses, to the Stork Club and the opera, where she sat with him in his box in her perpetual seated pose, elbow on knee, cigarette in hand. Couturiers sent her clothes. Cartier and

Tiffany lent her jewelry. Cynthia met her end when she fell off a chair in a beauty salon and shattered.

The guys in the motor pool left Jack a full tank of gas. He wished they had also checked the brakes and tightened up the steering. Driving Snoopy felt like wallowing on a waterbed at fifty-five miles an hour. On the ride east, Jack stayed in the right-hand lane, incurring, by their sidelong looks of disdain, the wrath of half his fellow motorists. The ones who did not transmit scorn were driving too fast to take their eyes off the road.

Never a cop around when you needed one, he thought. Ain't that the truth.

He got off the expressway at Nicolls Road and turned onto Horseblock. At the 7 Eleven store in Farmingville, Jack loaded up on chili dogs, chocolate milk and Oreos. Then he nursed the van up Blue Point Road to a minor peak near the top, from which he could observe and photograph the neat gray ranch with its red garage door. He opened the New York Telephone junction box and tapped into Zendt's private line with alligator clips the way Lomack had showed him. He ran the wires inside the van and closed the side door. Through several miniature, infrared telephoto lenses, Jack saw Zendt's living-room picture window magnified twenty times, the play of television light on the drawn shade, the red curtains. He aligned the Wolf's Ears and listened in.

Tony Zendt was apparently alone, watching a tape of a football game, using the remote fast-forward to speed untouched and silent through the commercials. The New York Giants were beating up on the Washington Redskins at RFK Stadium. John Madden was calling the game with Pat Summerall.

Jack unwrapped the first hot dog and swallowed half.

Tony was suddenly speaking to someone, a man with an English accent, and using an electric drill. Then a hammer. They were discussing angles of incidence, angles of refraction, throw weights and measures. Tony Zendt was talking to his dummies.

Jack felt a moment of heartache. It occurred to him that he could wind up like Zendt, stocking his life with phantom friends.

At 2123 hours the light on the panel of the telephone recorder blinked on.

"Hi, Mamma. It's me."

"Hel-lo, Tony. What's the matter?"

"Nothing's the matter, Ma. I just called to tell you I'm gonna take that vacation you're always saying I should. I'm going to California, leaving in a day or two."

"You're gonna stop in San Jose and see your sister?"

"What do you think?"

"What do you mean, what do I think? When it's you and family, I don't think nothing. It's better that way—I don't get disappointed."

Jack heard Tony exhale cigarette smoke.

"You got some time for me before you go? There's things I need you to do around the house, things I used to be able to do for myself."

"Maybe tomorrow, okay? I'll try, I promise."

"You know I don't like to bother you."

"I know, Mamma."

"How long you gonna be gone?"

"A couple weeks, maybe a month. I need a rest, Mom. Away from the Island. Things ain't been going too good for me lately."

"Go back to church. All your problems started when you stopped going to Mass."

"Nina was my problem, Mamma."

"You can say that again. She was a slut. I told you that. But does my Tony listen? My Tony thinks because he's a cop and I'm an old lady, I don't know about girls like her. My Tony thinks that—"

"Mamma. I'll see you tomorrow."

Jack heard Zendt make himself a cocktail and light another cigarette.

Zendt had been divorced from Nina Fowler almost ten years ago, around the same time Babe had given him the boot. But to hear the man whine, he was still not over the breakup; it was yesterday. This loss of love still shaped his life.

Jack played back the tape and wondered what else, on close psychological analysis, Dr. Alan Rensallin might surmise from Zendt's singsong lament to his mommy. Jack imagined Tony's report cards from grade school alluded to difficulty working and playing with others. And yet he'd been a cop for fifteen years, duly licensed by the state to carry firearms.

The phone rang.

"Tony, it's me."

"Yeah?"

"Your mother tells me you're taking a little trip."

"That didn't take her long."

"She happens to know what you're like, and she cares about her grandsons."

"Isn't that sweet? Did she also tell you that she called you a slut?"

"Of course not. She loves me. So Tony, who's gonna feed the troops while you're away? Who's gonna polish their barrels?"

"You're an asshole, Nina."

"Yeah, yeah. Just send me next month's check before you go lollygagging around the country like you don't have no obligations."

"Speaking of my obligations, how are the—"

"They're not here. I'll tell them you said hello."

"Fine."

"You should go away. You sound sick."

"I'm having problems with a woman. She seems to enjoy hurting me, Nina. Not like you, of course, but—"

"Get help, Tony. Your life is a fucking mess."

"Nobody fucks with me and walks."

"It's all hot air, Tony. You know it. I know it. The boys know it. This sounds like the time you told me you were gonna blow your brains out and didn't."

He gave a short, bitter laugh. "I remember what you said that night in the kitchen, when I had the barrel of the gun inside my fucking ear."

"Yeah? What was that?"

"You said, real soft and sincere too, 'Do it, honey. No one will care.'"

"You had just knocked out my tooth."

"And why did I do that? Huh? You junkie pig! I shoulda claimed the monkey on your back as a dependent."

Nina hung up.

At 11:35, Tony Zendt turned off his television set and walked into his bedroom. Jack heard sneakers

255

thrown into a closet, pants with change in the pockets tossed to the floor. The lights went out. Then Zendt either knocked out sixty push-ups or made big friends with himself.

Twenty minutes later, all Jack could hear from Tony Zendt's house were clocks ticking and gentle, rhythmic, solitary snoring.

Jack killed the interior lights and slid out into the darkness as quietly as if he were sneaking home drunk. After three hours in the stale air of the van, the night breeze felt good on his face.

A dog barked on the next block. Another answered. He put a baseball cap on his head and walked quickly along the opposite side of the street until he was even with Zendt's mailbox, then crossed over unnoticed.

It was garbage night on Blue Point Road, and Tony Zendt was nothing if not obsessively neat. His single rubber can was labeled in white paint ZENDT. Inside, his trash was neatly bagged and tied. Jack lifted it out, replaced the cover, then casually recrossed the street. A car was coming, from down below. The treetops lit up first, then the telephone pole. Jack hid behind the van, down on one knee, his hand groping his ankle for his gun. The car flew past, kids on a joyride, leaving on the wind a young girl's laughter.

Jack got back in the van and rolled silently downhill before starting the motor.

24

W HY COPS?" asked Claire, holding her lighter to the end of Angela Cortelli's cigarette.

They had just finished going over everything Angela had told Jack in his initial interview and were sitting in Claire's car behind the Spartacus Diner in Belmont, watching two Hispanic busboys lean on the dumpster and share a joint. It was the dawn of a clear bright Monday morning. Angela had nothing new to offer the investigation, and there were no inconsistencies to her story. The sky above the aluminum building facade was streaked with high red cirrus clouds. In the morning light Claire noticed the worry lines on Angela's forehead, how old and rough were her bony hands.

"I've asked myself that question a hundred times."

Angela wore a tight black waitress uniform and a button-down white sweater. Her makeup was heavy, her jewelry turquoise and silver, her perfume cheap.

"The adventure?" Claire asked.

"That's part of it, I guess. It all started with just one guy."

Claire nodded. What woman couldn't say that.

"He shot himself in the head when his wife threw him out."

"And then?"

"I was young then, maybe twenty-two, and so there was another and another, like an endless supply of horny men. Some stuck around longer than others. For a while I thought I was their queen."

Claire said nothing. It served no purpose to embarrass Angela any more than she already was.

"You like that Jack fella?"

Claire looked out her window. An elderly black man in a clerical collar was holding the car door open for his wife. She smiled up at him, took his hand, heaved herself out of the seat.

"I thought he was pretty hot myself," said Angela. "He tell you that?"

"No."

"Oh, yeah?"

"Forget him," Claire said with a wave. "Jack Mills is just good enough to wreck a girl's life, not good enough to go the distance. You know what I mean?"

Angela folded her hands in her lap. "My type exactly."

"Like Tony Zendt."

Angela looked startled.

"Tell me about him," said Claire. "Girl to girl."

"He's got his good sides and his bad."

"How long did you live with him?"

"About a year."

"Yes? And is there something else you want to tell me?"

Angela studied her hands. "He took us breaking up very hard."

"We're beginning to think so."

Angela bit the knuckle of her index finger and shook her head slowly. "For a while it was nice, traveling to his battles, camping out and drinking with his buddies. Then he hurt his back and he was here all the time, constantly breaking my chops. He was very jealous, as I'm sure you can imagine."

"Why?"

"He caught his wife with his next-door neighbor, before he met me."

"Go on."

"He used to watch me, follow me. He loved that kind of shit. I had to break off with him."

Claire lit cigarettes for both of them, handed one to Angela. "Then what?"

"When he gave me a black eye I made a complaint at the precinct. That's when I started up with Artie."

"Did you know a man named Richard Mazzarella?"

"You mean the other cop who got killed. I don't think I ever met him . . . but I might have."

"Completely bald."

Angela nodded sadly. "I knew him. They called him Dick."

"Did Tony ride a bike?"

"Sure," she said. "All the time, for his back. I think it's still downstairs in my storage bin."

"I doubt it," said Claire.

"No," said Angela. "You're wrong. I saw it there the other day."

"Let's look."

Riding down to the basement in the elevator, Angela jingled her keys like castanets. The chicken-wire storage room was lit by a single bulb and locked, filled with steamer trunks, packing crates, baby carriages, bikes. Angela produced a key and opened the door. "There," she said. "In the back. The silver Fuji."

Claire took a closer look. "This bike doesn't have dust on it. Does Tony have a key to this room?"

"He did, sure. He made copies of everything the day he moved in."

Claire bent over to examine the bike. Pinched between the greasy chainlinks were fibers that would match Artie Backman's car seat.

"I've got bad news for you," said Claire.

Angela bit her lip and began sobbing, her shoulders shaking. "Maybe I better show you something else," she said and led the way upstairs.

Her apartment looked and smelled like a greenhouse, one wall laden with roses in vases, wine decanters, juice bottles, milk cartons, pitchers. A stack of cards lay on her cocktail table. Claire riffled through them.

"Jesus."

"I thought it was the Right-to-Lifers," Angela said. "They gave me some shit outside the clinic, and I figured they followed me home or something."

"Why did you accept them? Why did you save them?"

Angela bit her knuckle again. "I couldn't let them die."

"What are you doing here? Impersonating a detective?" said Lomack. "I thought you were off."

"I took Snoopy out to Suffolk last night. Had a long but interesting evening."

Sergeant Lomack shook his head. "I do hope no one saw the van bouncing up and down."

"I went alone, boss. I staked out a house."

Lomack feigned surprise. "What initiative."

"You know a guy named Tony Zendt? A street cop, used to work the One-Three?"

"I know Zendt. He went out on three-quarters a few years ago."

"He was madly in love with Angela Cortelli. Artie Backman snatched her on the rebound, then turned her out to his friends." Jack held up Zendt's personnel photo. "Zendt's a fucking Section Eight. Listen to this."

Jack played back Zendt's phone conversations of the previous evening.

"Okay," Lomack said, "he's a pussy-whipped flake. But you'd better have more than that before you accuse this poor schmuck of murder. He never so much as drew his weapon in fifteen years on the street."

Jack made a T with his hands, signaling for time-out. "I picked his garbage."

"My, my," said Lomack. "We were going all out, weren't we."

"I found travel brochures from Grand Cayman Island. No American extradition."

"People shop around for vacations. People dream."

"I'm gonna call the airlines when I get done in here. I'll bet my ass he got a one-way ticket."

"Tell me the truth, Jack—this is not just a smoke screen to dodge one pissed-off county executive?"

"Zendt's the one, boss."

Claire arrived with Zendt's bicycle over her shoulder as Jack was completing his briefing of Lomack, and she added to the weight of the evidence.

"Goddamn," said Lomack. "Barbie and Ken come through, and apparently for Jack, not a moment too soon."

"You want my people to grab him?" asked Claire.

"He's our bad apple," said Lomack. "We'll get his official picture out to your boss and do a photo-pack identification at the rooming house on the kidnap charge. If it's a yes, we'll meet and scoop him up together. We can file the murder charges when we're absolutely sure about these bike fibers. Now we don't say anything to anybody, Jack. Not even Aaron. I want a media blackout until the wrap."

Jack nodded. Cops were prone to confession one on one, under soothing, fraternal circumstances. They would lose that chance should the building be surrounded by reporters.

"Come on, Let's go tell Barone," Lomack said. "Claire, you wait here."

The chief was not as happy as they had expected.

He stood up behind his desk and shouted: "What you're telling me is that this entire Greek fucking tragedy comes down to pussy, after we've just spent a month jerking off on people who can hurt us?"

Jack shrugged. "We'll know more when we talk to Zendt."

"Zendt's lawyers, you mean," said Chief Barone.

Lomack looked out the window, taking in the view.

Barone said, "I don't suppose we could say that Suffolk did not adequately protect the witness?"

"No," said Jack. "We could not."

"What is Suffolk doing to help us?"

"They got a team at Lucy's rooming house, another one on the way to Zendt's, an APB on Zendt's car. I'll make calls to the railroad and airport cops. You want the commissioner's office notified too?"

"Screw 'em," said Barone. "We don't even know what we have yet, or at least I don't."

Trankina stuck his head into the office. "There's a call on line two for Detective Mills."

"He'll take it," said Barone.

It was Claire. "My boss just called. We got a situation at Zendt's house. He and some friends started pegging shots out the window. Lucy's alive and with him, he walked her by the front picture window. Anticrime and uniform guys have the house surrounded and they're clearing folks out of the neighborhood as fast as they can. The hostage negotiators are on their way."

"I understand," said Jack.

"He's demanding to talk to you, yelling out the window that you drove him to this."

"I what?"

Barone punched the speaker-phone button.

Claire continued: "My boss wants you there forthwith. Zendt said he wanted to see you within the next hour or he was gonna do Lucy. He said he's got nothing left to lose."

"You don't have to go," said Barone, waving a hand at Jack. "This is technically a Suffolk County kidnapping. We ain't charged nobody with nothing yet."

"No," Lomack said. "We're going. Right, Jack?"

25

SERGEANT LOMACK studied Anthony Zendt's personnel file while his hands worked a handkerchief. He hated flying, even on 747s, much less an Air Bureau six-seater helicopter.

Claire asked if anyone minded if she smoked, and everyone said, "Yes!"

Each had changed into a blue Nassau County Police jumpsuit, not that any of them planned on jumping.

From on high, the Island's trees were bathed in fall colors, with the sound to the north and the ocean to the south, a dark green. The helicopter climbed. The sky above America's front porch was clear, and visibility ran to twenty miles.

Jack stared out the small side window, noting landmarks—the Jones Beach tower, Pilgrim State Hospital, Bald Hill, the striped power-station smokestacks at Northport, University Hospital at Stony Brook where he might soon be a patient. Bridgeport, Connecticut, passed slowly on the left, across the Sound.

Jack caught the sergeant's eye. "None of us ever

considered that a guy could care about a slut this much. That's what messed us up."

"Sometimes," said Claire, leaning forward, "you can be such a jerk."

Lomack took a deep breath.

Jack said, "Easy, boss. Almost there."

The chopper descended and set down safely on the Sachem soccer fields at twenty minutes to four. A black unmarked Plymouth with long antennae was waiting outside the flattened circle of grass. Claire, Jack and Lomack ran to it, ducking the rotor blades long after they had to.

A young detective sat behind the wheel of the car. An older man, thickset, with a military flattop, sat next to him, smoking a cigar. The new arrivals slid into the backseat of the car and introduced themselves.

"Captain Frank Bellini," said the older man. "I run Hostage Negotiations out here." His driver said nothing, just drove the car off the playing field while the chopper cranked up and skimmed off. "This is gonna be trouble," said Bellini. "My firearms guys are already itching for a killshot, and we ain't even got uncomfortable yet."

"What's happening?" said Lomack.

"What's happening is he's got a fucking army in there."

"Maybe not," said Jack.

"Come again?" said Bellini.

Jack described the basement arsenal, Tony's skill with electronics, his mannequins. He suppressed an urge to apologize for Tony.

"I don't know," said Bellini. "We've heard at least three distinct male voices since we set up the

sound truck—one of them an Englishman." Bellini
threw one arm over the back of his seat. "Around
forty-five minutes ago, when the squad dicks went
to knock on the door, rounds came flying out of
several windows, knocking out headlights and a
windshield."

"He's alone," said Jack. "He's got the house
rigged."

"How do you know that?"

"I listened to him set it up without knowing what
he was up to. From our snoop van," he added.

Bellini frowned, faced forward.

Sergeant Lomack asked, "What about crowd
control?"

"Civilians won't be a problem 'cause of the
geography. We got an outside perimeter set up a
quarter-mile out, two hundred feet below. It's cops
that'll jam things up. Last I heard the brass was
pouring out of headquarters, scrambling to get up
here in time to be a part of the circus. Nassau cop
goes nuts in Suffolk. Senator Tom Otto would be up
here already but he's busy reenacting a Chinese
immigration scam in Queens for Channel Eleven."

Lomack agreed with Bellini: Too many bosses
meant trouble.

Jack didn't mind a big crowd; he might get lost in
the surplus of heroes, maybe find someone to play
his role for a change.

Frank Bellini said, "I'm the only one to talk to
him on the phone so far. Maybe twenty minutes
ago, give or take. He told me Jesus was making him
take a stand against us. He said Jesus wants to
punish Mills, to show him the light of righteous-
ness. I did my best not to laugh out loud, and I

sensed that he was fighting it too. One highly unstable collection of atoms is Tony Zendt."

"Punish me for what?" asked Jack.

Bellini blew a cloud of ripe blue cigar smoke against the windshield. "You tell me. Until this afternoon, I'd never even heard your name."

The car turned north from Horse Block onto Blue Point Road and climbed a series of knobby hills. Four hundred yards from the Zendt house, yellow tape was strung across the road.

A uniformed cop with a clipboard logged them present at the scene and stepped aside, holding up the tape.

Two hundred yards from Zendt's house, the Suffolk County Police Mobile Command Post was set up for business behind the cover of several fir trees. Closer still were two brown Plymouths, their doors open, abandoned, their operators pinned down behind them. The little house looked like a bunker, garage door closed, shades drawn.

Around the blue-and-white bus stood a tense crowd of men in helmets and jumpsuits, smoking, holding radios, clipboards, shotguns and bullhorns. As Bellini parked the car, Mills thought he knew how French aristocrats felt about getting down from the tumbrils. He stifled an urge to grab a bullhorn and explain his involvement.

He did not have to. The word was out. The Suffolk cops moved out of their way as if the detectives from Nassau had something contagious.

Inside the command post, Claire Williamson stepped to the chalkboard and brought her superiors up to date on the situation. Present in their decorated blues were the Suffolk County Police commissioner, her father, the chief of patrol and, in a sharp business suit, the Suffolk County chief of detectives. Lieutenant Drexel, Bellini's second in command, wore a jumpsuit and flak jacket. While he listened to Claire, his eyes never left the monitors, which at that moment showed four camera angles of Tony Zendt's house.

Jack felt a lessening of tension in the pit of his stomach. He had help now. It's all of us good guys against one crazy bad guy. He was a number, not a name.

Claire gave him half a smile and continued her speech: "The suspect is heavily armed. A retired, decorated police officer with military combat training. Captain Bellini has previously established telephone contact with Mr. Zendt. These gentlemen are Sergeant Rodney Lomack and Detective Jack Mills from Nassau Homicide. The suspect's first and only demand at this time is an audience with Detective Mills."

Everyone looked at Jack: it was all he could do not to shrug.

Claire said, "Detective Mills is the case agent on the murder of retired Captain Arthur Backman and also involved in the investigation of Captain Mazzarella's murder. I worked the Suffolk end of the cases. I found the witness—now the hostage— Lucy Lallos, a fifty-nine-year-old female, white. The minimum level of protection, we now see, was not enough. Captain Bellini?"

Bellini tossed his cigar butt out the door and joined Claire in front of the blackboard.

"Well, Frank," said the commissioner, very much in control. "How's this one look to you?"

"Not good, sir," said Bellini. "In fact, we have a deadline to meet in twelve minutes. Zendt wants to talk to Mills or he said he'd kill the old lady right in front of us."

"And we believe him?" said the commissioner.

"Yes, we do."

"I see."

"Add to that the fact that we have absolutely no idea what sort of interior defense he might have assembled, although I'm guessing along the lines of the Alamo. Therefore an assault is out of the question. Just in case anyone was thinking of it."

"No one was thinking of it, Frank. We'll let you do it your way."

"I need more intelligence, sir. Badly. I need Zendt's shrink, if he's got one. His priest. The floor plan of his house. And I need time. Lots more time."

The commissioner said, "Summation?"

"Mr. Zendt is calling the shots."

"Suggestions?"

Jack said, "We can threaten to kill *his* mother."

Bellini ignored this and remarked to the commissioner, "Mills here will give us the floor plan and probably a whole lot more. Then I can make some intelligent decisions."

"And the deadline?"

"I want to hold off on letting him talk to Mills. I don't want to set him off, but I don't want him to think I'm a wimp."

"No one thinks you're a wimp, Frank," said Claire's father. "We just want to win without losing any cops."

"Let's not push it," said the commissioner. "Feel him out, but leave us time."

"He's waiting too, sir. The longer the better."

The commissioner looked to his underlings. His underlings had nothing to say.

"Make the phone call now."

Captain Bellini lit a fresh cigar, poured himself a cup of coffee, sat down at the main desk and dialed Zendt's house. The speakers in the command post played the single ring at high decibel.

Jack flinched.

"CNN News," said Tony Zendt.

"Very funny, Tony. Captain Bellini here."

"You find that lowlife scumbag yet?"

"Not yet, but we're doing our best. We need more time, Tony. I know that must be obvious."

"Ask his bimbo where he is. She must be out there, right? Sitting on someone's lap."

"Tony, even if they found him right this very minute, I couldn't get him here in time. You know that. I know that. How about you show some good faith."

"Please, Captain," said Zendt. "We weren't born yesterday."

"Then is there anything else I can do for you, anybody else you might like to talk to? A neighbor, a friend? Hell, pick a celebrity. Give me sixty more minutes and I'll have the pope at a phone booth in Vatican Square."

Zendt laughed, said nothing. The cops in the command post heard the sound of a cigarette lighter, the clatter of plastic on Formica. He's in the kitchen, thought Jack, at the rear of the house. It had been clean as a whistle, like the garage. He remembered the baby-food jar labeled TRASH. The picture tubes lined up like heads. The cordless phone. He could smell the gun oil of the basement museum. He thought of Lucy, that wacky old dame.

Bellini said, "Come on, Tony. Please?"

"You know what you can do, you can get my ex out here, and maybe Angela Cortelli, and hey, you can stop those fuckheads from moving around. You don't want to start losing them one by one."

A single shot rang out from the house, a bullet struck the grille of one of the stranded Plymouths. The firearms teams loosed a volley of their own, shredding the bedroom shade, exposing a member of the Second Wisconsin at parade rest, blowing away his head.

Via radio, Lieutenant Drexel ordered the cops to hold their fire.

Bellini shouted into the phone, "Hey, goddamn it! Lighten up!"

"You want a bloodbath, we'll have bloodbath," said Tony. "Your call, not mine."

"They're fucking scared, Anthony. What the hell do you expect?"

"I expect them to do what you tell them to do, Captain. Just as my men will. Now tell 'em to knock it off."

Frank Bellini made a hand signal to a cop at the door, and word spread around the inner perimeter for everyone to hold their places. "Okay?" he asked Tony Zendt. "Everything okay now?"

"Listen to yourself, Captain. You sound like Mister Rogers. Goddamn it, don't play me like no douchebag civilian. I wore the blue on meaner streets than yours and I expect to be treated accordingly."

Bellini said nothing.

"Ten minutes, Captain. Then Miss Lucy loses."

Bellini mashed his cigar in the aluminum ashtray. "You want to talk cop to cop, Zendt, I'll talk cop to cop. Ten minutes from now, your buttbuddy Mills won't be here. And we'll have us a fucking deadline. You'll get nervous, we'll get nervous. Maybe we'll rush the house, maybe we won't. Maybe we'll toss gas and save only Lucy. Maybe we'll chop up your dummies and piss on them. So don't start thinking to be a man you've got to kill an old lady. 'Cause you'll be wrong, Anthony, as wrong as you've ever been in your life. And if you do it anyway, you sick motherfucker, I will personally blow your head off."

"You're not supposed to threaten me," said Zendt. "You're not supposed to get caught in a lie. Rules tried and true, Captain. You're supposed to lick my balls and do my bidding. Bring me pizzas and shit. Time is on your side, remember? You should try to get an extension, not jeopardize the hostage."

"Are you finished?"

"You blow this one, baby, it ain't gonna be my fault."

The Suffolk County Police commissioner raised his eyebrows. He indicated to his entourage that it was time to let the true professionals take over. Established procedures were important; however, if rules were broken to achieve desired results, it was best done in private. They stood up in triplicate, and Jack felt more alone than ever. Claire stared at the floor, her chest rising with each inhalation. On the way out the door, her father kissed her cheek.

Sergeant Lomack fiddled with his holster and helped Drexel stare at the screens.

The voice of Tony Zendt said, "You ever blown one, Bellini? Ever bag the bodies and notify next of kin?"

"I know fucking-A-well what I'm supposed to say," said Bellini. "I'm supposed to offer you a lawyer, one of the chaplains, plane tickets to Disney World. It ain't gonna happen."

"Don't even bother. We got everything we need for months."

"And I've got years," said Bellini. "So what's the deal?"

"I told you before. The game we're playing is this: the old lady for Mills. He's the closest thing you got to a chaplain out there anyway. Just ask him."

Tony Zendt hung up. The speakers buzzed, fell silent.

Bellini spun around in his chair and looked at Jack.

Zendt's deal hung in the air of the command post like stale gas. The old lady for Mills. No cash, no future considerations, not even a player to be named at a later date. Bottom line, body for body.

"Think hard," said Bellini, "about something other than a swap."

"Believe me," said Jack. "I'm trying."

26

T HE SHADES in Tony Zendt's living room, kitchen and den rose simultaneously. But instead of the mannequins with guns Jack expected to see, on each windowsill was a television set connected to a VCR. The sets were on, volume high.

Word came back from the closest cops: Tony Zendt was showing home movies, entertaining the troops.

Gathered around the monitor screens in the command post, Bellini and the others could see that Zendt was running Commissioner Foley's news conference live in the living-room window, Chief Barone talking about the great cops of Nassau.

Jack Mills and Rodney Lomack appeared on the television in the kitchen window, getting out of the car at Backman's funeral, again and again, slow-motion. Then Zendt ran footage of Jack Mills teaching his daughter to play basketball. Jack and Claire entering the Landmark Café, followed by a windswept walk on the beach at Montauk, their body language painfully self-evident.

"You two make a handsome couple," said Lomack.

Jack gave a wry smile while Claire's face colored deeply.

"You're lucky you're not dead," said Bellini.

Then they watched a horror show from the den—the digging, the begging, the slow-motion murder of Arthur Backman, handcuffed, leaping like a fish in pain, gagging on his shield. The body of Richard Mazzarella in the trunk of a canary yellow Dodge. Again and again, as if these favorite scenes were on a continuous loop. Then the shades closed like curtains on a puppet show.

Lomack said, "You think this qualifies as spontaneous admission?"

Bellini kept his eyes on the monitors. "I don't think Tony much cares."

Lomack bent forward and whispered in Jack's ear, "We never swap cops for hostages, even loud-mouth pains in the ass, because we so rarely get them back. Got it?"

Jack nodded.

Two minutes before the deadline, Jack called Tony Zendt.

He said, in the cheerful tone one uses to drunken friends in emergency rooms, "Tony, buddy, what the hell are you doing?"

"Where are you, Mills?"

"At headquarters. I stopped by to pick up my check and got grabbed by half the squad. What the hell is going on out there?"

"Spare me the stroke-job, asshole."

"Now we're calling each other names?"

"That ain't the least of it, not by a long shot.

You'd better be on my front lawn in thirty minutes, or Lucy's dead on live TV."

"I can't get out to your house in thirty minutes. It's fucking rush hour. You got to give me two, two and a half hours."

Zendt said, "You're a big shot, Mills. Take a chopper."

In the pitch black subterranean dungeon she lay on her side, confronting her faith, alternating between hope and despair. She made an Act of Contrition, went once more around the rosary.

Dear Lord, she prayed, send Jack.

Lucy heard the crazy man laughing like an idiot up there, which made her more frightened than ever. She could hear almost everything that was happening on the main floor, except when the dehumidifier ran, and it was her belief that her captor was deteriorating rapidly, talking to people who were not there, arguing with someone, promising to let someone else live, speaking in tongues. She heard accents she did not recognize, and always the working, working—frantic working.

Lucy thought about her Irish childhood and her parents, about her sorry life at the rooming house, about her beloved husband, and she wondered if he had been good enough for heaven, where she expected to go if there was any justice at all. For the second time since that morning she soiled herself and cried.

Then she heard a loud shout, and someone groaning. She held her breath. Footsteps on the stairs, no longer concerned with secrecy or stealth. A key in a lock. The door opened. Light streamed around a SWAT cop in riot gear. The very miracle for which she had so humbly petitioned her savior.

"Thank God," she said.

The man kicked her feet. "Get up, bitch. Your fucking hero's coming."

Two local teams had already set up live remotes, and the crew from WCBS were marching up a nearby hill, cameras over their shoulders like cannon.

A traffic helicopter hovered overhead until it was chased away by the Suffolk Police chopper.

A sound expert advised Captain Bellini that the different voices were actually coming from one man, using different accents. "But unless he's got a bunch of big pets, there are at least three human hearts still beating in the house."

"Three?" said Bellini.

"At least."

"Gentlemen?" said Bellini.

The cops from Nassau shrugged.

Jack, Claire and Lomack stepped outside the command post into the gathering dusk. Twenty-four minutes remained until the new deadline, when Jack would have to be where he already was. Claire smoked a cigarette, then another. The phone ringing in the command post drew them quickly back inside. Their tap had picked up an outgoing call, which their register showed to be routed to a number Jack recognized, that of the Nassau County Police Homicide Squad. He said as much to Bellini.

"Oh, shit," said Bellini.

Lieutenant Drexel immediately pounded out the number on another phone.

The speakers said, "Homicide."

Jack recognized Quickstop Izzy Goldman's gravelly voice and lack of enthusiasm.

Zendt said, "Jack Mills, please."

"He ain't here."

A phone rang in the background, probably Drexel's call.

Izzy said, "He's on the road."

"This is his cousin. He's supposed to meet me for drinks this afternoon."

"He's out on a job. Left hours ago."

Zendt hung up.

Drexel hung up.

Tony Zendt called Jack's home phone number. The cops heard his answering machine take the call. "Hi," Jack's voice intoned. "I can't come to the phone right now . . ."

Click. Buzz.

The phone next to Frank Bellini's hand rang loudly.

"Captain Bellini here."

"Put fucking Mills on."

"I'm thinking of cutting your phone and electric, Tony."

"And we're thinking of cutting Lucy's throat. Put Mills on."

Bellini handed Mills the phone.

"Jack Mills."

"Nice try, punk."

"We're trying to bring this to a peaceful resolution."

"I see," said Tony. "You lied to me for my own good. Thanks a lot. Now, you gonna come and see me, you phony sack of shit?"

"You know we never do that."

"From right now, buddy, you got two minutes to make 'em change their minds. *Capisce?*"

"Listen, Tony. If you kill her it's over. We move in and you die."

"That's what you think."

"These guys out here are pissed, my man. They want to nuke your little theme park. It seems they don't like Nassau County problems spilling over the border."

"One minute and counting," said Zendt. "It's fish or cut bait."

Bellini looked at Jack, who wore the defeated expression of a doomed man.

"Uh, Captain, I'd like to volunteer to—"

Sergeant Lomack shook his head. "No, Jack. Sorry. That's not a part of your job description."

"Well, I sure don't want to, but . . ."

Zendt hung up.

The outside mikes picked up the sound of Zendt's garage door as it opened a foot and a half. The monitors showed a figure wrapped in blankets, head covered by a canvas sack. It rolled from the garage into the driveway, then crawled slowly like a caterpillar for the edge of the lawn, blindly lurching toward safety.

No one moved. Statues in the woods covered statues in the windows. A single shot rang out from inside the garage and reverberated through the hollow. The body in the blanket arched, quivered a moment, slumped. Blood spilled from the canvas bag, running down the drawstring.

The shades rolled down. The garage door closed.

Lieutenant Drexel, watching his monitor screen, said, "Jesus, Mary and Joseph."

Around the command post, the emergency services cops made ready to attack, strapping their body armor tight, checking and rechecking weapons. Inside, Frank Bellini was on the phone listening to Tony's phone ring unanswered. The interior of the van was filled with smoke, littered with Styrofoam coffee containers. The air shook with each new jangle. At last, Zendt picked up.

"We're coming in," said Bellini, "unless you come out. I'll leave it up to you."

"You're not going anywhere, asshole."

"Oh, no?"

"I got someone here wants to say hello to you guys."

They heard a woman's voice: "Claire? It's me, Lucy. Don't come in, please! Send in Jack Mills."

"When did you tape that?" said Bellini, scowling.

"You're the high-tech man, not me. I'm dealing in real life situations here, Captain."

"Let me see her," Bellini said.

"I do that, you'll know where I am. No doubt Mills has told you all about my various and sundry defenses."

"Put the woman back on. I want to ask her some questions."

Zendt thought it over. "Fine."

"Hel-lo?"

"Lucy, it's Captain Bellini of the Suffolk County Police Department."

"Hello, sir."

"Who was that he sent out of the house?"

"I don't know. A man. I never saw him but I heard him groaning—"

A grunt, a gap in conversation.

"You got it?" asked Zendt. "We agree she's alive?"

"I got it," said Bellini. "We're back to square one, not counting the mess you made in your driveway."

Tony said, "The mess *I* made? *That's* an interesting theory. Why don't you just send in Mills. I told you before I wouldn't kill him. He's a Long Island treasure, for God's sake. I'd go down in the books with Oswald and Hinckley and the guy who shot the Beatle."

"Mark Chapman," said Bellini. "Why should I believe you?"

"Because I've kept all my other promises."

"Not really. Not when you think about it."

"What?" said Tony. "Because I shot someone else instead of Lucy? You want me to fix that little oversight?"

"I was thinking of your oath as a police officer."

"Forget about it," Tony said. "No fucking way. Don't for one second assume that I was the problem. You don't know me, Frank Bellini. Mills don't know me. Three years ago he could have called for help and I would have come flying to his side. Things change; shit happens. Another one bites the dust."

"But—"

"My wife did me wrong; so fucking what? My girl did me wrong; ain't life a bitch? That ain't what's happening, Captain. You guys should start to believe in me."

"What do you want with Mills?"

"Conversation."

"Why?"

There was no answer.

"Then what? A plane to Cuba? Want me to free some Palestinians?"

"Then I'll surrender. Mills can walk me out the door."

"Really?"

Jack looked at Claire. Her eyes were like saucers.

Zendt said, "On what honor I have left as a gentleman."

Jack scanned the monitors: the house, the cop cars with their doors open, the lumpy blanket in the driveway, the spreading pool of blood.

"Give me an hour," said Bellini. "I've got to talk to my superiors."

"Half an hour," said Zendt.

"Hey!" Bellini protested.

"Twenty-nine minutes."

While the phone calls required to break ironclad rules were being made from county to county, Jack Mills called Wallace Wilson Benz at his home and explained the situation.

"Yes, I know. We've all been watching."

"Anyway, I was thinking you could find a bright spot for him, something to hang onto. Right now he thinks he's got nothing to win or lose. That's gonna make him very hard to take without someone getting hurt."

"Sorry, Mills. I no longer represent Anthony Zendt."

"But—"

"Do you remember when you were told that the party never forgets?"

"Yeah?"

"Have a nice fucking evening, Jack."

27

JACK WALKED Claire out of the command post and down the hill away from the house. The sun had set, yet the leaves flashed yellow and orange and red. A beautiful evening for almost everyone.

Claire took him by the arm. "That day in the woods, when I didn't take your picture? I'm sorry, now. I wish I had something to remember you by, in case—by going against the book—you get your silly face shot off."

He smiled, nodded, took a deep breath and leaned against the cool front fender of a police car. A crowd was gathered further down the hill. A Sabrett hot dog truck, under its yellow-and-brown-striped umbrella, was doing brisk business by the side of the road.

"There's got to be a better way," she said.

"I'm open to suggestions."

"You're all balls and no brains. The odds suggest that what you're about to do will be futile and deadly."

"You want to tell Lucy that?"

Claire shook her head. "No. I don't. But I don't

want to watch you die. It just seems that now, while there's still time . . ."

"That's the problem," said Jack. "This has nothing to do with time."

"You're the wrong man for this job, you know. The man who goes in there had better be ready to kill him. I'd do better."

"I'm ready," said Jack. "Don't worry about that."

Claire said she did not believe him, that he was just the sort of naive clown who would let the only opening pass.

"Now really," he said, "how could I be any less courageous than you already were, taking the rap for losing Lucy."

"Taking the rap ain't taking a bullet. Next Thursday I'll still get paid. My dad will still let me make him Sunday dinner."

He shrugged, trying not to listen to her.

"Are you showing off for me?"

"I don't know. Maybe myself."

She grabbed his arm and said, "Fuck that. Make Bellini find another way."

"I can do this," he said. "I'm only lousy at handling women, not men."

"You can't do this. Not really." She looked away from him, down the hill. He put his hands on her shoulders. Claire shook her head and said, "I'd kiss you good-bye, but I don't think your other ladies would appreciate the eight-by-ten splattered on the late edition."

"Let's leave them out of this."

She faced him, took his hand and shook it like a

man. "I love you, Jack. Make sure you come back out of there."

"Mills!" They were calling from up above. "We need you."

"No wires, no vest, no guns, no knives, no poison darts, no fucking hocus-pocus."

"Clear," said Bellini.

"Strip him down to his jockey shorts. No shoes."

"Clear."

"We make the switch in the front yard. The woman will come out when Mills hits no-man's-land. Anybody moves, I put two in his eyes."

"Clear."

"Ten minutes," said Zendt.

Then Frank Bellini handed over the phone to the former Mrs. Zendt, something she had agreed to on the condition that the speakers be turned off, that her sons, whom she would not leave alone, did not have to hear what Tony said. She did not mind if a tape was made. The teenaged boys said nothing, held their heads down. The youngest was weeping.

"Tony, it's Nina. I'm outside the house with the boys . . . Because they goddamned asked me to . . . I told them that . . . You'll never change. What? . . . Good-bye . . . I said good-bye." She held the phone an inch away from her ear and turned her head, scowling. "I don't have to listen to this, do I?"

Bellini severed the connection.

The Suffolk County Police chaplain heard Jack's confession and then left him alone in the front of the command post to say his penance and reflect upon all the sins of his past life. A moment later, while Jack was working his way out of the misdemeanors of adolescence and into the felonies of adulthood, Frank Bellini stuck his head in and asked, "You got clean underwear on?"

Jack chuckled softly.

"Good boy. Get ready."

Claire stepped out of the command post while Jack stripped down to his shorts. He was glad for all the workouts, for keeping in shape. He hoped he'd look as good as he had on the playing fields.

Lomack took his gun and wallet and handcuffs. Bellini told Jack to turn around, drop his shorts and spread his cheeks. He taped a thin stiletto in the crack and said, "Don't baby this when you yank it out." He pulled up the waistband and gave Jack a sharp pat on the rump.

Claire stepped back inside the bus as Bellini was telling Jack that they would give him all the time he needed. "If push comes to shove, Jack, give us any kind of signal you can and then hit the deck. We'll saturate from window level up for ten seconds, then you make your break."

Jack caught Claire's eye and smiled. "Don't nobody go nowhere. I'm coming out with a prisoner. Right?"

The house was lit up like a stage. In the surrounding darkness brother officers hugged fenders and trees, eyes locked into their sights.

The grass was soft and damp under his feet, the skin on his arms chilled in the evening breeze. It took tremendous physical effort to walk in the right direction. Running away would have been a snap.

Except the whole world was watching, everyone he had ever known. As he walked slowly under the guns, his shadow thrown out in front of him, the glare of the spotlights behind him, he saw the blood from the blankets had spread thirty feet to the street. Above the trees birds circled and the moon was rising.

The red front door of Tony Zendt's house swung open halfway.

Lucy Lallos appeared on the stoop in a pale housedress, her arms across her chest, squinting. She might have been a housewife, calling home the cat.

Jack smiled at her. "Come on out," he said softly. "Never mind how I'm dressed."

She was trembling, rubbing her wrists.

"Come on, Lucy."

Lucy took tiny steps, her head erect, her lips working on a prayer. The one time she pulled her gaze from his face was to look at the sky.

Tony Zendt screamed, "Mills!"

They froze.

"No fucking talking."

Jack called out, "Okay!"

"You just keep coming."

"Okay."

As Jack and Lucy Lallos passed on the lawn, exchanging fates, he thought of substitutions on the fly in lacrosse, one tired middle collapsing on the side of the field, one charging headlong into the fray—the roar of frenzied fans, the pounding of his heart.

"Bless you," she said.

He walked up the concrete steps, over the threshold and onto the living-room carpet, softly closed the door behind him with his bare foot. The house smelled of coffee, cigarettes and that slightly acid smell of a sickroom or a bunker, same as the command-post van. His eyes adjusted to the dark.

"Tony?"

A flashlight beam stabbed his chest, his face, checked the door and windows. Snapped off.

The living room was a glistening spiderweb of fishing line, running to the mannequins and their weapons through eyelets mounted on the floor and walls. The ceiling held a maze of mirrors, showing every window.

Tony Zendt was on the floor behind the couch, in a Suffolk County Police Department assault uniform, same as the men outside, pointing a revolver at Jack. A cordless phone was on the floor by his side. A computer terminal. Labeled pull-wires.

"Hi, hotshot," he said. "Glad you could make it. You should have knocked on the door last night. I was up."

"Do tell."

"Anyway, you're here now. I wasn't sure you were one of those jackass cops who think it's an honor to risk their ass. I guess you are as dumb as you look."

Jack dropped his hands at his sides. "You're a cop in trouble. I came to help you out."

"My brother," said Tony, making a face suggesting scorn. "Boy, was I happy when I heard that you caught the case. A dumb jock and an Uncle Tom. And then they added the fox like they were casting a movie."

"When you're ready, we can walk out together, and no one will hurt you."

"You got that part right."

"Incidentally, you're under arrest. You have the right to remain silent, the right to consult an attorney before questioning. If you cannot——"

Tony held up his hand. "Easy, now. This is my life we're doing, not yours."

Jack stared at Tony, sizing him up.

Tony said, "How long did they give you to kill me?"

"No one wants to kill you. Especially me."

"Now isn't *that* great news."

Jack shrugged.

Zendt motioned with his head for Jack to follow him, then duck-walked backward from the couch to the head of the cellar stairs, never taking his eyes off Jack.

Jack crouched low as he crossed the living room, hugging the wall, holding his breath, taking care not to trip a loaded dummy.

Zendt backed down the steps in front of him, aiming up, trailing wires. He ordered Jack to lock the door at the head of the stairs.

The eye-level windows of the finished basement were boarded and barred. The ceiling was dotted with high-hats on dimmer switches. The lights were low. The five-stool wet bar was attended by two mannequins in regimental dress.

An officer's club, Jack thought. Or a bunker, and he was the "smart" bomb.

There were three TVs on the bar, showing views of the front, kitchen and garage doors.

Zendt stepped behind the bar and offered Jack a seat as if they were neighbors hiding from their wives on a Saturday.

"Drink?" he said.

"Maybe later."

Tony smiled. "I wonder who'll live here next. I wonder if they'll have better luck than I did." He laughed loudly, threw his head back. "Have you ever considered the possibility that cops have such high divorce rates because they tend to marry sluts?"

"No."

"Fuck 'em, right?" said Tony. "Who cares?"

"What do you want me to tell you, Tony? Life is long and love is short."

"I hear ya. So what can I do about this thing with the captains?"

Jack leaned forward, put his elbows on the bar, his bare foot on the cold brass rail, thirty inches from his man. "You gonna tell me about that? You know you don't have to."

"Better to you alone than to twenty pricks who want to kick my ass."

"It's over, if you want it to be. I won't let anyone lay a glove on you."

Tony scoffed, "You gonna spend the night in jail with me too? And the second night, and the third?" He pulled a can of beer from his small refrigerator and put it on the bar. "Open it," he said.

Jack cracked it open, ignoring the pistol pointed at his head, unable to shake the odd notion that they were buddies, that this subterranean glimpse of death would pass. They would go upstairs and get back to their yardwork, their errands, the oil change—each to his honey-do list.

Tony cocked his head. "I hated Artie Backman. Besides fucking me over with Angela, he blackballed my promotion to the squad, once even had the nerve to say to my face that my kids would never call me detective. The man was scum, pure and simple."

"When I first thought of you as a suspect, it occurred to me that if you were jealous over Angela, you would have murdered Backman a couple of years ago, when Angela turned you down and he moved in."

"I was tempted," he said. "But when she told me she was pregnant, I asked her to marry me again. You know, to give the kid a name. I thought the time was right to save her. And you know what? She fucking laughed. Said its name was gonna be Garbage. I couldn't take that, you know?"

Tony plucked photographs out of his pocket and laid them on the bar like a pat hand. They were of Angela, taken at Louie's garage, with Louie and Artie and a bald man with a jagged scar on his calf—Dick Mazzarella.

"Artie Backman was selling her ass. It probably wasn't even his kid."

"So you bagged him."

Tony smiled, as if remembering a cherished moment, peered around his can of beer as he took a swallow, then set it down and wiped his mouth.

Jack said, "You got problems, Tony. Emotional problems. Everybody out there knows that."

"I got problems? What about you?" said Tony.

"Where do you get off telling me I'm fucked-up? We're not so fucking different. And they were assholes. I don't feel near as bad as I thought I would."

"Dead assholes," said Jack.

Tony elbowed the mannequin next to him— Monty, the Highlander. "God's teeth, man. Did we tell him we were sorry or what?"

Jack looked into the painted eyes for a response.

Zendt slapped the bar and laughed. "Angela thought you were cute, you know. She was gonna make you next."

"Pretty scary, Tony. You know what I'm saying?"

"You want to see scary, you shoulda been with me that day. With Backman."

"Where'd you grab him?"

"Angela's garage. I rode the train there, and I waited for him to park in the handicapped spot, just like he always did. Then I went upside his head with a nightstick, tucked him in the trunk of his car and came on out here. He woke up around North Ocean Avenue and started raising a racket, kicking the trunk. I knew about the Lilco road from all my bike riding. Do you believe that he begged?"

"Backman? Oh, yeah."

"Because you'd beg."

"Yeah."

"I ain't gonna make you beg, man."

"I appreciate that."

"I'll either do it or I won't, you know what I mean?"

Jack's throat was dry, calling for a beer of its

own, calling for a cessation of hostility and a case of Miller longnecks. He wondered what Jenny was up to, thought of Claire watching the house on the monitor, the cars, the body in the driveway. The blade between his cheeks. He wondered, remembering what Claire had said: Had his only moment passed?

Tony rested the barrel of the gun against his forehead and sighed. "The Dicktop never knew what hit him. Bang, zoom, off to the moon. He deserved more pain but I couldn't take the risk."

Jack nodded. "Now the big question, Tony."

Tony raised his eyebrows. "Oh, that."

"Who is lying out there in the driveway?"

Tony shrugged, a child with a dirty room. "This one you boys won't mind so much."

Jack said, "Louie?"

"He was walking his dog, right? So bingo, I scope off the mutt and now he's dragging meat. He freezes, expecting his. I pull up next to him, offer him a ride to the vet's. You know what he had the nerve to say? He says, 'Normally, Tony, I'd have to kill you. But you and me, we can make a deal.' Like he's some bad motherfucker instead of one dead wannabe. Of course, I couldn't take him out until I convinced you people to drop the tail on him. That broad you used was very good. I almost didn't notice her."

"If you loved Angela so much," said Jack, "and it certainly seems that way, why did you torture her with the roses?"

"For the kid. Someone had to."

"Tony, this isn't a little fucked-up, this is really fucked-up."

Tony flashed a wide smile. "Enough fucked-up? A Do-Not-Go-to-Jail card?"

"I'd say."

"Not sure I can do it, man. People think the nuthouse is fun, like Jack Nicholson had fun. That's a crock of happy horseshit."

"But you might actually get better."

"Listen to you."

Tony had lines of fatigue around his mouth. A silly smile crossed his face and he shook his head.

Jack sat quietly, sweat running down his sides into the waistband of his jockey shorts. He might make it out of here, they both might, if he could keep Tony calm. This could all work out.

"Are they all still out there? Nina and the boys?"

"I think so," said Jack. "You want me to have them moved away?"

He shook his head. "They've already formed their opinions."

"Anything you need, ask."

"Can't think of a thing."

"Really?"

"Other than maybe helping me escape."

Jack smiled.

Zendt indicated with his pistol that Jack should step away, they would go outside, and he came around from behind the bar and followed Jack back up the stairs, into the hallway on the main floor. Lights flashing around the edges of the window shades gave the living room the hellish atmosphere of a discotheque.

Zendt put his hand on Jack's shoulder and looked Jack in the eye, a look that said a bond had been formed, that it was all he had. "You really think they'll toss me in Matawan?"

"Like I said, I don't think you need to worry about jail."

28

Lieutenant Drexel sat hunched over the desk, headphones on, biting his thumbnail, hearing nothing. The initial assault team drew closer, one tree at a time. Lomack and Claire watched their tortuous progress on the infrared monitors.

At the rear of the command post, Frank Bellini debriefed Lucy Lallos, who was wrapped in blankets and shivering uncontrollably. Sobbing and stuttering, she said that Tony had kept her blindfolded in the basement. He had not fed her or allowed her to go to the bathroom. The other prisoner had been somewhere upstairs. She had heard him grunting when Tony walked her by the window. "He's got a knapsack packed to travel," she said.

Claire said, "I hate this shit. What the hell is he up to?"

"He talks to those dummies," Lucy said. "Quite a bit round the bend, I'd say."

"We were nuts to let Jack go in there," Claire whispered to Lomack. "That fucking wack isn't gonna surrender. I say we rush the house. Now."

Bellini asked Lucy what Zendt was wearing.

"If I'm not mistaken, sir, he was dressed pretty much like your men."

Claire bit her lip and looked at her watch.

Lomack asked her how long Jack had been inside.

"Twelve minutes," she said. "I don't like this at all."

"What do you got?" Bellini asked Drexel.

"Nothing. Dead silence. Wait a minute. Something about Matawan. Now something about jail."

"What the hell is Mills doing?" said Bellini. "Plea-bargaining?"

"Sounds like it," said Drexel.

"This one of your more experienced men, Sergeant Lomack?"

Lomack shook his head. "He's cherry."

"So you want to give me that gun?" asked Jack.

"You still don't get it, do you?"

"Get what?"

"Nobody's locking this boy up."

"I don't understand. What was downstairs about?"

"I had a couple things to get off my chest. I feel better. End of story."

"You don't possibly think you can escape."

"Watch."

Tony Zendt duck-walked across the strobe-lit living room and opened the door that led to the garage. "Come on," he said to Jack. "We're gonna see how much they value your life."

The garage was arranged for Tony's last stand, filled with one Trans Am, facing out, and five dangerous dummies pointing automatic weapons at the automatic door.

Tony said, "Welcome to the twenty-first century."

Jack knew then that anyone who rushed the house would die in a hail of bullets. "Thinking of taking a little ride?" he asked.

"They can keep the car."

"Tony, where do you think you're going?"

"Same place as you, Jack, hand in hand. Now get down and take cover. Wouldn't want you to catch your death."

Tony suddenly yanked a trip wire that he had trailed behind. A single shot rang out, perhaps a musket. A silent moment passed during which Jack thought about the cops outside, who, he guessed, were probably thinking that either the shot was his signal or that he was dead. He dove for the concrete floor and quickly wedged himself between the back wall of the garage and two stacks of knobby snow tires.

A mammoth volley of ordnance was the answer from the cops outside.

One Mississippi, he counted to himself.

Glass showered into the house. The doors and walls and ceiling splintered and shook.

Two Mississippi.

Dummies disintegrated. Hot rounds punched the tire next to Jack's head, and dust filled his eyes and lungs.

Three Mississippi.

He should get to a neutral corner.

Four Mississippi.

The knife up his ass.

Five Miss—

Tony was screaming, as if someone were holding a steam iron to the palm of his hand. Jack wanted to scream with him. The noise threatened to overpower his reason and patience, and he resisted an impulse to stand and race into the fire. He realized he had lost count. Started over, this time faster. One, two, three, four, five—

Sudden silence, inside and out.

Broken dummies on the dusty floor.

Tony's dark face next to his, a wide white smile. "So you see what I was saying? You ain't no big fucking deal."

The gun swung to Jack's face, freezing him, making him small in a world that was big, soft in a world that was hard.

"You don't actually need to kill me, Tony. I know how to play dead."

"Every cop knows that, Mills."

Jack bent over as if to dust his legs off, came up swinging the severed arm of an Iwo Jima vet, knocking the gun from Tony's hand.

"Hey!" He sounded put out.

While Tony reached for another pistol, Jack ran for the door that led back into the house.

"Freeze!" Tony screamed. "You fucking coward."

Jack scrambled down the dark hallway, snagged a toe on a trip wire, fell down hard at the feet of a British grenadier, 23rd Welsh Fusiliers, formally attired in scarlet waistcoat and high bearskin cap.

Zendt filled the doorway behind him. "Hold it right there, asshole."

Jack sprang to his feet and around behind the

soldier, cocked the soldier's Brown Bess, aimed at Tony and squeezed hard on the trigger. The flintlock made the sound of a rock dropped on concrete.

Jack cocked it again, pulled the trigger, same result.

"You fucked her, didn't you?" said Tony.

"No," said Jack, looking guilty anyway.

"Liar . . . stone-cold dead fucking liar." He raised his pistol.

"You're wrong."

"Go ahead," said Tony, looking at his watch, stepping closer. "I'll give you sixty seconds to reload, three times what he would take on a morning after too much grog."

Jack Mills had not the foggiest idea how to load a flintlock musket, but he did know to high-stick someone. He held the mannequin to his chest and charged Tony with a little bit o' steel, banging him up against a wall, grunting, smacking his own forehead into Tony's face. They made a sandwich of the soldier, looking deep into each other's eyes until warm blood pulsed across Jack's left wrist and Tony's pistol dropped to the floor.

They danced just so until Jack realized he was holding Tony up.

"Oh, Jesus," Jack whispered. "I'm sorry."

"Let me go. Please. I strike my colors."

"I never slept with her, man."

"Okay," Tony gasped. "It doesn't matter."

Jack released his hold.

Tony Zendt staggered back a step, pulled the bayonet from his gut, studied the blood on his shirt as if it belonged to someone else, then lurched to the open front door of his house with the ancient weapon in his hands. Jack moved to follow. Tony spun around, knocked him down with the rifle butt, walked outside and slammed the door behind him.

"Hey, Bellini." Tony's words echoed in the evening. One hundred disciplined gunmen held steady. Spotlights flashed in his face while blood poured from Tony Zendt like water out of a spigot.

"Put down the gun!" an amplified voice commanded.

Certain of his future, Zendt crouched, raised his empty musket, aimed at the lights and bellowed something unintelligible.

To the credit of the men on the perimeter, the shooting stopped as soon as the body hit the porch.

Captain Bellini declared the scene secure at ten o'clock that night. The bodies of Louie Allesi and Tony Zendt were bagged and trundled to the morgue wagon. The search boys moved in, the Suffolk County homicide detectives. Photos were taken, diagrams drawn, depositions made.

From the back of the command post, Bellini held a brief press conference in which he called the operation a clean kill, albeit a regrettable one. "Former Police Officer Anthony Zendt wasn't packing a full seabag," he told the reporters, "and what he had wasn't stenciled. There wasn't nothing nobody could have done."

Up front in the van, on television, Jack watched himself walking into the house in his underwear, Lucy fleeing like a nun, the interminable first barrage that riddled the house, then the second that finished off Tony Zendt. Cops in jumpsuits moving in, bouncing Zendt down the front steps, cuffing the corpse on the lawn. He watched Lucy Lallos hugging him while he was still undressed. He watched footage of Claire Williamson hugging him while he was still undressed.

Then the Suffolk County Police commissioner announced that he was recommending Detective Jack Mills for the Medal of Valor, which, he pointed out, had never been won by anyone from another jurisdiction who had lived. On the small screen flashed his police academy file photo, his Boys' Club publicity still, the last unamended copy of the poster, then slo-mo replays of perfect feeds from Julio Sanfilipo, the defending goalie raising his stick, the net's flick, the celebration. Nina Fowler, Anthony Junior and little William Zendt hid their faces from the cameras as a squad car drove them back down the crowded hill. The anchorman segued into a stock-market tally. Then a retrospective on Bo Jackson playing every sport known to man.

Jack picked up a ringing phone.

"Hi," said Babe. "It's me."

"Good to hear your voice."

"You okay?"

"Other than I killed a man," he said.

"I'm sure you had no choice."

"I've been trying not to throw up over everybody."

"Same old cast-iron stomach."

"Yup."

"Detective Williamson is beautiful, if you like your women in jumpsuits."

"Thanks, Babe."

He wondered if they would still be calling each

other years from now, after Jenny had gone off to college or was living on her own, or if he would suffer the pain of losing her again, his oldest friend who knew him best.

"You do have your clothes back on, right? They've yet to show you live and fully dressed."

"I'm dressed. I'm just hiding."

"Jenny wants to talk to you."

"You let her watch?"

"How was I supposed to stop her?"

"My God," said Jack. "What a sense of security I must give her."

"If you're fine, she's fine. You couldn't ask for any more than that."

He heard Jenny pick up the extension.

"Hi, Jenny," he said. "How was school?"

"Very funny, Daddy."

"You were all I was thinking of. But I *knew* I could make it out."

"You could have called and asked my opinion first."

"Next time."

He could see Claire through the window of the command post, one long leg sticking out of a squad car, smoking a cigarette and waiting.

The Babe hung up on her end, gently.

JOHN WESTERMANN

JOHN WESTERMANN brings to his fiction the gritty authenticity and graphic experience of his fourteen years as a highly decorated police officer in a tough coastal town on Long Island.

EXIT WOUNDS

HIGH CRIMES

SWEET DEAL

"Westermann has an extraordinary eye for the tawdry, writes unbeatably funny dialogue....a must for any devotee of raunchy burnt-out cop sagas... This wildly funny caper...is dark, anguished, and...authentic."
—<u>Publishers Weekly</u>

POCKET
BOOKS

Available from Pocket Books   726